Alphonse Daudet

The Novels, Romances, and Memoirs of Alphonse Daudet

Alphonse Daudet

The Novels, Romances, and Memoirs of Alphonse Daudet

ISBN/EAN: 9783337037086

Printed in Europe, USA, Canada, Australia, Japan

Cover: Foto ©Andreas Hilbeck / pixelio.de

More available books at **www.hansebooks.com**

THE NOVELS, ROMANCES AND MEMOIRS OF ALPHONSE DAUDET

PROVENÇAL EDITION

THIRTY YEARS IN PARIS
ULTIMA

SOCIETY OF ENGLISH AND FRENCH LITERATURE   NEW YORK

University Press

JOHN WILSON AND SON, CAMBRIDGE, U.S.A.

CONTENTS.

                                       PAGE

INTRODUCTORY NOTE ix

PAGES FROM MY LIFE AND MY BOOKS:

    I. The Arrival 1

    II. Villemessant 15

    III. My First Coat 29

    IV. History of My Books. — "Little What's-His-Name" 42

    V. The Literary Salons 57

    VI. My Drummer 74

    VII. History of My Books. — Tartarin of Tarascon . . 90

    VIII. History of My Books. — Letters From My Mill . 103

    IX. My First Play 117

    X. Henri Rochefort 125

    XI. Henry Monnier 143

    XII. The End of a Mountebank and of Murger's Bohemia 149

    XIII. History of My Books. — Jack 165

    XIV. Île des Moineaux. — A Meeting on the Seine . 186

    XV. History of My Books. — Fromont and Risler . . 192

    XVI. Turgénieff 207

Ultima.

ULTIMA 223

LIST OF ILLUSTRATIONS.

Alphonse Daudet and his Secretary . . . . *Frontispiece*

Henri Rochefort 125

Ivan Turgénieff 207

INTRODUCTORY NOTE.

WHEN this volume of fugitive articles, mainly reminiscent, was given to the public, in 1888, almost exactly thirty years had passed since the epoch-marking incident in Daudet's life to which the opening article is devoted. Ernest Daudet fixes for us the time of his brother's arrival in Paris as the early part of November 1857, when he was about seventeen and a half years old;[1] and his first appearance in print — the publication of *Les Amoureuses*, the volume of verses many of which he had brought with him from the provinces — did not take place until the following year. His journey to Paris and his arrival Daudet had already described in the first chapter of the second part of *Little What's-His-Name* — the chapter called *Mes Caoutchoucs*, with which the quasi-autobiographical part of that story ends. If we read Ernest Daudet's affectionate and admiring tribute to his brother in connection with the " history " of *Little What's-His-Name* in this volume, and with that story itself, we cannot fail, it seems to me, to be convinced that there have been few auto-

[1] *My Brother and I*, Chap. XVI.

biographies in the guise of fiction in which the general outline of the narrative is so closely in accord with actual fact, as in this case of Daniel Eyssette and Alphonse Daudet; and the result is that we have — the three supplementing one another — an extremely full and satisfactory biography of the novelist down to the beginning of his literary career. The first few years in Paris are described very briefly by the older brother, who has almost nothing to say of his brother's life after his marriage; and, as his little book was published in 1881, the last sixteen years of Alphonse Daudet's life are left untouched by him. He feels bound, he says, not to forestall the account which Alphonse may give for himself, either in his memoirs or in the story of his works. It is to be regretted that he exercised this self-restraint, for the only memoirs which his brother has left behind, so far as appears, are contained, with the histories of his books, in this volume and its companion — *Memories of a Man of Letters,* — and, vastly entertaining as these reminiscences are, and most illuminating as to his character and temperament and methods of work; and though they are written, as has been said, with infinite talent and with his unfailing humor, they are sadly lacking in material for anything like an adequate biography of the man.

Les Amoureuses, already referred to, was published in 1859, when Daudet was not yet twenty years of age, and many of the poems had been written long before; his next volume, *La Double*

Conversion, a " tale in verse," appeared in 1861. These, with the exception of some fugitive pieces, published in newspapers or written in albums, were his only ventures in the field of poetry, and the volumes are principally sought by collectors.

During the interval between the publication of *Les Amoureuses* and that of *La Double Conversion*, a very marked change had taken place in Daudet's position and prospects; he was no longer the timid, diffident Little What's-His-Name; he had become acquainted with Villemessant, had made his mark in the columns of *Le Figaro*, which, says M. Ernest Daudet, " was a sort of consecration for an author, a brevet accorded to talent; " and he had, in 1860, accepted a position in the office of the Duc de Morny, President of the Corps Législatif, then and until his death one of the most powerful men in France. Although Daudet had not then seen the last of his Bohemian days, he had gone beyond the point where, if ever, he was in danger of falling to the level of many of those with whom he was thrown in contact; he had passed among them and come forth unscathed, " having lost none of his talent, having left behind none of the bloom of his youth, the freshness of his soul, the uprightness of his heart." [1]

The publication of *Les Amoureuses* called forth an extremely eulogistic article in *Le Moniteur* by M. Édouard Thierry, and may be said to have

[1] *My Brother and I*, Chap. XVI.

opened the columns of the newspapers to its author. It was not long after that *Le Figaro* (November 24, 1859) published his first article as *chroniqueur fantaisiste*, a study entitled *Les Gueux de Province*, in which he described the miseries of provincial school ushers. "This page, glowing with reminiscences of his personal experience and written with great emotion," says an anonymous writer in Larousse, "placed Daudet in full communication with the public."

In 1862, Daudet's third volume was issued by the house of Michel Lévy Frères. It contained, under the general title of *The Romance of Red Riding Hood, Scenes and Fancies*, six sketches: *The Romance of Red-Riding-Hood, The Souls of Paradise, The Trumpet and the Trumpeter, The Eight Mrs. Bluebeards, An Examination for Charenton, The Nightingales of the Cemetery*. In some subsequent editions, the *Adventures of a Butterfly and a Beetle*[1] was included with these sketches.

"What other than that incorrigible poet Little What's-His-Name would be capable of writing stories so chimerical, so intangible as *The Adventures of a Butterfly*, etc., *The Romance of Red-Riding-Hood*, and *The Souls of Paradise?*" asks M. Jules Lemaître; and, after a very brief *résumé* of the last-named sketch, he continues:

"There you have a mystery which smells a little of heresy; for the Church teaches not only that the elect will forget the damned, but that the

---

[1] From *Little What's-His-Name*, Part 2, Chap. VIII.

damned will abhor the elect (I do not commend this as an amiable dogma). But there is in this heterodox fantasy, so compromising to St. Peter, an altogether appetizing mixture of ingenuousness, grace and passion." [1]

It was in the office of the President of the Corps Législatif that Daudet met M. Ernest l'Épine, who " managed M. de Morny's office," and in collaboration with whom he wrote the next of his published works, in a hitherto untried field. In 1862 Michel Lévy Frères issued the " *Last Idol*, drama in one act, in prose, by MM. E. l'Épine and A. Daudet." The play, was first performed at the Odéon February 4, 1862, and the occasion is described by M. Ernest Daudet.[2] Alphonse had been compelled to leave Paris because of the condition of his health, and had passed the winter in Algiers, where, as he tells us in this volume,[3] he received the news of the first performance and was so stirred thereby that he forgot health and prudence in his longing to see Paris once more. While the play was not an absolute failure, it achieved no marked success; a *succès de douces larmes* is the most emphatic expression I have seen applied to it, and the *douces larmes* of the masqueraders on their way to Bullier seem to have impressed the author most vividly at the performance he witnessed on the night of his arrival in Paris: Mardi Gras, 1862.

---

[1] *Les Contemporains, Études et Portraits Littéraires*, 2d Series.
[2] *My Brother and I*, Chap. XVIII.
[3] Chapter entitled " My First Play."

In 1863 *The Absent* made its appearance from the press of Dupray de la Mahérie. This thin volume of 43 pages is very rare, and is highly valued by collectors. A copy presented by the author is inscribed:

"This is the copy of Paul Arène, my little Abbé Galiani.
"ALPHONSE DAUDET."

In 1865 *The Absent*, which in its original form was called a *proverb*, was published by Lévy as a comic opera in one act, words by M. Alphonse Daudet, music by M. Ferdinand Poise. There are divers variations between the two, and the *dénouement* is not the same.

The opera was first performed at the Opéra-Comique, October 26, 1864.

The second of the plays written by Daudet and l'Épine in collaboration was published by Lévy in 1865, under the title of *The White Carnation*, comedy in one act, in prose. The play had originally been called the *Lily*, but both the title and the *dénouement* — an émigré shot by a platoon of soldiers and shouting " *Vive le Roi!*" the while — failed to please the censorship of the Empire, so that the *Lily*, momentarily a *White Dahlia*, finally became the *White Carnation*, and as such was performed at the Comédie-Française, April 8, 1865.

The Elder Brother, the last of the joint productions of Daudet and l'Épine, was published by Lévy in 1868. The play, a "drama in one act" had been produced at the Vaudeville, December 19, 1867, but obtained only a *succès d'estime.*

The same year (1868) was marked by the publication in book form of the first of those masterpieces upon which Daudet's fame rests secure. *Little What's-His-Name,*[1] *the Story of a Child* had appeared in serial form in the *Petit Moniteur Universel,* beginning with the number of the 27th November, 1866. The volume was published by Hetzel.

In 1881 MM. Dentu and Charpentier undertook an octavo edition of the " Complete Works " of Daudet, with illustrations, the publication continuing slowly until 1887, when the eighth, which proved to be the last, volume was issued. Each work was preceded by its history, written by the author especially for this edition. The first volume, *Fromont and Risler,* was published in 1881; *Jack, Jack* (conclusion) and *Robert Helmont* in one volume, and *Little What's-His-Name* in 1882; *Tartarin de Tarascon* and *Letters from My Mill* in one volume, in 1884; *Kings in Exile* in 1885, *The Nabob* in 1886, and *Numa Roumestan* in 1887. The " histories " written for this edition are to be found in the present volume and its companion, with two exceptions, namely that of the *Nabob,* and that of *Robert Helmont,* which latter has become a preface and occupies its appropriate place as such.

It is impossible to exaggerate the charm of these histories, which are absolutely unique and by the

[1] *Le Petit Chose.*

aid of which we seem actually to see the author at
work. I venture to suggest that it is the very
noticeable presence of that distinguishing quality
of all Daudet's work which has been well called
the " personal note,"[1] which makes these papers,
all things considered, the most entertaining and
absorbing of the contents of this volume, which
has itself been declared by some critics to be the
most entertaining of all Daudet's works.

Little What's-His-Name, we are told, is "an
echo of my childhood and my youth." A purely
bibliographical introduction is not perhaps a proper
place to make or to answer criticisms of the quality
of Daudet's work, but I cannot forbear a protest
against the criticism that the autobiographical
element in *Little What's-His-Name* is a blemish,
" because the real incidents of the author's life are
presented too much as they actually occurred."[2]
Who could say, without the assistance furnished by
Daudet himself and his brother, what incidents are
told as they actually occurred? And does the information given by them go beyond this: that the
first part of the *History of a Child* is, *in its general
outline*, and only therein, the history of a particular
child named Alphonse Daudet, even as the *Personal History and Experience of David Copperfield
the Younger* was " an echo of the childhood and
youth" of Charles Dickens?[3]

[1] Henry James in *Partial Portraits*, p. 210.
[2] Adolphe Cohn in the *Bookman*.
[3] On this point Daudet's own testimony cannot fail to be interesting, if not conclusive. On Monday, September 25, 1886,

The original edition of *Little What's-His-Name*, without an indication of the impression (of which there were some seven or eight), is very rare. " M. Daudet gave some complimentary copies to his friends. One was inscribed : 'To my friend Cladet, *alias* Popis, *alias* La Bataille.'　When this copy was offered for sale, some ten years ago, there was a rumor that it had been stolen.　On another copy we read : ' Copy belonging to my friend Duchesne, who did not steal it.'　Strangely enough — but it is a fact — these two copies are to-day in the same hands; the collector who owns them paid an average of 25 francs each." [1]

This first extended work of M. Daudet was re-printed by Hetzel in 1878, in the form of a special edition for children, with numerous illustrations. It also formed volume two of the *Works of Alphonse Daudet*, which Lemerre began to publish as an

Edmond de Goncourt writes in his Journal : " To-day in our daily ante-breakfast chat, Daudet deplored the fact that he wrote *Le Petit Chose* when he was too young. He told me all that he would put in it to-day, and added : ' I was unfortunate enough to meet some one to whom I read the beginning of my book, and who told me that it was childish. That impelled me to stuff it with imaginary details, and adventures, and prevented me from putting into it the whole of my real childhood in the Lyonnais.'"

[1] M. Jules Brivois, *Essai de Bibliographie des Œuvres de M. Alphonse Daudet, avec Fragments Inédits.* In the Preface to this little book, which is invaluable to all those who are interested in its subject, M. Brivois says: " I have tried to supplement, by a work of pure bibliography, the works of M. Alphonse Daudet — *Thirty Years in Paris* and *Memories of a Man of Letters*, published in 1888 — bringing my investigations down to the present day." Unluckily the present day was December, 1894.

édition définitive in 1879, two years before the appearance of the first volume of the Dentu-Charpentier edition referred to above. This Lemerre edition was much more complete than the Charpentier edition; it extended to eighteen volumes, the last of which [1] appeared in 1891.

Little What's-His-Name was followed in 1869 by *Letters from My Mill; Impressions and Memories*, whose " history," as it appeared in the Charpentier edition, will be found in this volume.

The original edition contained nineteen letters or tales. Subsequent reprints — Volume I. of the Lemerre edition (1879), Volume V. of the Dentu-Charpentier edition (1884), and a later duodecimo edition (Charpentier, 1887), contain, in addition, five tales originally published with *Robert Helmont*, in the series entitled *Études et Paysages*, namely *The Stars, The Oranges, The Locusts, Custom-House People* and *In Camargue*, and one, *The Three Low Masses*, which had first appeared in the second edition of *Monday Tales* (Charpentier, 1876).[2]

The *Letters from My Mill* were dedicated to Mme. Daudet (Mlle. Julie Allard), to whom the author had been married two years before.[3]

---

[1] *Thirty Years in Paris*, including much of the first edition of *Memories of a Man of Letters*.

[2] The *Three Low Masses* was afterward published with *La Belle Nivernaise* (1886); in this edition it is restored to the *Monday Tales*.

[3] " They (the *Letters from My Mill*) had to my mind an extraordinary charm," says Mr. Henry James; " they put me quite on the side of Alphonse Daudet, whatever he might do in the future.'

In this same year (1869) *The Sacrifice* was performed at the Vaudeville. With the exception of the unimportant comic opera, the *Absent* (1863), it was Daudet's first essay as a dramatist without the collaboration of l'Épine, and it was also the first play in which he had ventured beyond one act. It was published in the *Nouvelle Bibliothèque Dramatique* in 1869.

The second volume of "letters," so-called, *Lettres à un Absent*, was published in 1871 by Lemerre. It contained twenty-one sketches of which five now appear in *Memories of a Man of Letters*, namely, *The Francs-Tireurs, Les Évadés de Paris (An Escape), The Garden on Rue des Rosiers, The Summer Palace* and *The Shipwreck*. Of the remaining sixteen, seven — *The Surrender, The Dictators, A Mushroom Bed of Great Men, Rochefort and Rossignol, The Sentry-Box, The Knitters* and *A Year of Trouble* have never been reprinted in French, while the other nine were included in the second edition of the *Monday Tales;* and this, the author's latest arrangement, has been adhered to in this edition, only the seven sketches named above as having never been reprinted being included under the original title, and appended to *Letters from My Mill.*

The majority of the *Lettres à un Absent* had appeared in *Le Soir*, in February, March, April and May, 1871. *A Year of Trouble*, which was written by Mme. Daudet, may be found in the number of that journal for Sept. 23, 1871, with the sub-title : "Notes of a Parisienne."

The Defence of Tarascon, which is one of the most famous of all Daudet's shorter pieces, was reprinted on Japan paper by Lahure, in 1886, in a " *délicieuse plaquette*," of about fifty pages, illustrated by sixteen drawings engraved by the Gillot process and colored. Very few copies were printed and the book was never regularly offered for sale.

The Prodigious Adventures of Tartarin of Tarascon, after the diversified experience related by the author in his " history " of that work, were given to the world in 1872, in a volume bearing the imprint of Dentu. As we are told by M. Ernest Daudet, the materials for the Algerian portions of the story were gathered at the time of the trip to Algiers in 1861–62, which was brought so suddenly to a close by the news of the successful performance of *The Last Idol*. The author tells us that the book was not written until 1869, but in 1863 or thereabout *Figaro* published *Chapatin the Lion-Killer*, which was nothing less than *Tartarin* in embryo.

During the year 1872 Daudet made two more ventures into the dramatic field, resulting in the production of two plays, one of which is by common consent the worst, and the other in some respects the best of all his efforts in that line. *Lise Tavernier*, a drama in five acts and seven tableaux, was played at the Ambigu-Comique on January 29, 1872, and was published by Dentu. It can hardly be said to have obtained even what is somewhat vaguely called a *succès d'estime*, and was not deemed worthy a place in the single volume of plays included in the Lemerre collected edition.[1]

L'Arlésienne (*Woman of Arles*), a play in three acts and five tableaux, with symphonies and choruses by G. Bizet, was first performed at the Vaudeville, October 1, 1872, and was published by Lemerre. In his history of *Fromont and Risler*, Daudet has described the part played by the *Arlésienne* in determining the destiny of the more famous work; how, as he sat listening to a rehearsal, he reflected that the Parisians would soon weary of hearing him chatter about grasshoppers, the maids of Arles, the mistral, and his mill, and that it was time to arouse their interest by a work that would come nearer to them and their every-day life; how he then and there determined to place his next drama amid the laborious activity of that business quarter, the Marais; and how the resplendent failure of the little play, despite the " prettiest music in the world," led to his determination to write no more dramas and to transform *Fromont*, which was already mapped out in his brain, into a novel. *L'Arlésienne* did, in truth, " score a failure," and received only three performances at that time; but Daudet's generous appreciation of the music was not fully shared by the public, and Bizet was partly responsible with Daudet for the fate of the play. The judgment of

---

[1] See *My Brother and I*, p. 444.

1872 has been reviewed, however, in later years, and somewhat modified, and M. Ernest Daudet's estimate of the work seems to have been justified in the lapse of time. It was reproduced with more satisfactory results at the Odéon, May 5, 1885, which fact is recorded in a second edition of the play.[1] "We may safely predict," says a recent writer, "that great renown awaits the shade of Alphonse Daudet by reason of the *Arlésienne*."[2] The play is little more than an elaboration of the tale with the same name included among the *Letters from my Mill*.

In 1873, Dentu issued, under the general title of *Monday Tales* (*Contes du Lundi*), a volume containing a collection of thirty-one short sketches, most of which had previously appeared in one or another newspaper. Some of these are among the most familiar of all Daudet's works, and two, *The Last Class* and *The Siege of Berlin*,[3] have figured for several years in the list of books required to be read in preparation for admission to Harvard College.

Monday Tales. New Edition revised and considerably augmented. So reads the title-page of a

---

[1] "My copy," says M. Brivois, "bears the following autograph address: 'To Madame la Comtesse de Chambrun the touching and refined interpreter of Rose Mamaï. Her respectful and grateful *Alph. Daudet.*'"

[2] Gustave Geffroy, *Le Théâtre d'Alphonse Daudet*, in *La Revue Encyclopédique*, January 15, 1898.

[3] *The Siege of Berlin* first appeared in *Lettres à un Absent* (*supra*), to which collection it has been restored in this edition.

volume issued by Charpentier in 1876. It contains all the thirty-one tales included in the earlier edition, nine others taken from the *Lettres à un Absent*, and two previously *unpublished* pieces: *The Three Low Masses* and *The Harvest by the Seashore*, both of which are included in the *Monday Tales* by the present publishers. This edition was preceded by an advertisement by the publisher, stating in effect that, as the author did not propose to republish the volume entitled *Lettres à un Absent*, he had borrowed therefrom a few reminiscences of a purely anecdotal character.

Beginning in May 1873, F. Polo published a series of fifteen *livraisons* under the general title of *Contes et Récits*, containing in all thirty articles, of which only two, *Le Bon Dieu de Chemillé* and the *New Master* had not been previously published. The other twenty-eight were all taken from *Lettres à un Absent* and *Contes du Lundi*. *Le Bon Dieu de Chemillé* was reprinted with the first edition of *Robert Helmont* (1874) as one of the *Études et Paysages*, printed in this edition in the volume with *Port Tarascon*. *The New Master* was reprinted with *La Belle Nivernaise* in 1886.

An interesting detail is given by Brivois: in the first impression of the sixth *livraison*, at page 93, there is an engraving after a drawing by Gill, representing Bazaine playing billiards. In subsequent copies, in which this engraving is missing, we read in the middle of the page: "Illustration prohibited by the censorship." At this time Bazaine was at Île Sainte-Marguerite under sentence of twenty years' imprisonment for treason.   He escaped in the following year.[1]

Artists' Wives, a collection of twelve studies of marital infelicity from various points of view, was the next volume from Daudet's pen to be offered to the public.   It was published by Lemerre in 1874, and, so far as I have been able to learn, none of the twelve had previously appeared, even in newspapers.   The original edition was entitled *First Series*, but no other series has ever been published.

In the same year appeared *Robert Helmont*, with the exception of *Little What's-His-Name* and *Tartarin of Tarascon*, the longest single work thus far put forth by Daudet.   In the same covers were numerous tales, studies, etc., collected under the general title of *Études et Paysages*. The volume was published by Dentu; in 1888 the same publisher issued a new edition (octavo) of *Robert Helmont* alone, with many illustrations; and in 1891 a reduced copy (12mo) of the same, with the same illustrations.   With its former companions (*Études et Paysages*), — except those that had already been reprinted in *Letters from My Mill* (Volume I.), — and with *Artists' Wives*, it forms Volume VII. of the Lemerre collected edition; and, with the second part of *Jack*, Volume III. of the Dentu-Charpentier edition (1882) of the "Complete Works."   In this last-named volume it

---

[1] See *The Lesson in History* (*infra*), p. 359.

is preceded by its " history," written for this edition, which appears, in the shape of a *Preface* in the later editions and in the present edition in English.

Robert Helmont originally appeared in the *Musée Universel.* Of the *Études et Paysages*, none except *Le Bon Dieu de Chemillé*, had ever before been published, save in newspapers, and none, save those which were added to the *Letters from My Mill*, have ever been reprinted, except in the Lemerre collected edition, and in one or more of the collections entitled *Contes Choisis*, to which more extended reference will be made in the introduction to *Memories of a Man of Letters.* Among them were several, for example the *Death of the Duc de M——*, and *A Nabob*, which were afterward elaborated in the novels.

With the publication of the *Études et Paysages*, Daudet abandoned for many years, substantially forever, the style of composition which had given him even then, when he was but little past thirty, an enviable fame. *Tartarin*, though in form a continued story, is in reality but a succession of sketches in which, as his custom was, he describes, albeit with transparent exaggeration and with a more rollicking humor than usual, what he, the most ardent and loyal of Southerners,[1] had himself

---

[1] "'My Provence!' he said to me one day; 'people ask me if I love her, if I regret her! Why, I am dying of love and longing for her!'"

M. Auguste Marin in the *Revue Encyclopédique* of January 15, 1898.

seen and observed of one aspect of the Southern character.

Enough has been said of the confusing transfer of these shorter pieces from one collection to another to show how difficult a task it is to prepare an absolutely complete edition of them all. Although Daudet had not Balzac's extraordinary craze for revising and remodelling and transferring whole chapters and episodes from one novel to another, the sudden transformation of an *Étude* or *Paysage* into a *Letter from My Mill*, or of a *Lettre à un Absent* into a *Monday Tale* inevitably reminds one of the way in which, as the *Human Comedy* increased in bulk and scope, the different *Scenes* were transferred from one category to another, from *Parisian Life* to *Private Life* or to the *Études Philosophiques*. The collector who should attempt to secure all of Daudet's miscellaneous works in French, without duplicates, would be as badly off as one who had undertaken to collect a similar set of the writings of Rudyard Kipling. The list of publishers with whom Daudet had been associated in these first fifteen years of his literary career reaches the somewhat extraordinary number of nine or ten.

On the 25th of March, 1874, the newspaper called *Le Bien Public* began the publication of *Fromont and Risler*, and later in the year, when this publication was concluded, a *special impression* of the novel, printed in double columns, was made from the original type made up into pages, and issued from the office of that newspaper.

Such was the first appearance of the work with which Alphonse Daudet definitively won his great popularity, which endured without perceptible diminution to the day of his death, twenty-three years later, whatever the worshippers of the Academy may have dreamed for a moment, after the publication of *The Immortal* in 1888.

Close on the heels of this *special impression*, and in the same year, Charpentier[1] issued what we must call the original edition of *Fromont and Risler*. It was published at the sacramental price of 3 fr. 50, to be read on the back of all the familiar yellow-covered volumes of the " Bibliothèque Charpentier," and was worth in 1894 something like ten times that amount, according to M. Brivois, who records some interesting details concerning two copies. — " M. Paul de Boissy . . . once owned a copy at the head of which was the following interesting autograph : ' This copy of the first edition of *Fromont*, which I happened upon by chance, moves me deeply as I turn the leaves. My first great success — when I had my health, all my dear ones still living — ah ! how light-hearted I was and how proud to be alive, when this copy came from the printer !

" ' ALPHONSE DAUDET, 1890.'

" At the sale after the death of Adolphe Belot (April 1891), a copy of the fifteenth edition (dated 1876) was offered, bearing on the fly-leaf

---

[1] It is worth noting that this is the first appearance of this house as Daudet's publishers.

the following curious imprecation in the author's
hand:

> "' A MON (*sic*) ADOLPHE BELOT.
>
> "' *Vers pour être chantés.*
>
> "' Adolphe contempteur des Dieux,
> Tu mourras foudroyé par leur main vengeresse;
> Ils paieront d'un trépas odieux
> Ta violence et ta paresse.
>
> "' Mais Priape, Dieu des jardins,
> Touché par le constant homage de ton culte,
> Par ton amour des fleurs et des livres badins,
> Priera pour toi ces Dieux que ton cynisme insulte.
>
> "' *Musique de* LULLI ; paroles d' ALPHONSE DAUDET.' "[1]

Fromont was dedicated to " the two poets, Jules
and Léonide Allard. In testimony of my filial
respect." The two poets were Mme. Daudet's
father and mother, the latter of whom was, during
the novelist's later years, a cherished member of
his family.

---

[1] "To MY (*sic*) ADOLPHE BELOT.

> " *Lines to be sung.*
>
> " Adolphe, thou scorner of the Gods,
> Struck down by their avenging hand, thou 'lt die;
> They 'll pay thee with a death detestable,
> For all thy violence and indolence.
>
> " But Priapus, the god of gardens fair,
> Touched by the constant homage of thy adoration,
> And by thy love of flowers and sportive books,
> Will pray forgiveness for thee from these Gods
> Whom thou dost with thy cynic ways insult.
>
> " Music by LULLI ; words by ALPHONSE DAUDET."

A reprint of this original edition, issued in 1876 (the "fifteenth edition" mentioned in the foregoing quotation), bore the inscription: "*Ouvrage Couronné par l'Académie Française*," an honor accorded to none of the author's subsequent books.

In the Lemerre collected edition, heretofore mentioned many times, *Fromont and Risler* forms Volume IV. (1884), and in the Dentu-Charpentier edition, preceded by "the history of this book," Volume I. (1881).

Jack, the second in order of publication of the series of novels properly so called, and the longest of all M. Daudet's works, began to appear in the *Moniteur Universel*, in June (15th), 1875, although, as the author himself tells us, he had not then completed the story and did not complete it until late in October. It had taken him nearly a year, and yet it was the "most quickly written" of all his books.

Jack was issued in two volumes by Dentu in 1876. It filled two volumes (5 and 6) of the Lemerre collected edition (1885) and Volumes II. and III. (with *Robert Helmont*) of the Dentu-Charpentier edition of the "Complete Works" (1882), wherein it was preceded by its "history," written especially for this edition.

I suspend at this point the chronological sketch of Daudet's works, to take it up anew, with the publication of the *Nabob*, in the introduction to

the *Memories of a Man of Letters*.   A word or
two may be said, however, concerning the various
papers contained in *Thirty Years in Paris*, and
concerning the later sketches printed therewith in
this volume.

As to the former, they were written at divers
times, most of them probably, always excepting
the " histories of my books," before 1881 ; and the
greater number, if not all, had been published
prior to the first appearance of this volume, in
1888.   Writing in 1881, M. Ernest Daudet says :
" He (Alphonse) has spoken in the pages of his
memoirs which have already been published of
the first weeks of his sojourn in Paris, with a penetrating melancholy."   And he proceeds to quote
that passage of the first chapter which begins with
the words : " With the exception of my brother, I
knew no one." [1]

The article on Villemessant, we are told in a
note, was written in 1879; an episode taken from
Little-What's-His-Name, entitled *The First Coat*,
was published in the volume with *La Belle Nivernaise* (Marpon and Flammarion) in 1886.

The histories of *Little-What's-His-Name* and
the other books were written, as we have seen,
especially for the Dentu-Charpentier edition of
Daudet's " Complete Works," begun in 1881.

The article on the *Literary Salons* first appeared
in the *Novoë Vremya* of St. Petersburg in 1879;
Daudet's introduction to Mmes. Ancelot, Wal-

---

[1] *Infra*, p. 7 ; *My Brother and I*, p. 408.

dor, and Chodsko belongs to the very early years of his residence in Paris, when he was known solely as the author of *Les Amoureuses.*[1]

In the history of *Numa Roumestan*[2] we are told that some features of the character of Valmajour in that novel are authentic, — for example, the little phrase: "It came to me, at night," etc., "taken down word for word, from his ingenuous lip," and that the original of the character was "that Draguignanais whom my dear and great Mistral sent to me one day with these words: 'I send Buisson, *tambourinaire*, to you; pilot him.'" "But," says Daudet, "the real truth, which I could not tell in his lifetime for fear of injuring him, I may tell now that death has burst his drum, *pécaïre!* and stuffed with black earth the three holes of his flute. Buisson was only a bogus *tambourinaire*, a petty bourgeois from the south, a town clarinetist or bugler," etc. — An episode of *Numa Roumestan*, under the title of *My Drummer*, was published in the third collection of *Contes Choisis*, in 1884, but the story of Buisson seems never to have appeared, unless in some newspaper, until the publication of *Thirty Years in Paris.*

In connection with the history of the *Letters from my Mill*, where he tells of his visits to his friends the *Félibres* and of their journeyings together, it may be said that in 1868 Daudet's name appears as the translator (from Provençal into

---

[1] See *My Brother and I, p.* 412.
[2] *Memories of a Man of Letters.*

French) of Roumanille's *Lou Mège de Cucugnan,*[1] published by the *Librairie Internationale;* and that he himself occasionally ventured to write in the mellifluous *langue d'oc* is evidenced by the " epigraph" prefixed to *Arlatan's Treasure*, printed in this volume.

A most interesting account of some of the escapades in which Daudet took part with the brotherhood of Provençal poets, as given by Mistral in *Armana prouvençau*, a " popular almanac," is reproduced by M. Auguste Marin in an article entitled *La Jeunesse de Daudet*, in the *Revue Encyclopédique* of January 15, 1898.   Only a short time before his death, he says, Daudet sat one day at 'his desk, turning the leaves of a copy of the almanac, fresh from Provence and exhaling an odor of seaweed.

" Whenever his eye caught a forgotten word, a picturesque phrase, in the little pamphlet composed by *trouvères*, who transform themselves into writers once a year without laying aside the hammer or the plough, he uttered a joyful exclamation; all his youthful memories throbbed at his temples; he found anew the accent of the soil with which to speak of Mistral, Roumanille and Aubanel. . . .

" Mistral relates that the author of *Les Prunes* (Daudet had then published nothing save a volume of poems, *Les Amoureuses*) was secretary to the Duc de Morny, a sort of ' honorary secretary'

---

[1] *The Physician of Cucugnan.*

evidently, for he went but once a month to see if his master, who presided over the Senate, was in good health and humor. Daudet was a comely youth, dark but with little color, with a silky beard just sprouting, and rampant hair. It was this too independent hair which disturbed the duke: 'Well, poet,' he would say, 'how about that underbrush, when are we going to have it cut?'

"'*Next week*,' the poet would reply.

"But when the next week came the hair was more bushy than ever; it overgrew the forehead and the cheeks; it became a wild tangle; and the duke fell instead of the hair. But this independent attitude was not assumed by Daudet with his haughty superior alone. He was fond of playing *casse-cou;* he plunged headlong, says Mistral, into everything that savored of life, light, noise and merriment.

"One evening, when they were supping together at the *Chêne-Vert*, a cabaret in the outskirts of Avignon, Daudet discovered that there was dancing at a neighboring house, at the foot of the terrace where the two friends sat at table. He gave one leap, from a height of three metres, through the trellis-work which concealed the dancers, and dropped, like the devil, into the midst of the ball. Another time, while crossing the bridge over the Bartelasse, he began to run along the parapet, at the risk of falling into the stream, and to horrify some worthy bourgeois who stopped to look, he cried: 'Tonnerre! it was from here that we threw

Brune's dead body into the river! yes, Maréchal
Brune's! and let this serve as an example to the
Frenchmen and Allobrogi who would harass us
anew!'

"But the anecdote in which the future author of
the *Letters from My Mill* is most fully revealed, is
that of a walk through Arles, and a dinner at
'Trenquetaille,' — a revel!   They (Mistral and
Daudet, with Anselme Mathieu and the painter
Grivolas) had taken it into their heads to have a
feast *à la Provençale*, and they went about in
search of a signless inn, through the narrow streets
of Arles, where the old houses are whitewashed to
the first floor and are always clean and fresh;
where the ' Arlesian queens ' smile at the passers-
by from behind the light curtains at their doors.
When they reached La Poissonnerie, toward nightfall, they asked an old woman, who was knitting
stockings, if she knew of a little inn in the neighborhood where one could dine cleanly and *à la
bonne apostolique*.   The gossip, scenting a *galéjade*,
called the neighbors, who showed their shrewd
faces crowned with the white *cravate au chignon*.
And each one commended the comely wayfarers
to some inn whose name showed that they were
laughing at them.   But a stout man, who sat on a
stone smoking his pipe, saw by the piteous manner
of the four comrades that they were not making
sport of the fishwives, and he offered to take them
to the cabaret on the other side of the Rhone, at
which the boatmen generally stopped.

"'I own my own boat,' he said, 'and I have followed the sea many years.'

"'Have you made long voyages?' said Daudet, as they followed the worthy man.

"'Oh! I have sailed mostly on small coasting craft; but if the Holy Marys had n't always had an eye on us, many's the time we should have gone to the bottom, shipmates! I am Captain Gafet, at your service, when you want to go down the river.'

"They crossed the Rhone to the inn of Trenquetaille, where fifteen or twenty boatmen were already seated in front of a roast kid. The hostess, dismayed at the sight of such well-dressed guests, put some eels on the fire none the less, and, to whet their appetite, placed on the table some fine Bellegarde onions, a dish of peppers in vinegar, goat's-milk cheese wrapped in a walnut leaf, salted mullet roes and some bits of delicious codfish broiled over the embers.

"Daudet, who had never in his life been present at a Camarguese debauch, bravely attacked a great red onion, ate it with cheese and codfish, and consumed it; and as his companions were not to be outdone, Captain Gafet was kept busy filling the glasses, remarking that onions made one drink and kept the thirst alive.

"Meanwhile the boatmen, having made an end of their kid, were finishing their meal, according to the custom of Rhone watermen, with a plate of greasy soup. Having poured in a glass of wine, each man held his plate in both hands and drank the mixture so. Then they began to sing. Daudet must needs do his part, a lively ballad, as old and light as the good wine. But the hostess was terribly afraid that she would be reported to the police for permitting such an uproar at night.

"'The police, the guard,' cried Daudet, 'oh! they have no terrors for us. Go and fetch the register in which you write the names of those who lodge in your inn; you'll see who we are!'

"And the wine-inspired singer, whose rustic tastes were so in evidence, wrote on the blank page: 'Alphonse Daudet, secretary to the President of the Senate; Mistral, Chevalier of the Legion of Honor; Anselme Mathieu, *Félibre* of Châteauneuf-du-Pape; Grivolas, master-painter of the School of Avignon.'

"'Now,' said he with dignity to the old woman, 'if any one undertakes to make trouble for you, whether he be commissioner, gendarme, or sub-prefect, you need only put these fly-tracks under his nose. And if he molests you, just write to Paris. *Baste!* I will undertake to make him dance!'

"'We took our leave,' Mistral adds, 'accompanied by public veneration, like princes who have just made themselves known. But on Trenquetaille bridge, which was then a bridge of boats, —

"'"Suppose we dance a farandole," says Daudet. "That's the only proper way to cross a bridge in Provence."

" ' Suddenly — we were half way across the Rhone — just before us, in the half-light, appears a procession of sweet damsels of Arles, each with her mate, walking slowly along, chattering and laughing. The rustling of the silk dresses, the amorous cooing of the pairs, in the placid evening air impregnated with the warm breath of the Rhone, all were caressing to the senses.

" ' " A wedding-party," said the captain, who had not left us.

" ' " A wedding-party?" echoed Daudet. With his imperfect sight he did not know the source of all this noise. "An Arlesian wedding! A wedding by moonlight! A wedding on the Rhone!"

" ' And like a madman, our *Levantine* darted forward, threw his arms around the bride's neck, and, if you please, such kisses!

" ' Ah! my friends in the Lord! Twenty resolute young blades surrounded us, pressed us close, brandishing their fists and shouting:

" ' " Into the Rhone!"

" ' But Captain Gafet rushed into the mêlée. " *Qu'es aco ?* " he said, most opportunely. " Don't you see that they 've been drinking at Trenquetaille, to the health of the married pair, and that it would be bad for them to drink any more?"

" ' " *Vivent les mariés!* " they shouted, one and all, with great good-will. Thanks, to the brawn and presence of mind of honest Gafet, whom all the young men knew, we were allowed to cross the bridge.'

"He was a true, a pure Provençal, and Mistral writes in his graceful way: 'The lioness will never bear a grudge because her cub scratches her a little, in play.'

"Alphonse Daudet knew," adds M. Marin, "that only the Tartarins, the Roumestans and the Aunt Portals harbored malice against him in a country where 'everybody is a little Tarasconian.'"

As we have already seen, the play referred to in the title of the next of these papers is *The Last Idol*, written in collaboration with M. l'Épine and performed for the first time in the spring of 1862, in the absence of the author, but in the presence of M. le Duc de Morny, in whose department of the government both of the authors were employed. This paper had never been published in book form until the appearance of *Thirty Years in Paris;* the charming reminiscence of his Algerian wanderings, interrupted in the valley of the Chelif by the arrival of the Spahi with the telegraphic message for "Sidi Daoudi," which had been following him from camp to camp all the way from Milianah, is well worthy a place among the *Études et Paysages.*

Dealing as it does with a man still conspicuously prominent in contemporary French politics, the article on Henri Rochefort has a more intense *present* interest than most of Daudet's work. It was no longer ago than the election of M. Loubet to the presidency of the Republic that the founder of *La Lanterne* forced himself upon public attention as he has never failed to do on any occasion of more than ordinary interest for many years past. The paper was written for the same St. Petersburg journal in which the *Literary Salons* first appeared; it was published also in *Le Voltaire* of May 23, 1879.

The brief portrait of Henri Monnier, who is hardly known outside of France except as the creator of Joseph Prudhomme, was first published in *Thirty Years in Paris.* The same is true of the article on Desroches — *The End of a Buffoon*, etc. — a wonderfully lifelike description of the life which he saw at such close quarters during his early years in Paris, and which Henri Mürger, writing with an even more intimate acquaintance of his subject, pictured so vividly to an earlier generation in his *Scènes de la Vie de Bohème.*

The pretty little retreat under the willow-tree on the river by the *Île des Moineaux*, where Daudet first met Léon Pillaut, will be found described in *The Little Parish Church;* it was Lydie's "bathroom," one of the spots haunted by Richard after her flight with the prince; but the sketch as it appears in this volume had never before been printed.

It has always seemed to me that the "history" of *Fromont and Risler* is the most absorbingly interesting of all Daudet's narratives of the genesis of his various books; perhaps because it is the first of them that he wrote, and for that reason contains more general information as to his method of work, and because the particular book to which it relates was his first venture in the direction of novel-writing; perhaps, too, because it contains that affectionate tribute to his wife which he epitomized in the dedication to the *Nabob.* He had been married in 1867, and his thirty years of married life were never clouded by a suggestion of infelicity of any of the varieties so powerfully described by him in *Artists' Wives.* — "Not a page which she has not revised and retouched, on which she has not cast a little of her lovely gold and azure dust," says Daudet, speaking of her share in his work.[1]

In the *Journal des Goncourt* there are one or two sympathetic references to Mme. Daudet. "1874, Friday, 5 June. Yesterday Alphonse Daudet came with his wife to lunch with me. A partnership which resembles that between my brother and myself. The wife writes, and I have reason to suspect that she is an artist in style."

"1885. Sunday, 25 January. — To-day Daudet and his wife came to see me. . . .

"Daudet talked of the first years after his marriage, told me that his wife did not know that there was such a place as the *mont-de-piété,* and that, when she found it out, a sort of modesty prevented her from mentioning it and she never taunted him with a: 'You have been there!' —

---

[1] See, too, *My Brother and I*, pp. 447-448.

The pleasantest part of the story is that this young woman, brought up in bourgeois fashion, never betrayed the slightest fright in her new existence, in the society of that circle of eaters of dinners, squanderers of five-franc pieces and borrowers of pantaloons.

"'Why, upon my word,' cried Daudet, 'the dear woman spent nothing, nothing at all, on herself. We still have our little account-books of those days, where, among louis taken by me or somebody else, there is an occasional entry, here and there, of *omnibus* 30 *centimes*, for her.' — Mme. Daudet ingenuously interrupted him, saying: 'I really think that I was not fully developed in those days; I did not understand.'"

The *portrait intime* of Turgénieff was, as the footnote tells us, written in 1880 for the *Century Magazine*. In his volume entitled *Partial Portraits*, Mr. Henry James draws a no less sympathetic portrait of the Russian novelist's private character, and emphasizes even more strongly the attractive traits described by Daudet. The concluding paragraph, beginning: "As I correct the proofs of this article, — " was first published in the *Temps* of November 10, 1883, the year of Turgénieff's death. It inadvertently conveys the impression that the *Souvenirs* to which it refers were written *by* his friend, whereas they were souvenirs *of* Turgénieff written by his secretary, one Pavlovsky, — a series of alleged private conversations between himself and his employer. As the pretended strictures upon Daudet were, to say the least, of doubtful authenticity, — for their publication was, at the best, such a shameless breach of confidence that the person who perpetrated it might justifiably be suspected of exaggeration, if nothing worse — it would seem that Daudet would have been well advised to let the matter pass without notice. Perhaps he would have done so, except that the supposititious criticisms created a sensation and were made a handle upon which to hang attacks upon him. I have been assured by one who was the friend of both men that the incident was never considered to have any real importance or to throw any new light upon Turgénieff's character.[1]

GEORGE B. IVES.

[1] In the description of Edmond de Goncourt's last hours, entitled *Ultima*, printed in the volume with *Memories of a Man of Letters*, there is a further reference to this subject, indicating that Goncourt also was maltreated in the same work.

THIRTY YEARS IN PARIS.

PAGES FROM MY LIFE AND MY BOOKS.

———◆———

I.

THE ARRIVAL.

SUCH a journey! Merely thinking of it thirty years after, I can still feel my legs encased in iron fetters, and I am seized with cramps in the stomach. Two days in a third-class railway carriage, dressed in thin summer clothing, and in bitterly cold weather. I was sixteen years old; I came from a long distance, from the very heart of Languedoc, where I was usher in a school, to devote myself to literature. When my ticket was paid for, I had just forty sous left in my pocket; but why should I be alarmed? I was so rich in hopes that I forgot to be hungry; despite the seductions of the bakeshop and the sand-wiches displayed on the lunch counters at railway stations, I would not part with my silver coin, carefully stowed away in one of my pockets. Toward the end of the journey, however, when our train, groaning and tossing us from side to side, was whirling us across the melancholy plains of Champagne, I was very near being ill. My travelling companions, sailors who passed their time in singing, offered me a flask. Worthy fellows! How jolly their rough songs were — and how good their fiery eau-de-vie, to a boy who had not eaten for twice twenty-four hours!

That saved and revivified me; my fatigue inclined me to sleep. I dozed — but with periodical awakenings when the train stopped, and relapses into drowsiness when it went on again.

The noise of wheels rattling over cast-iron plates, an enormous arched roof of glass, flooded with light, doors slamming, baggage-trucks rumbling, a restless, busy crowd, custom-house officials — Paris!

My brother was waiting for me on the platform. Being a practical youth, in spite of his tender years, he was fully alive to his duties as an older brother, and had engaged a hand-cart and a porter.

"We will go and load your luggage."

It was an imposing sight, that luggage! A wretched little valise, studded with nails, with many patches, and heavier than its contents. We started for the Latin Quarter along the deserted quays, through the sleeping streets, marching behind our little cart pushed by the porter. It was barely daylight; we met nobody but workmen with faces blue with cold, and newspaper carriers who deftly slipped the morning papers under the house doors. The gas-jets were extinguished; the streets, the Seine and its bridges, all appeared

to me in a sort of twilight through the morning
mist.   Such was my entrance into Paris; clinging
to my brother, with anguish at my heart, I shud-
dered involuntarily from sheer terror; and still
we followed the little cart.

"If you 're not over-anxious to see our rooms,
let us go and have some breakfast first," said
Ernest.

"Oh! yes, let us eat."

I was literally starving to death.

Alas! the creamery, a creamery on Rue Corneille, was not open; we had to wait a long while,
walking about the neighborhood to keep ourselves
warm, and making the circuit of the Odéon, which
made a deep impression on me with its vast roof,
its portico and its temple-like aspect.

At last the shutters were thrown back; a waiter,
half-asleep, admitted us, dragging his feet heavily
along in their loose slippers, and grumbling like
stable-boys awakened at posting stations to har-
ness the fresh horses.   That breakfast at daybreak will never fade from my memory; I have
only to close my eyes to see again the little room
with its bare white walls, with its rows of pegs
driven into the rough plaster, the counter piled
with napkins arranged in circles, the marble
tables, without cloths, but shining with cleanliness; glasses, salt-cellars, and tiny little decanters
filled with a wine in which there was not the
slightest trace of grape-juice, but which I considered excellent, such as it was, were already in
place.

"*Three of coffee,*" the waiter ordered of his own motion when he saw us. As there was nobody but himself in the restaurant or kitchen at that early hour, he answered himself: "*Boum!*' and brought us "three of coffee," — that is to say three sous' worth of a delicious balsamic coffee, sweetened to a reasonable degree, which disappeared in short order, simultaneously with two little rolls served in a wicker basket.

Then we ordered an omelet; for it was still too early for a cutlet.

"An omelet for two, *boum!*" roared the waiter.

"Well cooked!" cried my brother.

I bowed with respectful admiration before the self-possession and grand manners of that sybarite of a brother of mine; and at dessert, what plans, what confidences we exchanged, as we sat eye to eye, our elbows on the table before a plate of nuts and raisins! A man becomes a better man when he has eaten. Adieu melancholy, adieu anxiety! that simple breakfast intoxicated me as thoroughly as champagne.

We went out arm-in-arm, talking very loud. It was broad daylight at last. Paris smiled upon me from all its open shops; even the Odéon assumed an affable air to greet me, and the white marble queens in the Luxembourg garden, whom I saw indistinctly through the railings, standing among the leafless trees, seemed to nod their heads gracefully to me and to bid me welcome.

My brother was rich. He performed the duties of secretary to an old gentleman who was dictating his memoirs to him, at a salary of seventy-five francs per month. We must needs live on that seventy-five francs pending the time when glory should fall to my lot, must share that little room on the fifth floor of the Hôtel du Sénat, Rue de Tournon; almost a garret, but in my eyes a superb apartment. A Parisian garret! The mere sight of the words *Hôtel du Sénat* standing forth in great letters on the sign flattered my self-esteem and dazzled me. Opposite the hotel, on the other side of the way, there is a house dating from the last century, with a pediment and two couchant figures, which always look as if they proposed to fall from the top of the wall into the street.

"That's where Ricord lives," said my brother, "the famous Ricord, the Emperor's physician."

The Hôtel du Sénat, the Emperor's physician — those high-sounding phrases tickled my vanity, fascinated me. Oh! the first impressions of Paris!

The great restaurants on Boulevard Saint-Michel, the new buildings on Boulevard Saint-Germain and Rue des Écoles had not yet driven the studious youth from the Quarter, and, despite its pompous name, our hotel on Rue de Tournon could hardly boast at that time of an atmosphere of senatorial gravity.

There was a whole colony of students there, a horde from the south of Gascony, excellent fellows, a little vainglorious, self-assured and jovial, great connoisseurs in beer-mugs and tedious lec·

tures, who filled the stairways and corridors with
their deep bass voices. They passed their time
talking on all conceivable subjects and arguing
without respite. We met them rarely, except on
Sunday, and even then only by accident, that is
to say when our purse permitted us to indulge in
the luxury of a *table d'hôte* dinner.

It was there that I first saw Gambetta. He
was already the man we have since known and
admired. Happy in being alive, happy in being
able to talk, that loquacious Roman, grafted on a
Gallic stock, made himself giddy with the clatter
of his harangues, made the window-panes tremble
with the outbursts of his thunderous eloquence,
and generally ended with a loud roar of laughter.
He held sway even then over the multitude of
his comrades. He was a personage of importance
in the Quarter, especially as he received three
hundred francs monthly from Cahors — an enormous sum for a student in those far-away times.
We became intimate afterward. But I was as
yet only a provincial, arrived overnight, with the
rough surface hardly worn off. I confined myself
to staring at him from the end of the table, with
profound admiration and without a shade of envy.

He and his friends were intensely interested
in politics; in the Latin Quarter they were
already laying siege to the Tuileries, whereas my
tastes, my ambitions turned toward conquests of
another sort. Literature was the single goal of
all my dreams. Sustained by the unlimited confidence of youth, poor but radiant with hope, I

passed that whole year in my garret, writing verses. That is a common and affecting story. Paris counts by the hundreds the poor young devils whose only fortune is a few rhymes ; but I do not believe that any one ever began his career in destitution more complete than mine.

With the exception of my brother, I knew no one. Short-sighted, awkward and shy, when I stole out of my garret I invariably made the circuit of the Odéon, I walked under its galleries, drunk with awe and with joy at the thought that I should meet men of letters there. At Mme. Gaut's shop, for instance. Mme. Gaut, who was quite old but had surprisingly sharp, bright eyes, allowed the public to look through the new books displayed on her shelves, on condition that they did not cut the leaves.

I can see her now, talking with the great novelist Barbey d'Aurevilly; she, knitting a stocking, the author of *Une Vieille Maîtresse* with his hand on his hip "à la Mérovingienne," and the collar of his wagoner's cloak, lined with fine black velvet, thrown back, so that every one may appreciate the splendor of that outwardly modest garment.

Some one approaches — it is Vallès. The future member of the Commune passed Mme. Gaut's shop almost every day, on his return from "Mère Morel's" office, where he was in the habit of going daily to work and read. Bilious, sneering, eloquent, always dressed in the same wretched frock-coat, he talked in a harsh, metallic voice, with his lowering Auvergnat face enveloped in a beard as stiff as a brush, which reached almost to his eyebrows. That voice made me nervous. He had just written *L'Argent*, a sort of pamphlet dedicated to Mirès and embellished with a five-franc piece by way of vignette; and, pending the time when he should become Mirès's partner, he had become the inseparable comrade of Gustave Planche, the old critic. The Aristarchus of the *Revue des Deux Mondes* was at that time a corpulent old man with a forbidding manner, an inflated Philoctetes, who dragged one leg and limped. One day I had the audacity to spy upon them through a window in the café on Rue Taranne, hoisting myself up to the glass, and rubbing it clean with my fingers; it was the café next to the house, now pulled down, in which Diderot lived for forty years. They were sitting on opposite sides of the table; Vallès was gesticulating earnestly, Planche absorbing a decanter of eau-de-vie, glass by glass.[1]

And Cressot! the meek, the eccentric Cressot, whom Vallès afterward immortalized in his *Réfractaires ;* it would be hard for me to forget him. I have often seen him in the Quarter, gliding along the walls, with his sad, distressed face, and his long skeleton-like body wrapped in a short cloak.

Cressot was the author of *Antonia*, a poem.

---

[1] Planche died in 1857, the same year that Daudet arrived in Paris. Jules Vallès was at one time his secretary, and after his death published a monograph, "full of affectionate memories."

What had that poor Gringoire to live upon? No one knew. One fine day a friend in the provinces left him a little property; that day Cressot ate a square meal, and died of it.

Another face of that period is engraved in my memory, that of Jules de la Madelène, one of the best *poctæ minores* of our prose literature, the too little known author of creations which excel in lines genuinely antique: the *Âmes en Peine* and the *Marquis de Saffras*. Aristocratic manners, a fair head recalling Tintoret's "Christ," refined, somewhat sickly, features, eyes overflowing with melancholy and weeping for the sunshine of Provence, his home. His story was whispered from ear to ear, — that of an enthusiast and hero of good stock. In June, 1848, he was wounded on the barricades and left for dead in the ranks of the insurgents. Picked up in the street by a bourgeois, he remained in hiding in his rescuer's house, where the family nursed him and restored him to health. When he was fully cured, he married the daughter of the house.

Nothing more is needed to kindle the ambition than to meet famous men, to have the good luck to exchange a few words with them. "I, too, will make my mark!" you say to yourself with full confidence.

With what ardor I would climb my five flights — especially when I had succeeded in effecting the purchase of a candle, which would enable me to work all night, to elaborate, by its dim light, poems, outlines of dramas, succeeding one another in an endless line on sheets of white paper. Presumption gave me wings; I seemed to see the future throw its doors wide open before me, I forgot my poverty, I forgot my privations; as, for instance, on that Christmas Eve when I dashed off rhymes in a frenzy, while the students below were holding high festival with a vast deal of noise, and Gambetta's voice, rumbling under the arches of the stairway, echoed by the walls of the corridor, made my frost-covered window rattle.

But in the street my former terrors regained the mastery. The Odéon, in particular, impressed me with dread; it seemed to me all through the year as cold, as imposing and inaccessible as on the day of my arrival. Oh, Odéon, — Mecca of my aspirations, goal of my inmost ambition, — how many times did I renew my hesitating, secret attempts to cross the august threshold of the little low door through which thy artists enter! How many times have I watched Tisserant pass through that door in all his glory, his shoulders stooping beneath his cloak, with a meek, slouching air, copied from Frédérick Lemaître! Behind him, arm-in-arm with Flaubert, and as like him as a brother, Louis Bouilhet, author of *Madame de Montarcy*, and frequently Comte d'Osmoy, to-day a deputy. Those three were then writing a fanciful play, which never saw the boards. Behind them, and following them, came a group of four or five giants, of military carriage, all Normans, all cut on the same cuirassier pattern, with light moustaches. That was the cohort of

Rouennese, Bouilhet's lieutenants, who applauded to order at first performances.

Then Amédéc Rolland, Jean Duboys, Bataille,[1] a younger trio, enterprising, bold, trying to creep in through the little door in their turn, the tail of Tisserant's enormous cloak, as it were.

All three died like Bouilhet at the very outset of their literary careers, and that is why the galleries of the Odéon, when I walk there at twilight, seem to me to be peopled with friendly shades.

Meanwhile, having completed a volume of poems, I went the rounds of the publishers; I knocked at Michel Lévy's door, at Hachette's; where did I not go? I insinuated myself into all the great publishing houses, immense as cathedrals, where my boots squeaked frightfully and made a horrible noise notwithstanding the carpets. Clerks of bureaucratic mien scrutinized me with a cold and self-sufficient air.

"I would like to see M. Lévy — about some manuscript."

"Very well, monsieur; be good enough to give me your name."

My name duly given, the clerk would, in a leisurely way, put his lips to one of the orifices of the speaking-tube; then, putting his ear to the other, —

---

[1] In the sketch entitled *At the Salpêtrière*, page 345 of this volume, Daudet speaks of Duboys and Bataille as two of his best friends, who died insane. For Duboys see also page 45. He died in 1873.

"M. Lévy is not in."

M. Lévy was never in, nor M. Hachette; no one was ever in, always by favor of that insolent speaking-tube.

There was also the Librairie Nouvelle, on Boulevard des Italiens. There, there were no speaking-tubes, no red tape, quite the contrary. Jacotet, the publisher, who was then issuing his small one-franc volumes, — an idea of his own, — was a short stout man bearing some resemblance to Balzac, but without Balzac's forehead, always on the move, overwhelmed with business and with dinner-parties, constantly revolving some colossal project in his brain, and with gold burning holes in his pockets. That eddying whirl led him to bankruptcy in two years, and he crossed the Alps and founded the newspaper *L'Italie.* But his shop served the purpose of a salon for the intellectual aristocracy of the boulevards; there one might see Noriac, who had just published his *Cent-et-Unième Régiment*; Scholl, proud of his great success, *Dénise*; Adolphe Gaiffe, and Aubryet. All these habitués of the boulevard, irreproachably dressed, discoursing of money and women, gave me a feeling of bewilderment when I saw my own person reflected with theirs in the panes of the show-window, with my hair as long as a bagpiper's and my little Provence hat. As for Jacotet, he constantly made appointments to meet me at three in the afternoon at Maison d'Or.

"We will have a talk there," he would say, "and sign our contract on the corner of a table."

What a joker! I hardly knew where to find his "Maison d'Or!" Only my brother had a word of encouragement for me when I returned home in despair.

One evening, however, I brought home with me glorious news and exceeding joy! The *Spectateur*, a legitimist journal, had agreed to put my talents to the proof as a news-writer. One can readily imagine the ardor and care with which I wrote my first article; even to the point of laboring over the penmanship! I carried it to the office, it was read and found satisfactory, and sent to the composing-room. I waited, hardly breathing, for the number to appear. Presto! Paris is turned topsy-turvy, some Italians have fired on the Emperor.

We were wild with terror, the newspapers were prosecuted, the *Spectateur* suppressed! Orsini's bomb blew up my article.

I did not kill myself, but I thought of it.

And yet heaven took pity on my misery. The publisher whom I had sought in vain suddenly appeared under my nose, — Tardieu, on Rue de Tournon, at my very door. He was a literary man himself, and some of his works had been successful: *Mignon* and *Pour Une Épingle*, compositions of the sentimental order, written in rose-colored ink. I made his acquaintance by chance one fine evening, when I was strolling near our hotel and he was sitting in front of his shop. He published my *Amoureuses*. The title proved attractive and so did the dainty exterior of the

volume.   Some newspapers spoke of my work and
of me.   My timidity took flight.   I walked
boldly under the galleries of the Odéon to see
how my book was selling — and I even ventured
after a few days to accost Jules Vallès!   I had
appeared.[1]

[1] *Les Amoureuses* were published in 1857–58.

II.

VILLEMESSANT.[1]

SOMETIMES — when my personal necessities and the hazards of my wanderings coincide — I go to be shaved or have my hair cut at Lespès's. A curious and distinctively Parisian spot is that great barber's shop, occupying the whole corner of the Frascati building, on Rue Vivienne and Boulevard Montmartre! Its clientage is *All-Paris;* that is to say, that infinitely small fragment of Paris which leads its life between the Gymnase and the Opéra, Notre-Dame de-Lorette and the Bourse, and fancies that it alone exists; hangers-on of the greenroom, actors, journalists, to say nothing of the restless, busy legion of worthy *boulevardiers*, who do nothing at all. Twenty or thirty permanent attendants shave and curl them all.

Superintending everything, with one eye on the razors and the other on the jars of pomade, the master, Lespès, prowls about here and there, an active little man whom the fortune he has made — for he is very rich — might have fattened, were it not that a certain disappointed ambition keeps him in a suitably feverish frame of mind.

[1] Written in 1879.

It was in that house, predestined in very sooth, that *Le Figaro* had its offices twenty years ago, on the same entresol where Lespès shaves his clients. There were the passage way, the subscription department, the counting-room, and, behind an iron-wire grating, the round eye and hooked nose of Père Legendre, always vexed, rarely good-natured, like a parrot playing the rôle of cashier. There was the editorial office (*The Public not admitted !* on the soiled glass panes of the door), a few chairs and a large table covered with an enormous green cloth. I can see it all distinctly at this moment, and I can see my bashful self, seated in a corner, holding tight under my arm my first article, rolled and tied with fatherly care. Villemessant had not arrived and they had told me to wait: I was waiting.

There were half-a-dozen of them around the green table that day, clipping from newspapers and writing. They laughed and talked and consumed cigarettes; the infernal caldron bubbled gayly. Among them was a short man with a red face beneath a mass of perfectly white hair, standing on end, which suggested Riquet à la Houppe. It was M. Paul d'Ivoy, the famous news-writer, kidnapped from the *Courrier de Paris* by a lavish use of gold; Paul d'Ivoy, in short, whose fabulous salary — it was fabulous for the time, but would seem smaller now — was the envy and admiration of the literary breweries. He wrote with a smile on his face, like a man content with himself; the sheets of paper rapidly grew black under his pen; and I watched M. Paul d'Ivoy write and smile.

Suddenly there is a sound of heavy footsteps, a cheerful, hoarse voice: Villemessant! The pens scratch busily, the laughter ceases, the cigarettes are hidden; Paul d'Ivoy alone raises his head and dares to gaze familiarly upon the god.

VILLEMESSANT. — Very good, my children; I see that we are getting on. (*To Paul d'Ivoy, affably.*) Are you satisfied with your article?

PAUL D'IVOY. — I think it rather good.

VILLEMESSANT. — So much the better; it happens very nicely, as it will be your last.

PAUL D'IVOY (*pale as a ghost*). — My last?

VILLEMESSANT. — Just so! I am not joking — your copy is something terrible; there's only one opinion on the boulevard; you've been hanging around our necks long enough.

Paul d'Ivoy had risen: "But, Monsieur, our agreement?"

"Our agreement? Very good! Try going to law about it, that will be amusing; I will have your articles read aloud in court, and we will see if any agreement can compel me to stuff such idiotic trash into my newspaper!"

Villemessant was the man to do as he threatened, and Paul d'Ivoy did not go to law. But none the less that way of shaking his editorial staff out of the window, like an old rug, sent a shiver down my back, unsophisticated creature that I was. I would have liked to be a hundred

feet underground with my unfortunate manuscript, rolled in such an absurd way. That was
an impression I have never forgotten. I met
Villemessant frequently afterward and he was
always very agreeable to me, but I always felt
when I saw him the unpleasant thrill of terror
which little Hop-o'-my-Thumb must feel when
he meets the ogre.

Let me add, in order to do him justice, that,
later on, at the death of that same Paul d'Ivoy
whom he had so brutally dismissed, it was Villemessant — an ogre with the lining of a Saint-
Vincent de Paul — who insisted upon assuming
the expense of his children's education.

"Is he kind? — is he cruel?" It is difficult to
answer the question, and Diderot's comedy seems
to have been written with him in mind. Kind?
He certainly was! Cruel, too, according to the
day and hour; and a painter might make two
portraits of him, without falsifying a line or a
tone — one fatherly, the other pitiless; one all
black, the other all rose-color — which would in
no wise resemble each other, but would both
resemble the subject.

If one wished to relate characteristic anecdotes
of that strange dual personality, he would find
only too many to select from.

Before the war I made the acquaintance of a
worthy man, the father of a family, who was a
clerk at the central Post Office on Rue Jean-
Jacques Rousseau. He remained in Paris during
the Commune. Had he some trace of sympathy

with the insurrection in the depths of his heart?
I would not swear that he had not. Did he say
to himself that, as letters continued to arrive at
Paris, it was necessary, after all, for some one to
assort and distribute them? That also is possible. Perhaps, too, with a wife and grown-up
daughters it was not an easy matter for him to
move at a moment's notice. At that time Paris
contained no small number of poor devils in such
a plight, barricaders by force of circumstances,
insurgents without knowing why. However that
may be, despite M. Thiers's orders, my friend
remained at his office, behind his railing, assort-
ing his letters amid the roar of battle as if nothing were happening; he refused to accept promotion
or increase of pay from the Commune. When
the Commune was overthrown, however, he found
himself none the less — fortunate to escape a
court-martial — thrown on the street, penniless,
discharged from his post as he was on the eve of
retirement with a pension. Thereupon a pitiful
yet comical existence began for him. He had
not dared to inform his family of his dismissal
from the government service; every morning his
daughters laid out the freshly starched shirt — a
government clerk must be neat! — and carefully,
merrily, as before, tied his cravat and kissed him
on the doorsteps at the regular hour, imagining
that he was going to his office. His office? Ah!
it was a long distance away, was the office, cool
in summer, well warmed in winter, where the
hours passed so placidly. Now he must tramp

around Paris, in the rain, through the snow, seeking employment which he never found, and go home at night, with death in his heart, to lie and invent stories about a deputy chief who did not exist, about an imaginary office-boy, forcing himself to assume a cheerful air. (I made use of the poor man as the model of Père Joyeuse in *The Nabob ;* he too was in quest of employment and told fibs to his daughters.) I met him sometimes, and it was heartrending. His distress led me to go to Villemessant. Villemessant, I thought, will surely find him some little corner in the managerial department of *Figaro.* Impossible: every place was filled. And a Communard, too, fancy! A fine outcry there would be if it were discovered that Villemessant employed a Communard in his offices. But the story of the daughters, the clean shirts, the cravat bows, had touched the excellent ogre, so it seemed.

"I have an idea!" he said; "how much did your protégé earn a month?"

"Two hundred francs."

"Very well! I will give you two hundred francs a month for him until he has found a place. He can still pretend to be going to his office, his daughters can still tie his cravats for him." And he concluded his speech with the everlasting: "It will be very pleasant!"

It was very pleasant, in truth: for three months the good man received his little income. After three months, having found a place at last, he practised such strict economy and kept himself on such short commons, that one fine morning he came to me with the six hundred francs and a beautiful letter of thanks for M. de Villemessant, whose name I had divulged to him, and whom, despite their disagreement in politics, he nobly called his benefactor. I carried the money to Villemessant.

"It's very pleasant! But I gave him that money! and now he wants to return it to me. It's the first time that ever happened to me. And a Communard, too! It's very pleasant."

How Villemessant shouted and laughed, and how enthusiastic he was! He threw himself back in his chair. But now follows a touch which will complete the man's portrait. Overjoyed, delighted, both by the kind deed he had done and by the very natural pleasure that we feel — however sceptical we may be — in the discovery that we have not been deceived and have not wasted our kindness on an ingrate, Villemessant, as he talked, amused himself by playing with the six hundred francs and arranging them in six little piles on the table. Suddenly he turned to me:

"Why! I say, Daudet, the money's a hundred sous short!"

It was, in fact, a hundred sous short, a wretched gold piece overlooked in a fold of the coat-lining. At the height of his enthusiasm the practical man of business appeared.

Such is that man's complicated nature; a shrewd calculator, very malicious in reality beneath an appearance of good-fellowship and

impulsiveness that would make one believe that
Toulouse is a near neighbor of Blois and that the
turrets of Chambord are located on one of the
arms of the Garonne![1]

In private and even in public life, Villemessant
has made familiarity a principle — in his treatment of others, be it understood! for he exacts a
full measure of respect when he himself is concerned. On the day following one of those
intensely bitter *echoes*, which he was in the habit
of inserting in his newspaper, at the last moment,
while the presses were at work, Villemessant was
summoned to the office of the president of the
Corps Législatif. (This took place under the
Empire.) He was requested to explain — I do
not think I can be mistaken — the famous " Morny
is in the affair," which old *boulevardiers* must
remember. The duke was very angry, or pretended to be, but the man from Blois was not
disconcerted.

"What! Monsieur le Duc, you did not send
for me to present me with a decoration? That
garde de Paris, with his sealed missive and his
helmet, can boast of having caused me a thrill of
emotion — my editors are already preparing to

---

[1] Villemessant resuscitated *Figaro* in 1854. In 1868 he founded
Le Diable à Quatre, and while not relinquishing his control of
Figaro allowed M. Jules Richard to adopt in its columns a tone
somewhat more agreeable to the government. In 1873 he offered
Figaro for sale and announced his determination to retire from
journalism, but did nothing of the kind. In 1874 the Governor of
Paris suspended *Figaro* for a fortnight.

Villemessant died in 1879, having apparently retained his con-
trolling interest in the journal to the end.

illuminate. Upon my word, this is very pleasant!"
— And in an instant, an amusing story, an
anecdote, an exceedingly shrewd, intensely Parisian remark, enveloped in a loud laugh; and, with
all the rest, an air of profound concern, a keen
and very manifest pleasure in saying: "Monsieur
le Duc!" — and the grievance was forgotten.

Elsewhere, at Persigny's[1] for example, familiarity was less successful; and on a certain day
Villemessant found that his most bewildering
buffoonery congealed in the cold official atmosphere and fell stiff and lifeless. But Morny, for
his part, forgave everything; that man doted on
Villemessant, and, thanks to his all-powerful
protection, *Figaro* was able to indulge in innumerable tricks. What respect, therefore, what
veneration he had for the president! I looked
forward to the time when they would build a little
chapel to him in the walls of the editorial sanctum,
as to the protecting genius of the place, as to a
household god. All of which did not prevent the
Figaro's publishing, one morning, in a prominent
place, apropos of the Duc de Saint-Rémy's plays
— that was the name assumed by the duke as a
man of letters — an article by Henri Rochefort, as
corrosive as a test-tube filled with acid, as sharp

---

[1] Jean G. V. F., Comte, afterwards Duc de Persigny, 1808-1872,
Bonapartist conspirator and politician. He was concerned in the
Bonapartist plots of Strasbourg in 1836 and Boulogne in 1840,
and was one of the leading conspirators in the *coup d'état* of 1851.
He held various important posts under the Second Empire : Min-
ister of the Interior 1852-54 and 1860-63, and Ambassador in
London 1855-58 and 1859-60.

and unpleasant as a handful of needles left in an easy-chair.[1]

"Why has this M. Rochefort a grudge against me? I never injured him in any way!" said the duke, with the artless vanity which not even the most sophisticated statesmen escape when they have dipped their finger in ink ; and Villemessant, assuming a distressed expression, exclaimed : —

"It 's horrible! Such an article would never have passed me — you see how distressed I am. But on that particular day I did n't go to the office, and the rascals took advantage of it ; I did n't read the proofs."

The duke thought whatever he chose of the excuse; but the article made a sensation. People showed it to one another, snatched it from one another's hands. That was all Villemessant wanted.

From this incident we see (and herein lies the unity of that apparently many-sided and contradictory character) that Villemessant was, before and above all else, the editor of his newspaper.

---

[1] As to the relations between Morny and Rochefort, see the article upon the latter in this volume, page 138. The Duc de Morny was born in 1811 and died in 1865. He was an officer in the army from 1830-32. He entered public life in 1842, was chosen to the Corps Législatif from Puy-de-Dôme in 1849, and was one of the most prominent actors in the *coup d'état* of 1851. He was Minister of the Interior 1850–52, and President of the Corps Législatif from 1854 until his death, serving also as Ambassador to Russia in 1856–7.

As the Duc de Mora he plays a prominent part in Daudet's novel of *The Nabob*. He also appears under the same name in the sketch : *Memoirs of a Chief Clerk*, in this volume.

After the gropings in the dark at the outset, volleys fired here and there, somewhat at random, feelers put forth to all the points of the compass, —when the course was once laid, he took his bearings and sailed straight. His newspaper became his life.

The man and his work resemble each other; and one may fairly say that no man was ever shaped more exactly to the measure of his destiny. Marvellously active, restless, lively, displacing a vast quantity of air, and, withal, sober in his habits, as men used to be sober, which astonishes those of the present day; a non-drinker, a non-smoker, fearing neither loud talk nor blows nor adventures; unscrupulous in reality, always ready to throw his prejudices overboard; never having had any very profound political beliefs, but fond of making a show of platonic legitimism and of a certain respect which he considered becoming to him, Villemessant was the very man who was needed to command that audacious corsair, which roamed the seas for twenty years, under the royal flag studded with fleurs-de-lis, doing business to some extent on its own account.

He was tyrannical and capricious; but probe the affair to the bottom and the interest of the newspaper will always afford an explanation of his tyranny and his caprice. We are at the *Café des Variétés* or the *Café Véron* at eleven o'clock on a Thursday, in the year of grace 1858. *Figaro* has just appeared, Villemessant is breakfasting. He talks, tries experiments with anecdotes which he will put in the next number if they raise a laugh, which he will forget if they fall flat. He listens and asks questions. — "What do you think of So-and-So's article?" "Charming!" "And such talent, eh?" "Extraordinary talent!" With radiant face Villemessant points to the paper: "Where is .So-and-So? Send for So-and-So! Extraordinary talent! He's the only man! All Paris is talking about his article!" — And behold, So-and-So is congratulated, petted, and has his salary raised. Four days later, at the same table, the same guest declares the same So-and-So's article tedious, and Villemessant draws himself up once more, not radiant now, but in a rage, not to increase his salary but to settle his account. Doubtless the scene between Villemessant and Paul d'Ivoy, which so scandalized my pristine innocence, was the result of one of these consultations between the fruit and the cheese.

Of what consequence was an editor to Villemessant? When one had gone another turned up; and the last comer was always the best. According to him, *every man has his article inside of him ;* the only thing is to get it out. Monselet embroidered a fascinating legend upon that theory: Villemessant meets a chimney-sweep in the street; he takes him to the offices of *Figaro*, washes his face, seats him in front of a sheet of paper, and says to him: "Write!" The sweep writes, and his article proves to be delightful. So it is that All-Paris, illustrious or obscure, which can hold a pen, has passed through the columns of *Figaro.* So it is that some worthy fellows — seeing the story of Saint-Aulaire's quatrain repeated in their favor — have had their quarter of an hour of celebrity, by virtue of a lucky find of fifteen lines. Afterward, the miracle not being repeated, it was discovered that they were empty, had been emptied by Villemessant. I have known a Paris filled with people thus emptied. What an epoch of innocence, when one was emptied by the discharge of fifteen lines!

Not that Villemessant despises literature: far from it! Although himself unlettered, he has the respect of a peasant for his curé's Latin for those who write well, who *hold their tongue*, as he expresses it. But he realizes instinctively, and not without reason, that they are the people of bulky tomes and of the Academy. To cakes of that weight and that shape he prefers for his shop the dainty Parisian puff-cake. He said one day to Jouvin, in my presence, with the cynical frankness for which his outspoken manner wins forgiveness:

"You work over your articles; they are the work of a literary artist, as everybody agrees, remarkable, learned, admirably written, and I publish them. But nobody reads them in my paper."

"Nobody reads them? Upon my word!"

"Do you want to make a wager? Daudet here will be a witness. I will print Cambronne's remark [1] in the middle of one of your most finished pieces, and I have lost my wager if any one discovers it!"

My impartiality as a witness compels me to say that Jouvin refused to bet.

[1] See the article on Cambronne in Larousse. See also Victor Hugo's LES MISÉRABLES: *Cosette*, Book I. Chap. XV.

III.

MY FIRST COAT.

How did I come by that coat? What tailor of primitive times, what unlooked-for M. Dimanche[1] decided, on the faith of fantastic promises, to bring it to me one morning, all glaringly new, and artistically pinned in a cambric handkerchief? It would be very difficult for me to tell. Of the honest tailor I remember nothing at all — so many tailors have crossed my path since then ! — nothing, unless it be, in a luminous mist, a pensive brow and a heavy moustache. But the coat is here, before my eyes. Its image is still engraved in my memory, after twenty years, as on imperishable brass. Such a collar, young men, and such lapels ! And, above all, such skirts, cut like the mouthpiece of a flute ! My brother, a man of experience, had said: "A man must have a coat if he wants to make his way in the world!" And the dear fellow relied much on that garment for my renown and my future.

Augustine Brohan had the honor of christening that first coat of mine. These are the circumstances, worthy to be handed down to posterity:

---

[1] A creation of Molière; introduced in the most comical scene of *Don Juan*. The name became proverbial as the type of the timid creditor who lends money but dares not demand repayment.

My volume had blossomed, virginal and fresh in its rose-pink covers. Some newspapers had mentioned my rhymes. Even the *Officiel* had printed my name. I was a poet, no longer in manuscript, but published, launched, displayed in shop-windows. I was astounded that the crowd did not turn to look when my eighteen years sailed through the streets. I really felt on my brow the gentle pressure of a paper crown made of reviews clipped from the journals.

One day some one proposed to procure me an invitation to Augustine's evenings. Who was that SOME ONE? Why, SOME ONE, *parbleu!*—You can see him from here, the sempiternal SOME ONE who resembles everybody else, the obliging, providential person, who, although he amounts to nothing in himself, goes everywhere, takes you everywhere, the friend of a day, the friend of an hour, whose name nobody knows, an essentially Parisian type.

You can imagine whether I accepted! To be invited to Augustine's,—Augustine, the famous actress, Augustine with the laughing white teeth of Molière and with a suggestion of the more modern poetic smile of de Musset;—for, although she played soubrette parts at the Théâtre Français, de Musset had written his comedy of *Louison* at her house;—Augustine Brohan,[1] in fact, whose

---

[1] Augustine Brohan was a brilliant and versatile actress, who succeeded Rachel at the Conservatoire. She was a member of the company of the Comédie Française from 1847. She lived until 1893.

wit Paris eulogized, and quoted her *bons-mots*, and who already wore in her hat, not as yet dipped in ink, but cut with a sharp knife and all ready for use, the quill of the hue of the bluebird with which she was to sign the *Lettres de Suzanne*.

"Lucky dog!" said my brother, as he helped me to put on my coat, "now your fortune is made."

Nine o'clock was striking; I started.

Augustine Brohan lived at that time on Rue Lord-Byron, at the upper end of the Champs-Élysées, in one of those dainty houses which poor little provincials, of poetic imagination, see in the dreams inspired by novelists. An iron fence, a small garden, a flight of four steps under an awning, a reception-room full of flowers, and in another instant the salon, a green salon brilliantly lighted, which I can see now so distinctly.

How I ascended the steps, how I entered, how I presented myself, I have no idea. A servant announced my name, but that name, mumbled as it was, produced no effect on the assemblage. I remember nothing but a woman's voice, which said:

"Good, a dancing man!" It seemed that dancing men were lacking. What an entry for a lyric poet!

Terrified, humiliated, I slunk out of sight in the crowd. How describe my dismay! In a moment another adventure: my long hair, my sulky, lowering eye aroused public curiosity. I heard whispering about me: "Who is it? — just

look at him!" and everybody laughed.   At last
some one said:

"It's the Wallachian prince!"

"The   Wallachian   prince? — ah!   yes,   of
course."

It was evident that a Wallachian prince was
expected that evening.   I was identified, and they
left me in peace.   But you can hardly conceive,
all the same, how my usurped crown weighed
upon me all the evening.   First a dancing man,
then a Wallachian prince!   In heaven's name,
did not those people see my lyre?

Luckily for me, a piece of news which was suddenly repeated from mouth to mouth from one
end of the salon to the other, caused the little
dancing man and the Wallachian prince to be
forgotten at the same instant.   Marriage was
then very much in vogue among the female con-
tingent of the drama, and it was at Augustine
Brohan's Wednesdays, where the fine flower of
official journalism, of finance and of the higher
circles of the Imperial government assembled
about the pretty *sociétaires* or *pensionnaires* of the
Théâtre Français, that most of these romantic
matches were planned.   Mlle. Fix, the clever
actress with the long Jewish eyes, was soon to
marry a great banker and to die in childbirth;
Mlle. Figeac, a Catholic and romanticist, was
already dreaming of having her future warerooms
on Boulevard Haussmann solemnly blessed by a
priest, as a ship is blessed when launched; Émilie
Dubois, even the fair-haired Émilie, although

destined by her fragile beauty to play *ingénue* rôles forever, had visions of orange-flowers beneath the protecting shawl of Madame, her mother. As for Madeleine Brohan, Augustine's beautiful and majestic sister, she was not marrying, not she! but was in the act of unmarrying herself and of giving Mario Uchard the necessary leisure and materials for writing the four acts of *La Fiammina*. What an explosion there was, therefore, in that atmosphere charged with marital electricity, when this report was circulated: "Gustave Fould has married Valérie," — Gustave Fould, the son of the Minister; Valérie, the charming actress! That is all far away now. After flights to England, letters to the newspapers, pamphlets, a war *à la Mirabeau* against a father as inexorable as the *Friend of Mankind*,[1] after the most romantic of romances, capped by a most commonplace *dénouement*, Gustave Fould, following Mario Uchard's example, wrote the *Comtesse Romani*, and described his misfortunes in eloquent language on the stage. Mlle. Valérie has forgotten her name of Mme. Fould and signs with the pseudonym of "Gustave Haller" volumes entitled *Vertu*, with a beautiful picture on the delicate blue cover, — great passions calming themselves in a bath of literature. But that evening, gossip and excitement were rife in Augustine's green salon. The men, the government officials shook their heads

---

[1] The father of the great Mirabeau so styled himself. His character is drawn with characteristic energy by Carlyle in his *French Revolution*.

and rounded their mouths into the shape of an O
to say: "It's a serious matter! very serious!"—
One could hear such remarks as: "Everything is
going by the board." "Respect is a thing of the
past." "The Emperor ought to intervene — sacred
rights — paternal authority." The women, for
their part, openly and merrily took sides with the
lovers, who had fled to London. "Whose affair is
it if they suit each other?" "Why should n't the
father consent?" "He's a minister, but what
then?" "Since the Revolution, thank God!
there's no Bastille, or For-l'Évêque!"— Imagine
everybody talking at once, and above and around
the hurly-burly, like embroidery, the sparkling
laughter of Augustine, a short, plump creature,
and the merrier on that account, with eyes on a
level with her face, pretty, short-sighted eyes,
bright as diamonds, and always wearing a look of
surprise.

At last the excitement subsided and the quad-
rilles began. I danced; I could not avoid it. I
danced very badly, too, for a Wallachian prince.
The quadrille at an end, I became a wall-flower,
foolishly held in check by my myopia, not bold
enough to sport a monocle, too much of a poet to
wear spectacles, and always afraid to make the
slightest movement lest I should strike my knee
against the angle of a piece of furniture, or plant
my nose between a woman's shoulders. Ere long
hunger and thirst took a hand; but not for an
empire would I have ventured to approach the
buffet with the crowd. I watched for the moment

when it should be deserted. Meanwhile I mingled with the group of politicians, maintaining a
serious expression, and pretending to look disdainfully upon the amusements of the small salon,
whence there came to me, with the sound of
laughter and of little spoons tinkling in porcelain
cups, a subtle odor of steaming hot tea, of Spanish wines and sweetmeats. At last, when the
dancing began again, I summoned courage. Behold me at last in the refreshment room; I am
alone.

A bewildering spectacle, that buffet! in the
light of the candles, with its glasses, its decanters, a white, dazzling pyramid of crystal, cool to
look upon, like snow in the sunlight. I take a
glass, fragile as a flower; I am very careful not
to grasp it tightly, for fear of breaking the stem.
What shall I pour into it? Come! courage, for no
one sees me! I find a decanter, by feeling, without attempting to choose. It must be kirsch; one
would say it was liquid diamond. Here goes then
for a *petit verre* of kirsch; I love its odor, which
makes me dream of tall trees, — its bitter, slightly
wild odor. And behold me pouring out the transparent liqueur, drop by drop, like a gourmand.
I raise the glass, I put out my lips. Horror!
Pure water! What a wry face! Suddenly there
is a twofold burst of laughter: a black coat and a
pink dress flirting in a corner, whom I have not
noticed and who are amused at my mistake. I
try to replace the glass; but I am confused, my
hand trembles, my sleeve catches on something or

other. A glass falls, two, three glasses! I turn, my coat-tails take a hand, and the white pyramid falls to the floor, with the scintillation of thousands of stars, the roar of a hurricane, the countless crashings of a crumbling iceberg.

The mistress of the house comes running in at the crash. Luckily she is as near-sighted as the Wallachian prince, and he is able to escape from the buffet unseen. My evening is spoiled, however. That massacre of glasses and decanters weighs upon me like a crime. I think of nothing but taking my leave. But Maman Dubois, dazzled by my principality, clings to me, insists upon it that I must not go without dancing with her daughter, — what do I say! with her two daughters. I excuse myself as well as I can. I escape from her, I am about to leave the house, when a tall old man, with a shrewd smile, the face of a bishop and a diplomat, stops me on the wing. It is Doctor Ricord, with whom I exchanged a few words a moment ago, and who, like the others, believes me to be a Wallachian. — "But, Prince, as you live at the Hôtel du Sénat, and we are near neighbors, wait for me. I have a seat for you in my carriage." — I would be glad to accept, but I came without an overcoat. What would Ricord say to a Wallachian prince without furs, and shivering in his dress-coat? Let us be off at once; let us trudge home on foot, through the snow and fog, rather than disclose our poverty. Still short-sighted and more confused than ever, I reach the door and am stealing away, not without getting entangled in the hangings. "Does not Monsieur mean to take his overcoat?" a footman calls to me.

Behold me, at two o'clock in the morning, a long way from home, wandering through the streets, famished, frozen, and hardly a sou in my pocket. Suddenly hunger inspired me, a happy thought flashed through my mind: "Suppose I go to the market!" I had often heard of the market and of a certain Gaidras, open all night, who furnished a succulent cabbage stew for three sous. *Parbleu*, yes, I will go to the market. I will take my seat there, like a vagabond, a night prowler. My pride has vanished. The wind is freezing cold, my stomach is hollow. "My kingdom for a horse!" said the other fellow; but I, as I trot along: "My principality, my Wallachian principality for a good bowl of soup in a warm place!"

Externally it was a genuine hovel, that establishment of Gaidras, buried under the pillars of the old market, dirty and wretchedly lighted. Very often since then, when *noctambulism* was fashionable, we have passed whole nights there, a party of great men *in futuro*, with our elbows on the table, smoking and talking literature. But the first time, I confess, I nearly drew back, notwithstanding my hunger, at sight of those black walls, that thick smoke, those people at the tables, snoring with their backs against the wall, or lapping up their soup like dogs, those caps of sidewalk Don Juans, the enormous white felt hats of the market men, and the coarse, healthy blouse of the market-gardener beside the greasy rags of the prowler about the barriers. I entered, however, and I must say that my black coat found company at once. They are by no means rare in Paris, black coats after midnight in winter, without overcoats, and hungry for three sous' worth of cabbage soup! Delicious cabbage soup, by the way; as fragrant as a garden, and smoking like a crater. I ate two portions, although the habit, inspired by healthy suspicion, of fastening the forks and spoons to the table with a chain, embarrassed me a little. I paid, and with my heart strengthened by that substantial fare I resumed my journey to the Latin Quarter.

You can imagine my return, the return of the poet trotting up Rue de Tournon, with his coat collar turned up, and with the elegantly-attired ghosts of a fashionable party dancing before his eyes, — which are heavy with fatigue and drowsiness, — blended with the famished figures of the market, and kicking his boots against the corner of the Hôtel du Sénat to knock off the snow, while the white lanterns of a coupé light up the front of a venerable mansion opposite, and Dr. Ricord's coachman calls: "Gate, please!" Life in Paris is made up of such contrasts.

"An evening wasted!" said my brother the next morning. "You were supposed to be a Wallachian prince, and you did n't start your volume. But there 's no reason to despair yet. You can make up for lost time at your party call." — A party call for a glass of water — what irony![1] It took me quite two months to make up my mind to that call. One day, however, I conquered my irresolution. Beside her regular Wednesdays, Augustine Brohan gave more select morning receptions on Sunday. I betook myself resolutely to one of them.

In Paris a self-respecting morning reception does not dream of beginning before three or even four o'clock in the afternoon. I, ingenuous creature, took the word "morning" seriously, and made my appearance at precisely one o'clock, supposing that I was late even then.

"How early you come, Monsieur," said a page of five or six years, fair-haired, in a velvet jacket and embroidered breeches, who was riding through the verdant garden on a tall mechanical horse. That young man made a profound impression on me. I saluted the fair hair, the horse, the velvet, the embroidery, and, being too shy to turn back, I ascended the steps. Madame was finishing her toilet and I had to wait, all alone, half an hour. At last Madame appears, blinks at me, recognizes her Wallachian prince, and, for the sake of saying something, begins: "So you 're not at La Marche, Prince?" — At La Marche, I, who had never seen a horse-race or a jockey!

At last I began to feel ashamed, the blood

---

[1] It is impossible to translate this passage so as to make clear the play upon words in the French. The phrase used for "party-call" is *visite de digestion*. Then follows — "Digestion of a glass of water — what irony!"

rushed suddenly from my heart to my brain; and
then that bright sunlight, that perfume of a garden
in springtime entering through the open window,
the absence of solemnity, that good-natured, smiling little woman, and a thousand other things
gave me courage, and I opened my heart, I told
everything, I confessed everything in a breath:
that I was neither Wallachian nor prince, but a
simple poet, and my adventure with the glass of
kirsch, and my supper at the Market, and my
pitiful return home, and my provincial terrors,
and my myopia, and my hopes, — all heightened
by my Southern accent.   Augustine Brohan
laughed like a madwoman.   Suddenly the bell
rang.

"Ah! my cuirassiers," she said.

"What cuirassiers?"

"Two cuirassiers who are sent to me from the
camp at Châlons, and who have, it would seem,
an amazing aptitude for acting."

I started to retire.

"No, no, stay; we are going to rehearse the
Lait d'Ânesse, and you shall be the influential
critic.   Here, beside me, on this couch!"

Enter two tall fellows, bashful, tightly girthed,
crimson-coated (one of them, I believe, is acting
somewhere to-day).   They arrange a screen, I
take my position, and the rehearsal begins.

"They don't do badly," said Augustine Brohan
to me in an undertone, "but what boots!— Monsieur le Critique, do you smell the boots?"

That semblance of intimacy with the cleverest

actress in Paris raised me to the seventh heaven
of delight. I threw myself back on the couch,
shaking my head, smiling with a knowing air.
My coat fairly split with joy.

The most trivial of these details seems to me of
enormous consequence to this day. But just see
what perspective will do: — I had told Sarcey the
comical story of my début in society. Sarcey
repeated it one day to Augustine Brohan. And
that ungrateful Augustine — whom I have not
seen, by the way, for thirty years — swore with
perfect sincerity that she knew nothing of me but
my books. She had forgotten it all! yes, all of
the details that filled so large a place in my life,
— the broken glasses, the Wallachian prince, the
rehearsal of the *Lait d'Ânesse*, and the cuirassiers'
boots!

IV.

HISTORY OF MY BOOKS. — "LITTLE WHAT 'S-HIS-NAME." [1]

NOT one of my books was written under such capricious, such chaotic conditions as this. Neither plan nor notes, but a frantic improvisation on long sheets of wrapping-paper, rough and yellow, on which my pen stumbled as it ran, and which I threw fiercely on the floor as fast as they were blackened. The scene was two hundred leagues from Paris, between Beaucaire and Nîmes, in a large country house, isolated and deserted, which some relatives had obligingly placed at my disposal for a few months in winter. I had gone thither in search of the concluding scenes of a drama, the *dénouement* of which did not run smoothly from my pen: but the peaceful sadness of those vast fields of mulberry and olive trees, of undulating vineyards extending to the Rhone, the melancholy of that retreat in the heart of nature, were hardly adapted to the conventional requirements of a dramatic work. Probably, too, the air of the province, the sunshine lashed by the mistral, the proximity of the town where I was born,

---

[1] *Le Petit Chose* appeared in 1868, just after Daudet's marriage.

the names of the little villages where I played as an urchin — Bezouces, Redessan, Jonquières — stirred a whole world of old memories within me, and I soon laid aside my drama to undertake a sort of autobiography: *Little What's-His-Name, the Story of a Child.*

Begun in the early days of February, 1866, that work was continued energetically, without stopping for breath, until the second fortnight of March. Nowhere, at no time in my life, not even when a capricious inclination for silence and solitude caused me to shut myself up in the chamber of a lighthouse, have I ever lived so entirely alone. The house stood at some distance from the road, among the fields, separated even from the farmhouse appurtenant to it, whose various noises never reached my ears. Twice a day the *bailo's* (farmer's) wife served my meals at one end of the enormous dining-room, the shutters at all the windows save one being tightly closed. That Provençale, indistinct of speech, dark, flat-nosed like a Kaffir, unable to understand what strange necessity had brought me to the country in the middle of winter, could not shake off a certain distrust and fear of me, but would set down the plates hurriedly, and run away without a word, avoiding a backward glance. And hers was the only face I saw during that Stylite existence, my only distraction being a promenade toward evening in an avenue of tall plane-trees, shedding their bark to the wailing of the wind, in the melancholy light of a cold red sun, whose early setting the frogs saluted with their discordant croaking.

As soon as the rough draft of my book was finished, I began at once upon the second copy, the painful part of the work, especially antipathetic to my nature as an *extemporizer*, an inventor; and I was working ·zealously at it with all my courage, when one morning the voice of the *bailesse* called to me vehemently in the local patois: "*Moussu moussu, vaqui un homo.*" (Monsieur, monsieur, here's a man!)

The man was a Parisian, a newspaper man sent down to attend some meeting of local interest in the neighborhood, and, knowing that I was there, he came to seek news of me. He lunched with me, we talked newspapers, theatres, boulevards; the Paris fever attacked me, and at night I started for the capital with my intruder.

That abrupt breaking off of work in the middle, that laying aside of the book when the casting was half done, gives an accurate idea of my life in those days, open to all the winds of heaven, with only brief flights, impulses instead of wishes, never following aught save its caprice and the blind frenzy of a youth which threatened never to end. Having returned to Paris, I allowed my manuscript to lie for a long time and turn yellow in the bottom of a drawer, unable to find in my minutely subdivided existence the necessary leisure for a work requiring time and thought; but in the following winter, being annoyed by the thought of that unfinished book, I took the violent course of tearing myself away from the distractions, the uproarious invasions which, at that time, made of my defenceless house a veritable gypsy camp, and I took up my quarters with a friend, in the small apartment then occupied by Jean Duboys on the entresol of Hôtel Lassus, Place de l'Odéon.

Jean Duboys, whose plays and novels had given him some celebrity, was a kindly, gentle, timid soul, with a childlike smile in a Robinson Crusoe beard, an unkempt, ragged beard, which seemed not to belong to that face. His work lacked character; but I loved his kindly disposition, I admired the courage with which he harnessed himself to interminable novels, cut up beforehand into regular slices, of which he wrote each day so many words, lines and pages. At last he had succeeded in having a great play called *La Volonté* (*The Will*) produced at the Comédie Française; and, although it was manifested in execrable verses, that *will* made a profound impression on me, who so utterly lacked anything of the kind. So that I went to cling to the skirts of its author, hoping to gain a taste for work from the contact with that indefatigable producer.

It is a fact that for two or three months I worked steadily at a small table near his, in the light from a low, arched window which formed a frame for the Odéon and its porch, and the deserted square, all gleaming with frost. From time to time Duboys, who was working at some magnificent Jack-in-the-Box affair, would stop to describe the plots within plots of his novel, or to develop his theories concerning "the cylindrical motion of mankind." Indeed there were in that methodical and mild-mannered scribbler certain symptoms of the visionary, the *illuminé*, just as there was in his library a shelf reserved for the Cabala, for the Black Art, for the most curious lucubrations. Eventually that crack in his brain grew larger, allowing insanity to enter; and poor Jean Duboys died a madman at the close of the siege, leaving unfinished his great philosophic poem, *Enceldonne*, wherein all mankind was to revolve upon its cylinder. But who could have suspected at that time the melancholy destiny of that estimable, placid, sensible youth whom I watched enviously as he covered with his fine, regular handwriting the innumerable sheets of a novel for a petty newspaper, and assured himself by a glance at the clock from hour to hour that he had done his whole stint?

It was very cold that winter, and notwithstanding the baskets of coal consumed in the grate, we saw, during those toilsome vigils, indefinitely prolonged, the frost coat the window-panes with fanciful arabesques. Without, shivering shadows wandered through the opaque fog on the square; they were the audience coming from the Odéon, or the flock of young men and women on their way to Jardin Bullier, shouting and yelling to guide one another. On the evenings of masquerade balls, the narrow stairway of the hotel shook beneath a reckless downward scampering, accompanied every time by the jingling of the little bells on a fool's cap. The same fool's cap would ring out its carnival peal on its return when the night was far advanced; and often, when the hotel attendants were sleeping soundly and delayed admitting it, I could hear it shake its bells with a discouraged movement, with diminishing vigor, which made me think of Edgar Poe's *Cask of Amontillado*, of the poor imprisoned wretch, weary of imploring, of crying out, and betraying his presence only by the last convulsive movements of his cap. I have retained a charming impression of those winter nights during which the first part of *Little What's-His-Name* was written. The second part did not follow it until much later. Between the two an event intervened, totally unexpected by me, but most serious and decisive: I married. How did that come about? By what witchcraft was the inveterate Bohemian I then was, caught and laid under a spell? What charm was able to tether the everlasting caprice?

For months the manuscript was neglected, left lying in the bottom of the trunks that accompanied us on our wedding-journey, spread out upon hotel tables before an empty inkstand and a dry pen. It was so pleasant under the pines of Estérel, so pleasant to fish for sea-urchins near the cliffs of Pormicu! Afterward, the installation of the little household, the novelty of that domestic existence, the nest to build and to decorate, — so many pretexts for not working!

It was not until summer. had come, under the dense foliage of the Château of Vigneux, whose Italian roof and lofty trees we could see spread out before us in the plain of Villeneuve-Saint-Georges, that I returned to my interminable novel.   Six delightful months, far from Paris, at that time turned topsy-turvy by the Exposition of 1867, which I would not even go and see.

I wrote *Little What's-His-Name* partly on a moss-covered bench in the depths of the park, disturbed by rabbits leaping and snakes crawling among the underbrush, partly in a boat on the pond in which were reflected all the changing hues of the summer sky, and partly, on rainy days, in our room, while my wife played Chopin, whom I can never hear without imagining the dripping of the rain on the swaying green branches of the hornbeams, the harsh cries of the peacocks, the tumult in the pheasant house, amid the odors of tree blossoms and damp wood.   In the autumn the book, finished at last, appeared as a *feuilleton* in Paul Dalloz's *Petit Moniteur*, was published by Hetzel, and attained a measure of success, notwithstanding all that it lacks.

I have told how this, my first serious work, was undertaken, without reflection, on the wing as it were; but its greatest fault is that it was written prematurely.   One is not mature enough at twenty-five to review and comment on his life. And *Little What's-His-Name*, especially in the first part, is in substance only this, an echo of my childhood and my youth.

Later I should have been less afraid to pause at the childish fancies of the beginning, and should have developed more fully those far-off memories which contain our initial impressions, so vivid and profound that all that comes after renews them without excelling them. In the more rapid movement of life, the onward flow of days and years, incidents fade from sight, are effaced by others, disappear, but that past remains, standing erect, luminous, bathed in the rays of dawn. You may forget a recent date, a face seen yesterday; you always remember the design of the wall-paper in the room in which you slept as a child, a name, a tune of the time when you did not know how to read. And how far memory travels in these backward journeys, striding across empty years, hiatuses, as in dreams! For instance, I can remember, in my third year, a display of fireworks at Nîmes in honor of some Saint-Louis, and that I was carried in somebody's arms to the top of a pine-covered hill. The slightest details of that event are still present in my memory, the murmur of the trees in the night wind — my first night out of-doors, doubtless — the noisy delight of the crowd, the "Ahs!" ascending and bursting with the rockets and suns, whose reflection lighted up the faces about me with a ghostly pallor.

I can see myself, at about the same period, mounted on a chair in front of a black table at the Brothers' school, and tracing my letters with chalk, proud of my precocious learning. And then there is the memory of the senses, those sounds, those perfumes which come to you from the past as from another world, without the slightest trace of any accompanying event or emotion!

At the rear of the factory where *Little What's-His-Name* passed his childhood, near abandoned buildings whose doors were noisily slammed by a breeze of solitude, there were some tall rose-laurels, in the open air, giving forth a bitter fragrance which haunts me still after forty years. I would that there were a little more of that fragrance in the first pages of my book.

The chapters on Lyon are too short; I allowed many vivid and delightful sensations to escape me there. Not that my childish eyes could have grasped the originality, the greatness of that manufacturing city, with its suggestion of mysticism due to the permanent mist which rises from its rivers, permeates its walls and its people, and imbues the productions of its writers and its artists — Ballanche, Flandrin, de Laprade, Chenavard, Puvis de Chavannes — with a vague Germanic melancholy. But if the mental individuality of the province escaped me, the enormous hive of toil of the Croix-Rousse, humming with its hundred thousand looms, and, on the hill opposite, Fourvières carolling and marching in procession through the narrow lanes of its slope, lined with religious images and stalls for the sale of relics, left on my mind an ineffaceable impression, for which a place was reserved in *Little What's-His-Name.*

The points that I consider to be faithfully depicted in the book are the ennui, the sense of banishment, the distress of a Southern family lost in the Lyonnese fog, — the change from one province to another, change of climate, customs and language, the mental distance which facility of communication does not lessen. I was ten years old at the time, and being already tormented by the longing to go outside of myself, to become incarnate in other people, due to a dawning mania for observing and annotating mankind, it was my chief amusement, during my walks, to select some passer-by and follow him about through Lyon, wherever his saunterings or his business led him, to try to identify myself with his life and comprehend his secret preoccupations.

One day, however, when I had escorted in that way a very beautiful lady in a bewitching costume as far as a low house with drawn blinds, the ground floor occupied by a *café chantant*, where hoarse voices were singing to the accompaniment of harps, my parents, to whom I confided my surprise, forbade my continuing my wandering studies and observations of real life.

But how could I, while I was marking the stages of my adolescence, fail to say a word of the religious paroxysms which shook *Little What's-His-Name* violently between his tenth and his twelfth year, of his revolts against the absurdities and mysteries in which he was compelled to believe, revolts followed by fits of remorse, of despair which caused the child to prostrate himself in dark corners of the deserted church, whither he

furtively crept, dreading and ashamed to be seen?
Above all, how could I have attributed to the
little man's exterior aspect that gentleness and
air of good-breeding, without mentioning the
devilish existence into which he abruptly plunged
about his thirteenth year, in a desperate longing
to live, to exert his strength, to tear himself away
from the unrelieved gloom, the tears that stifled
him beneath his parents' roof, darkened from day
to day by financial ruin.   It was the effervesc-
ence of the Southern temperament and imagination
too sternly compressed.   The delicate and timid
child was transformed, became bold, vehement,
ready for all sorts of mad freaks.   He played
truant, passed his days on the water, in the crowd
of skiffs, barges and tugs, rowed about in the rain
with a pipe between his teeth and a flask of
absinthe or eau-de-vie in his pocket, escaped a
thousand deaths, from the paddles of a steamboat,
from collision with a coal-barge, from the current
which threw him against the piles of a bridge or
under a towing rope, drowned, fished up, his head
split open, cuffed by bargemen who were annoyed
by the awkwardness of the little monkey too weak
to handle his oars; and in that fatigue, those
blows, those perils, he was conscious of a savage
joy, a broadening of his existence and of the dark
horizon.

In some of the *Monday Tales* there are some
sketches of that troubled period, made at a later
date; but how much more valuable they would
have been in the *Story of a Child.*

Even then that harebrained *Little What's-His-Name* possessed a strange faculty which he has never lost, the gift of seeing himself, of judging himself, of surprising himself red-handed in all sorts of crimes, as if his footsteps were always attended by a pitiless and redoubtable spy. Not what is known as conscience, — for conscience preaches, scolds, takes a hand in all our acts, modifies them or arrests them. And then we can put that excellent conscience to sleep with ready excuses or subterfuges, while the witness of whom I speak never relaxed his severity, never interfered in anything, simply watched. It was like an inward glance, impassive and fixed, a lifeless, cold *double*, who, during *Little What's-His-Name's* most violent outbreaks, kept an eye upon everything, took notes, and said the next day: "This is for us two to settle!" Read the chapter entitled: "He is Dead! Pray for Him!" an absolutely true page of my life. My older brother's death was announced to us in just that way, and in my ears there still rings my poor father's cry when he divined that his son was dead; so heartrending, so poignant was that first loud outcry of human grief within my hearing, that all night, as I lay weeping in my despair, I surprised myself repeating: "He is dead," in my father's tone. In that way was revealed to me the existence of my *double*, of the implacable witness who, in the midst of our mourning, had retained, as on the stage, the faithful echo of a death-shriek, and tried it upon my despairing lips. I regret, on re-reading my book, to find therein not a word of these confessions, especially in the first part, where the character of Daniel Eyssette resembles me so strongly.

Yes, he is myself, that *Little What's-His-Name*, compelled to earn his living at sixteen in that horrible calling of school-usher, and performing its duties in the heart of a province, of a region of smelting-furnaces, which sent me vulgar little mountain imps, who insulted me in their harsh, brutal Cevennese patois. Defenceless against the persecution of those little monsters, surrounded by bigots and pedants who despised me, I underwent the degrading humiliations of the poor man.

In that depressing prison-house I had no other sympathy than that of the priest whom I have called Abbé Germane, and of the horrible "Bamban," whose absurd little face, always smeared with ink and mud, looks mournfully into mine while I write these lines.

I recall another of my pupils, a refined, unusual character, to whom I became attached and for whom I set special tasks, solely for the joy of seeing that youthful intellect develop like a bud in the spring. The child, being deeply touched by my interest in him, had made me promise to pass my vacation with him in the country. His parents would be so glad to know me, to thank me. And so, on the day of the distribution of prizes, after a great triumph which he owed to me in some degree, my pupil came and took my hand,

and politely led me to his people, — father, mother, fashionably-dressed sisters, — all of whom were engaged in loading the prizes on a great break. I must have cut a sorry figure in my threadbare clothes, or have had something about me to offend the eye; for the family barely glanced at me, and the poor little fellow went away, with tears in his eyes, heartily ashamed because of his own disappointment and mine. Humiliating, cruel moments, which wither, which degrade life! I trembled with rage in my little room under the eaves, while the carriage bore away the child, laden with wreaths, and the vulgar bourgeois who had wounded me in such a das tardly way.

A long time after I left that dungeon at Alais, it often happened that I woke in the middle of the night, weeping bitterly; I had dreamed that I was still an usher and a martyr. Luckily that cruel début in life did not poison my mind; and I do not curse too bitterly that wretched time which enabled me to endure lightly the trials of my literary novitiate and my first years in Paris. Those were hard years, and the story of *Little What's-His-Name* conveys no idea of them.

There is almost nothing taken from real life in the second part except my arrival without shoes, my blue stockings and my rubbers, and my brother's welcome, the ingenious devotion of that Mère Jacques, whose real name is Ernest Daudet, who is the radiant figure of my child-

hood and early youth. Aside from my brother
all the characters are purely imaginary.

I had a plentiful supply of models, however,
and models of the most interesting and rarest
types; but, as I said just now, I wrote that book
when I was too young. One whole stage of my
existence was too near me; I was not far enough
away to see it distinctly, and, not seeing it, I invented. For instance, *Little What's-His-Name*
was never an actor; indeed he was never able to
say a single word in public. The porcelain trade
also is unfamiliar to him. Pierrotte and her
black eyes, the lady on the first floor, Coucou-
blanc her negress, are done with spirit, as the
painters say; but they lack the relief, the real
articulation of life. So it is with the literary silhouettes, in which some people have fancied that
they could detect insulting personalities of which
I never dreamed.

Let me point out, however, one other of the
realities of my book — the chamber under the
eaves, over against the steeple of Saint-Germain-
des-Prés, in a house now demolished, so that my
glance is unsatisfied whenever I seek with my
eyes, as I pass, the scene of so many follies, of so
much misery, of so many long vigils of toil or of
gloomy, desperate loneliness.

V.

THE LITERARY SALONS.[1]

I DO not think that there is a single one left to-day. We have other salons, more "in the swim," as they say: political salons, — Madame Edmond Adam's, Madame d'Haussonville's, all white or all red, where prefects are made and ministers unmade, and where Messieurs the Princes or Gambetta sometimes appear on great occasions. Then there are the salons where the guests enjoy themselves, — I dare not say try to enjoy themselves. Memories and regrets! they sup and play cards, they renew the parties at Compiègne as far as they can: attractive conservatories, a fragile shelter, beneath whose crystal roof blooms in all its trivial splendor the odorless flower of a purely superficial and worldly life. But the genuine literary salon, the salon where, around a charming and mature Muse, men of letters, or those who deem themselves such, assemble once a week to repeat little poems, dipping little dry cakes in a little tea, — that species of salon, I say, has definitively disappeared. Although I am not an old man, I have known some of those blue salons of

[1] Written in 1879, for the *New Times* (*Novoe-Vremya*) of St. Petersburg.

Arthenice,[1] which are to-day relegated to the provinces, more out of fashion than the guitar, the
"void in the soul" and album verses.

Suppose we breathe upon our memories of
twenty years since. *Pouf! pouf! pouf!* The
dust rises in a fine cloud, and in that cloud, as
distinctly as if for a fairy spectacle, the amiable
features of good Madame Ancelot[2] assume form
and substance.   Madame Ancelot lived at that
time on Rue Saint-Guillaume, a short provincial
street in the heart of Paris, overlooked by Haussmann, where the grass grows between the pavements, where the rumbling of carriage wheels is
never heard, where the tall houses, too tall for
their three floors, allow only a cold and distant
reflection of the daylight to find its way.   The
old, silent mansion, with the shutters of its bal-
cony windows always closed, its front door never
open, had the air of having slept for centuries
beneath a magician's wand.   And the interior
fulfilled the promises of the street front: a white-
walled hall, a dark, echoing stairway, high ceil-
ings, broad windows surmounted by paintings set
in panels.   It was all faded and pale, seemed
really to have ceased to live, and in the midst of

---

[1] Arthenice was an anagram of Catherine, Marquise de Ram-
bouillet, whose salon was so famous in the later years of the
17th century.   The anagram was invented by Malherbe.

[2] Madame Ancelot, born at Dijon in 1818, was a dramatist and
author of some pretensions.   She wrote at first in collaboration
with her husband, "seeking only the pleasure of expressing her
ideas," but after her comedy, *Un Mariage Raisonnable*, was produced at the Français in 1835, she worked independently.

it, in her proper frame, Madame Ancelot, dressed
in white, plump and wrinkled like a little red
apple, — in a word, exactly as we picture to ourselves the fairies in children's tales, who never
die, but who grow old for thousands of years.
Madame Ancelot loved birds, therein again resembling the good fairies.   All around the salon, covering the walls, were tiers upon tiers of cages,
chirping like the show-window of a bird-fancier's
on the quay.   But the very birds seemed to be
singing old-fashioned tunes.   In the place of
honor, well in sight and in an excellent light, was
a large portrait by Baron Gerard, hung at the
proper angle, representing the Muse of the domi-
cile with her hair dressed like a child's, in a
costume cut after the fashion of the Restoration,
and smiling with the smile of those days; the
pose was three-quarters profile, as if about to fly,
à la Galatea, the better to show a bit of a marvellously white and well-rounded shoulder.   Forty
years after the portrait was made, at the time of
which we write, Madame Ancelot still wore low-
necked dresses, but truth compels us to say that
she no longer displayed the white, well-rounded
shoulders painted by Baron Gerard.   But what
cared the good woman for that?   She imagined
in 1858 that she was still the fair Madame
Ancelot of the year 1828, when Paris was applauding her play, *Marie, ou les Trois Époques*.   Indeed, there is nothing to give her warning; everything about her fades and grows old with her: the
roses in the carpets, the ribbons of the hangings,

persons and memories; and while the century
advances, that arrested life, that household of
another age, motionless as a vessel at anchor,
bury themselves silently in the past.

A simple remark would break the spell. But
who will pronounce those sacrilegious words, who
will dare to say: "We are growing old!" The
habitués of the house less than others, for they too
are of the same epoch; they too fancy that they are
not growing old. There is M. Patin, the illustrious M. Patin, lecturer at the Sorbonne, playing
the young man yonder by the window, in the
corner at the left. He is a little man, as white
as snow, but so jauntily curled and perfumed, and
quivering with circumspection, as befits a University man of the First Empire. And Viennet,
the Voltairian fabulist, as long and skinny as the
heron of his dull fables. The god of the salon,
surrounded, admired, petted, was Alfred de Vigny,
a great poet, but a poet of another age — a strange,
superannuated creature, with his archangel's expression and his weeping white hair, too long for
his short figure. When he died, Alfred de Vigny
bequeathed his parrot to Madame Ancelot. The
parrot took his place in the centre of the salon,
on a varnished perch. The old habitués stuffed
him with sweetmeats; he was de Vigny's parrot!
Some jokers dubbed him Eloa,[1] because of his
long beak and mystic eye. But I am getting ahead
of my story; at the time when I was presented at

---

[1] De Vigny, author of *Cinq-Mars*, died in 1862. He published
in 1822 *Eloa, ou la Sœur des Anges.*

Madame Ancelot's, the poet was still alive, and the parrot's shrill little old-fashioned note was not yet added to the formidable chirping which, by way of protest, I imagine, arose from all the cages when M. Viennet attempted to repeat a few verses.

Sometimes the salon renewed its youth. On those days we met there Lachaud, the famous advocate, with Madame Ancelot's daugher, whom he had married: she a little inclined to melancholy, he stout and sleek, with a fine head worthy of a Roman, of a jurist of the Later Empire. Poets: Octave Lacroix, author of the *Chanson d'Avril*, of *L'Amour et son Train*, acted at the Théâtre Français; he made a very deep impression on me, although he was most benignant in appearance, being Sainte-Beuve's secretary. Emmanuel des Essarts came there with his father, a distinguished writer, librarian at Sainte-Geneviève. Emmanuel des Essarts was at that time a very young man, had hardly made his début in literature, and still wore, if I remember aright, the green palm-leaf of the Normal School pupils in his buttonhole. He fills now the chair of Literature in the Faculty of Clermont, which does not prevent his publishing one or two volumes a year on an average, in which are some fine poems. A delightful professor, as you see, with a sprig of myrtle in his cap. And then the ladies, — lady poets like Madame Anaïs Ségalas, and from time to time a newly discovered young Muse, with an azure eye, hair like refined gold, in the then somewhat out-of-date attitude of the Delphine Gays and Elisa Mercœurs.   One fine day appeared the fair Jenny Sabatier, whose real name was Tirecuir,[1] a most prosaic name for a Muse.   I too, was sometimes asked for verses like the others, but it seems that I was timid and that my voice showed it. — "Louder!" Madame Ancelot would always say, "louder; Monsieur de la Rochejacquelein does n't hear!" — There were half-a-dozen of them like that, deaf as Etruscan pots, unable to hear a word, but always very attentive, with the left hand in a circle around the ear by way of speaking trumpet.   Gustave Nadaud, for his part, always made himself heard.   Short and thickset, with a turned-up nose and a large, expansive face, affecting an amiable rusticity which did not lack charm in that drowsy circle, the author of *Les Deux Gendarmes* would seat himself at the piano, sing at the top of his voice, pound the keys, and wake everybody.   How popular he was in consequence!   We were all jealous of him. — Sometimes, too, an actress anxious for a start would come there and recite poetry.   There was a tradition that Rachel had recited several stanzas in Madame Ancelot's salon; a picture near the mantelpiece attested the fact.   People continued to recite stanzas there, but they were not Rachels.   That picture was not the only one; they came to light in every corner, all from the hand of Madame Ancelot, who did not disdain to handle the brush in her hours of leisure, and all devoted

[1] Draw-leather.

to her salon, destined to perpetuate the memory of some momentous event in that miniature world. The curious can find reproductions of them (made, O irony! by E. Benassit, the most cruelly sceptical of painters), forming a sort of autobiography: *Mon Salon*, by Madame Ancelot, published by Dentu. Each one of the faithful has his or her counterfeit presentment therein, and I think that mine is somewhere there, rather in the background.

That slightly heterogeneous party assembled every Tuesday on Rue Saint-Guillaume. They arrived late, and for this reason: on Rue du Cherche-Midi, two steps away, there was a rival salon, Madame Mélanie Waldor's,[1] set up there as if for the express purpose of serving as a permanent protest. The two Muses had formerly been intimate friends; indeed, Madame Ancelot had to some extent launched Mélanie in society. Then one day Mélanie shook herself free, and raised altar against altar: a repetition of Madame du Deffand's experience with Mademoiselle de Lespinasse. Mélanie Waldor wrote; we have had from her hand novels, poems, and a play, *La Tirelire de Jeannette!* Alfred de Musset, one day when he was in a savage humor, wrote some crushing, superb lines about her, a highly-spiced blend of Arétin and Juvenal, which, in default of anything better, will bear the Muse's name to

---

[1] Madame Waldor was older than Madame Ancelot, having been born in 1796. She was a very prolific writer of history, novels, sketches of manners, poetry and dramatic works.

posterity, on the wings of secret publications. Pray, what had Mélanie Waldor done to the *enfant terrible?* I remember her very well, all in velvet, with black hair — the hair of a century-old crow who persists in not growing gray — stretched out on her couch, languid and drooping, with attitudes indicative of a broken heart. But the eye kindled, the mouth became viperous at once when *She* was mentioned. *She* was the other, the enemy, dear old Madame Ancelot. There was war to the knife between those two. Madame Waldor purposely chose the same day, and about eleven o'clock, when you tried to steal away, in order to run across the street, cold glances nailed you at the door. You must needs remain, wag your tongue, blackguard Père Ancelot and outdo yourself in scandalous little stories. Opposite, they took their revenge by repeating innumerable mysterious legends concerning Madame Waldor's political influence.

How much time was wasted, how many hours frittered away in those venomous or absurd little trifles, in that atmosphere of moss-grown little poems and rancid little calumnies, on those pasteboard Parnassuses, whence no stream flows, where no bird sings, where the poetic laurel has the color of the green leather badge of a chief of department! And to think that I too have climbed the slopes of those Parnassuses! One must see everything in one's youth! That will last as long as my coat.

Poor dear coat, how many narrow halls it

rubbed with its skirts in those days, how many stair-rails it polished with its sleeves! I remember sporting it in Madame la Comtesse Chodsko's salon. The countess's husband was an excellent old scientist who seldom appeared and who counted for little. She must have been very beautiful; she was a tall, straight, thin woman, with an imperious, almost ugly manner. It was said that Murger, being deeply impressed by her, took her for the model of his *Madame Olympe*. Murger did, you know, undertake a brief journey in the first society, and that particular social circle was the one he discovered in his innocence. Somewhat confined quarters, truly, for the first society, and a little too far from the ground, that third floor suite on Rue de Tournon, consisting of three cold, bare little rooms, with windows looking on the courtyard. People came there, however, and the company was by no means commonplace. It was there that I first met Philarète Chasles,[1] restless genius, nervous pen, of the race of the Saint-Simons and Michelets, whose astounding *Mémoires*, quarrelsome, mischievous, made up of thrusts and parries, and filled, as it were, from the first chapter to the last, with the incessant clash of foils and crossed swords, appeared recently, and are allowed to pass almost unnoticed in the hurly-

[1] Philarète Chasles was one of those whom the late James Russell Lowell called Balzacidae. He wrote a very long and elaborate preface to the second edition of Balzac's *Peau de Chagrin* (*Magic Skin*), which is reprinted in M. de Lovenjoul's *Histoire des Œuvres de Balzac*. His miscellaneous works fill eleven volumes.

burly of a Paris that is really too indifferent to anything unconnected with painting or politics. A man of letters to the core, but tormented all his life, as Balzac was, by an appetite for a broader life and for dandyism, he lived, a librarian, at the very threshold of the Academy, which, no one knows why, would have none of him; and he died of cholera at Venice.

I also met there Pierre Véron, Philibert Aude-brand, and an interesting couple, very interest-ing, and at the same time very congenial, whom I ask your leave to introduce to you. We are in the salon, let us sit down and watch: the door opens, enter Philoxène Boyer and his wife. Phi-loxène Boyer! another of those extraordinary youths, the terror and chastisement of families, chance productions which no theory of atavism explains, seeds brought no one knows whence, on the wings of the wind, across the seas, and some fine day blooming in a field of cabbages, in the midst of a bourgeois kitchen-garden, with their outlandishly irregular foliage, and their flowers of strange and gorgeous coloring! The son of that Boyer who knew more Greek than any man in France of his time; born between two pages of a lexicon; knowing nothing, in his childhood, of walks or of gardens outside the learned garden of Greek roots; fed on Greek, oiled with Greek, Philoxène with his Greek name seemed inexor-ably destined to see that name inscribed on marble, beside the Eggers and Estiennes in the Pantheon of Greek scholars. But Père Boyer reckoned

without Balzac. Philoxène, like all schoolboys
of that day, had Balzac in his desk; so that, having inherited a hundred thousand francs from his
mother, he could not come soon enough to Paris
to squander the hundred thousand francs as Balzac's characters do. His project was carried out
in the most orthodox fashion: bouquets given
away, tips of gloved fingers kissed, duchesses sub-
jugated, girls with golden eyes purchased, —
nothing was left undone, and the whole was
crowned by a wild revel after the style of the one
described in *La Peau de Chagrin*. The *peau de
chagrin*, that is to say, the hundred thousand
francs, had lasted just six months. The Hellen-
ist's son had enjoyed himself prodigiously. With
empty pockets and his brain full of rhymes, he
declared that he proposed thenceforth to carry on
the trade of poet. But it was written that Philoxène, so long as he lived, should be *a victim of
books*. Having left Balzac, he fell in with Shakespeare; Balzac had consumed only his five-franc
pieces, Shakespeare consumed his life! — One
morning, perhaps as the result of a dream, Philoxène awoke, absolutely infatuated with the
works of Shakespeare. And as that self-willed,
fragile creature, of mildly vehement disposition,
could do nothing by halves, he devoted himself
to Shakespeare body and soul! To study Shakespeare, to learn him by heart, from his least
known sonnets to those of his plays of which the
authorship is most disputed, was a mere nothing,
and it took only a few months. But Philoxène

aimed higher than that: proposing to write a
book upon Shakespeare, a complete, definitive
book, a monument, in short, worthy of the god, he
conceived the impossible project of reading, in
the first place to extract its quintessence, everything (everything, I say, not excepting the most
insignificant article or the most trivial document)
— everything that had been published concerning
Shakespeare from two hundred years ago down
to our own times.   A mass of dusty folios suffi-
cient to build a Babel: and the Babel, alas! was
soon built in Philoxène's brain.   I have seen him
in his own home, no longer master of himself,
overflowed on all sides by Shakespeare.   Five
thousand, ten thousand volumes on Shakespeare,
of all sizes, in all languages, rising to the ceiling,
blocking the windows, crushing the tables,
encroaching on the chairs, piled up, toppling
over, consuming air and light, and in the midst
of them Philoxène, taking notes, while his brats
howled about him.   For he had married, with no
very clear idea why, and had had children between
the reading of two books.   Over-excited by his
fixed idea, talking to himself when he was alone,
with his eyes fixed on the horizon, lost in reverie,
he walked through Paris like a blind man.   His
wife, a gentle creature, inclined to melancholy,
followed him everywhere, acted as his Antigone.
I used to see them at the Café de la Régence,
always together.   She would prepare his absinthe
with great care, a mild absinthe, barely tinged
with greenish opal, for the enthusiastic poet

needed no stimulants. She was always seen, too, in the front row at the conferences held by Philoxène in the hall on Quai Malaquais, always upon Shakespeare. Sometimes the word would not come — a painful spectacle! — the orator would seek it, clench his fists in vain. Every one felt that in that overcrowded brain ideas and sentences jostled one another, unable to come forth, like a frantic crowd around a door in a conflagration. The wife, divining the word, would whisper it gently, maternally. The sentence would come forth and fly away; and at such times that painful improvisation, that frantic gesticulation, were illumined by vivid flashes, eloquent outbursts. There was a genuine poet at the core of that gentle monomaniac. Philoxène ended his life sadly, working at obscure tasks to earn his livelihood and buy books, always dreaming of his great monograph, but never able to write it. For he wished to read everything concerning Shakespeare; and every day books appeared in England, in Germany, which went beyond him and compelled him to postpone his first line until the morrow. He died, leaving no effects save two short plays written in collaboration with Théodore de Banville, an unfinished *Polichinello*, original in design, which was afterwards retouched by adapters, and a volume of verse collected and published by the exertions of his friends. They obtained a small stamp office for his widow. After long mourning her poet, the worthy, simple-hearted woman married again two years ago.   Guess whom she married?   The postman!

Was I not justified in directing your attention to Philoxène and his wife? For my own part, I can never forget them, and I can still see them, reserved and shy, in the corner of the little salon; he twitching nervously, she with her knees pressed closely together, marvelling; while Pagans, recently arrived from the land of citron, sings his Spanish ballads; while Madame la Comtesse Chodsko serves light, weak tea — genuine exile's tea! — to superb Polish dames, with their luxuriant hair twisted in heavy masses on the neck, gleaming hair of the color of parched corn; and while worthy Père Chodsko, as the clock strikes twelve, appears in the doorway, with the regularity of a cuckoo, with a candlestick in his hand, casts a circular glance on the assembled company, mutters with a marked Slavic accent a "Good-evening, Moussiou," to the men who are presented to him, then disappears, automatically, between the folds of a portière.

The desire to display my coat carried me even farther sometimes, way to the other extremity of Paris, on the other side of the Seine.   I followed the quays a long, long while, inhaling the odor of wild beasts, listening to the lions roar behind the iron fence of the Jardin des Plantes; I crossed a bridge, I gazed by gaslight or moonlight at the fanciful pediments and curiously pierced turret of the ruins of the Hôtel de Lavalette; and so I arrived at the Arsenal, — at the old Arsenal, to-day a library, with its long iron railing, its stoop, its doorway of the time of Vauban, whereon bombs are carved, — at the Arsenal, still full to overflowing with souvenirs of Charles Nodier.[1] Nodier was no longer there: the famous little green salon, from which romanticism took its flight, which has seen Musset, Hugo and George Sand weep over the adventures of Brisquet's dog, the little green salon, more celebrated, and justly so, than Arthenice's blue salon, was occupied now by M. Eugène Loudun. The spirit of revolution, the spirit of freedom, no longer fluttered in its curtains. After the champions of romanticism, poet workmen, Christian rhymers had found their way into that eighth castle of the King of Bohemia. Of the old romanticists a single one remained, unswervingly faithful at his post, as stanch and straight in his frockcoat as a Huguenot cavalryman in his coat of mail.

That one was Amédée Pommier, a wonderful workman in *bons-mots* and rhymes, a friend of the Dondeys and Pétrus Borels, the author of *L'Enfer*, of *Crâneries et Dettes de Cœur*, excellent books with flaming titles, a feast for men of letters, a terror to the Academies, and full of lines as noisy and as brilliant in coloring as an aviary of tropical birds.

Amédée Pommier was poor and dignified. He lived in close retirement, earning his living by

---

[1] A most attractive picture of Nodier's life at the Arsenal will be found in the first chapter of the elder Dumas's *Woman with the Velvet Necklace.*

making translations for Hachette, which he did not sign. It is an interesting fact that it was in collaboration with Amédée Pommier that Balzac, always possessed with the idea of writing a great classical comedy, undertook *Orgon*, five acts in verse, as a sequel to *Tartufe.*[1]

In that green salon at the Arsenal I also met M. Henri de Bornier. He often repeated some very clever little poems, one of which I have always remembered; each couplet ended with this refrain:

"Eh! eh! je ne suis pas si bête!"[2]

No such fool, indeed! for M. de Bornier wrote *La Fille de Roland*, which achieved a great success at the Théâtre Français, and will carry its author into the Academy. On certain evenings there was a great clearing of decks, screens were produced, chairs without arms and chairs with arms arranged in lines, and we acted charades. I have acted in charades there, I confess it! and I can see myself at this moment in a Turkish bazaar, as a Circassian girl, swathed in long white veils. I had Madame de Bornier for my companion in slavery. M. de Bornier, in turban and belted tunic reaching to the knees, made an apology for a sultan, and purchased us. As for the slave-merchant, he was, by your leave, no less a per-

---

[1] Of *Orgon*, M. de Lovenjoul says in his *Histoire des Œuvres de Balzac*, "that it was never published and never acted."

[2] "Ha! ha! I'm no such fool!"

sonage than M. L——, senator, former minister,
then much in the public eye, and afterwards con-
victed of financial irregularities.   The fall of the
Empire treated us to many surprises; and this
great Parisian highroad sometimes develops
strange windings!

VI.

MY DRUMMER.[1]

I WAS at home one morning, still in bed, when some one knocked.

"Who is that?"

"A man with a great box!"

I supposed that it was some package from the railway station; but, instead of the porter I expected to see, a short man with the round hat and short jacket of Provençal shepherds appeared before me. Jet black eyes, mild and restless, a face at once ingenuous and obstinate, and, half lost beneath heavy moustaches, an accent perfumed with garlic, probably not southern. The man said to me: "I am Buisson!" and handed me a letter, on the envelope of which I at once recognized the beautiful, fine handwriting, regular and placid, of Frédéric Mistral the poet. His letter was short.

"I send you my friend Buisson; he is a drummer, and goes to Paris to exhibit his talents; pilot him about."

---

[1] *Mon Tambourinaire.* — The *tambourin* is a species of drum (*tambour*), smaller and longer than the ordinary drum, and is beaten with a single drum-stick to accompany the shrill notes of a *galoubet* (flute), which is held to the mouth with the other hand.

Pilot a drummer! These Southerners stick at nothing. Having read the letter, I turned to Buisson again.

"So you 're a drummer?"

"Yes, Monsieur Daudet, the best of all drummers; I 'll show you!"

And he went to fetch his instruments, which he had discreetly deposited on the landing behind the door, before entering my room; a small, square, flat box, and a huge cylinder covered with green serge, similar in dimensions and shape to the monstrous affairs which the hurdy-gurdy men trundle through the streets. The little flat box contained the *galoubet*, the simple rustic flute which goes *tu-tu* — while the drum goes *pan-pan !* The veiled cylinder was the drum itself. Such a drum, my friends! the tears came to my eyes when I saw it unpacked: an authentic drum of the age of Louis XIV., touching and laughable at once by reason of its huge size, groaning like an old man if one so much as touched it with the end of the finger, made of fine walnut embellished with light carved work, polished, delicate, light, resonant, and made supple, as it were, by the mellowing hand of time. Buisson, solemn as a pope, fastened his drum to his left arm, took the flute in three fingers of his left hand — you must have seen the instruments and the attitude in some eighteenth century engraving or on a plate of Vieux-Moustier ware — and, wielding the little ivory-tipped drumstick with his right hand, he touched up the big drum, which, with its quavering note, its constant locust-like humming, marks the time and plays the bass to the sharp, piercing chirp of the flute. — *Tu-tu ! Pan-pan !* — Paris was far away and so was the winter. — *Tu-tu! pan-pan ! tu-tu!* — Bright sunlight and warm perfumes filled my room. I seemed to be transported to Provence, on the shore of the blue sea, in the shade of the poplars of the Rhône; serenades with voice and instruments arose beneath my windows, they sang Noël, they danced the Olivettes, and I saw the *farandole* wind in and out under the leafy plane-trees on the village squares, over the wild lavender on the scorched hillsides, in the white dust of the highroads, disappearing to appear again, more and more excited and wild, while the drummer followed slowly, never quickening his pace, — very sure that the dance will not leave the music behind, — grave and solemn, and limping a little with a movement of the knee to push the instrument forward at every step.

There are so many things in an air upon a drum! Yes, and many others, too, which you might not have seen, perhaps, but which I certainly saw. The Provençal imagination is made that way; it is of tinder, kindles quickly, even at seven o'clock in the morning, and Mistral was right to rely upon my enthusiasm. Buisson, too, became excited. He told me of his struggles, his efforts, and how he had stopped flute and drum half-way down the slope as they were falling into the abyss.

Some savages, it seems, wished to perfect the

galoubet, to add two holes. A *galoubet* with five holes! what sacrilege! He clung religiously to the *galoubet* with three holes, the *galoubet* of his ancestors, without fear of rivalry, however, in respect to the richness of the chords, the animation of the variations and trills. "It came to me," he said modestly and with a vague suggestion of inspiration, with that peculiar accent which would make the most touching of funeral orations ridiculous, — "it came to me one night when I was sitting under an olive-tree listening to a nightingale, and I thought: 'What, Buisson, the good Lord's bird sings like that, and you can't do with three holes what he does with just one hole?'" Rather an idiotic way of putting it! But it seemed charming to me that day.

A true Southerner never really enjoys his emotion unless he can induce somebody else to share it. I admired Buisson: one could not help admiring him. Behold me, therefore, on my journey through Paris, exhibiting my drummer, putting him forward as a phenomenon, enlisting my friends, arranging for an evening party at my house. Buisson played, described his struggles, said again: "It came to me." He was decidedly fond of that phrase, and my friends pretended to be overcome with admiration when they went away.

That was only the first step. I had a play in rehearsal at the Ambigu Theatre, a Provençal play! I mentioned Buisson, his drum and his flute, to Hostein, then manager, with such eloquence as you

can imagine!   For a week I pestered him. At last
he said to me : —

"Suppose we bring your drummer into the
play? It lacks a nail; he may perhaps serve to
hang success on."

I am sure that the Provençal did not sleep that
night. The next day we all three took a cab, he
and the drum and I; and at "noon for the fourth,"
as the notices of rehearsals put it, we alighted
amid a group of idlers, attracted by the strange
aspect of the machine, at the shamefaced, low door
which, in the most sumptuous theatres, affords a
far from triumphal entry to authors, artists, and
employés.

"Good God, how dark it is!" whispered the
Provençal, as we followed the long corridor, damp
and windy, like all theatre corridors. — "Good
God, how cold and dark it is!"—The drum
seemed to be of the same opinion, and banged
against all the angles of the corridor, against every
step of the spiral stairway, with ominous vibrations
and rumblings. At last we arrived, limping, on
the stage. The rehearsal was in progress. It is a
horrible thing to see the theatre at such a time, in
the privacy of its undress uniform, without the excitement, the life, the paint, and the illumination of
the evening: people full of business, walking softly
and speaking low, depressing shades on the banks
of the Styx, or miners in the depths of a mine; an
odor of dampness and of escaping gas; men and
things, — men running hither and thither and
scenery jumbled fantastically together, everything

of the color of ashes in the grudging light of infrequent lamps and gas-jets, veiled like Davy lamps; and to make the darkness denser, the impression of being underground, intensified from time to time as a door opens up above, on the second or third floor of the dark auditorium, and admits a ray of daylight as if through the distant opening of a well. That spectacle, being entirely a novel one to my compatriot, disconcerted him a little. But the rascal soon recovered himself and courageously allowed himself to be stationed all alone in the darkness at the very rear of the stage, on a cask which they had prepared for him. With his drum there were two casks, one on top of the other. In vain did I protest; in vain did I say: "In Provence drummers play while walking, and your cask's an impossibility;" Hostein assured me that my drummer was a minstrel, and that a minstrel could not be imagined otherwise than as sitting on a cask on the stage. The cask it is, then! Indeed, Buisson, full of confidence, had already climbed upon it, and said to me as he moved his feet about to establish his equilibrium: "It makes no difference!" So we left him with his flute at his mouth and his drumstick in his hand, behind a virgin forest of flies, uprights, pulleys, and ropes, and took up our positions, manager, author, and actors, at the front of the stage, as far away as possible, to judge of the effect.

"It came to me," sighed Buisson, "one night, under an olive-tree, while I was listening to a nightingale."

"All right! all right! play us something," I cried, irritated already by his eternal phrase.

Tu-tu! Pan-pan!

"Hush! he's beginning."

"Now we will see what the effect is!"

Great God! what an effect was produced upon that sceptical audience by that rustic, piping music, quavering and thin as the noise of an insect, buzzing away in a corner! I saw the actors, always delighted professionally by the failure of a comrade, slyly and ironically curl their clean-shaven lips; the fireman, under his gas-jet, writhed with silent laughter; even the prompter, aroused from his usual somnolence by the singularity of the episode, raised himself by his hands, and stuck his head out of his box, so that he looked like a gigantic turtle. Meanwhile Buisson, having finished playing, reverted to his phrase, which he apparently considered pretty.

"What! the good Lord's bird sings like that, and you can't do with three holes what he does with just one?"

"What's this fellow of yours saying with his chatter about holes?" said Hostein.

Thereupon I tried to explain the significance of the matter, the importance of having three holes instead of five, the originality of the idea of one person playing two instruments. "I must say," observed Marie Laurent, "that it would be more convenient with two."

To support my argument I tried to give an idea of the *farandole* step on the stage. No one paid any attention to it, and I began to realize vaguely the cruel truth that, in order that others might share the impressions, the poetic memories, which the drum and its simple old airs aroused in me, it was essential that the musician should bring with him to Paris a hill-top, a patch of blue sky, a bit of Provençal atmosphere. — " Come, children, let's go on, let's go on ! " — And, with no further heed to the drummer, the rehearsal proceeded. Buisson did not stir, but remained at his post, assured of his triumph, honestly believing that he was already a part of the play. After the first act I felt a pang of remorse at leaving him on his cask at the rear of the stage, where his figure could be indistinctly seen.

" Come, Buisson, down with you at once ! "

" Are we going to sign the contract ? "

The poor devil believed that he had produced a tremendous effect, and he showed me a stamped paper prepared beforehand with the characteristic foresight of a peasant.

" No, not to-day; he will write to you. But take care, *sapristi !* your drum knocks against everything and makes a great racket ! "

I was ashamed of the drum now : I feared that somebody would hear it ; and what joy, what a sense of relief I felt when I had stowed him away in the cab once more ! I dared not go to the theatre again for a week.

Some time after, Buisson came to see me again.

" Well, what about that contract ? "

" Contract ? Oh, yes ! that contract. Well, Hostein is hesitating ; he does n't understand."

" He 's a fool ! "

From the harsh and bitter tone in which the sweet-tempered musician uttered those words, I realized the full extent of my crime. Intoxicated by my enthusiasm, my praise, the Provençal drummer had lost his head, gone daft; he took himself for a great man in all seriousness, and was confident — had I not told him so, alas ! — that great triumphs were in store for him in Paris. Just try, I pray you, to stop a drum when it is rolling thus, with a great noise, among the rocks and bramble bushes, on the downward slope of illusion ! I did not try; it would have been mere folly and a waste of time.

Moreover Buisson now had other and more illustrious admirers : Félicien David and Théophile Gautier, to whom Mistral had written when he wrote to me. Poetic, dreamy souls, easily charmed, quick to forget their surroundings, the author of travels in the Orient and the musician of the land of roses had had no difficulty in imagining a landscape in harmony with the rustic melodies of the drum.

The first, while the flute mimicked the nightingale, fancied that he saw once more the shores of his native Durance and the crumbling terraces of his hills of Cadenet; the other let his dreams wander farther away, and found in the dull, monotonous beating of the drum some delicious reminiscence of nights on the Golden Horn and the Arabian *derboukas.*

Both conceived a sudden and ardent fancy for Buisson's real talent, out of its element though it was. For a fortnight the newspapers were full of extravagant articles; they all had something to say of the drummer, the illustrated journals published his picture, in a majestic pose, his eye flashing with triumph, the light flute between his fingers, the drum slung over his shoulder. Buisson, drunk with glory, bought newspapers by the dozens and sent them to his province.

From time to time he came to see me and told me of his triumphs: a punch at an artist's studio, evening parties in society, in Faubourg Saint-Germain — his mouth was full of his *Faubourg de Séint-Germéin* — where the rascal made beplumed dowagers dreamy and pensive by repeating shamelessly his famous sentiment: "It came to me one night under an olive-tree, as I listened to a nightingale."

Meanwhile, as it was important that he should not grow rusty, but should preserve, despite the innumerable distractions of artistic life, his mellowness of touch and purity of phrasing, our ingenuous Provençal conceived the plan of rehearsing his serenades and *farandoles* late at night, in the heart of Paris, in his room on the fifth floor of the furnished lodging-house in the Bréda Quarter. *Tu-tu! Pan-pan!* The whole quarter was stirred to its depths by those unusual noises. The neighbors rebelled, they entered a complaint; but Buisson continued with renewed vigor, spreading harmony and insomnia abroad with a turn of his hand, until the *concierge*, at the end of his forbearance, refused him his key one night.

Buisson, robing himself in his artistic dignity,
sued for his rights before the justice of the peace,
and won.   The French law, which is very harsh to
musicians and banishes hunting-horns to the cellars
throughout the year, allowing them only on Mardi
Gras, — one day out of three hundred and sixty-
five to blow their coppery blasts in the free air,
— the French law, it seems, had not foreseen the
drum.

After that victory, Buisson was daunted by nothing.   One Sunday morning I received a card: he
proposed to display his talents, that afternoon, in
a grand concert at the Salle du Châtelet.   Duty
and friendship called: I went to hear him, therefore, not without a feeling of depression due to a
secret presentiment.

It was a superb audience, the hall filled from pit
to arched ceiling; evidently our newspaper articles
had told.   Suddenly the curtain rose: general
agitation, profound silence.   I uttered a cry of
horror. In the centre of the vast stage, so vast
that six hundred ballet-dancers can perform freely
upon it, Buisson, with his drum, arrayed in a coat
that was too small for him, and gloves that made
him resemble the insects with yellow claws whom
Granville, in his fanciful sketches, represents puffing desperately at fantastic instruments, — Buisson
made his appearance alone.   I saw him, with my
opera-glass, waving his long arms and moving his
shoulders up and down; the poor devil was evidently playing, beating his drum vigorously and
blowing with all the strength of his lungs; but no

perceptible sound reached the audience. It was too far, everything was swallowed by the stage. It was like a cricket singing his serenade in the middle of the Champ de Mars! And it was impossible for any one to count the holes at that distance, or for him to say, " It came to me," or to talk about the good Lord's bird!

I was red with shame; I saw bewildered faces all about me, I heard voices muttering: " What's the meaning of this wretched joke? " The doors of the boxes began to slam, the hall gradually became empty; however, as it was a well-bred audience, there was no hissing, but they left the drummer to finish his tune in solitude.

I waited for him at the stage door to console him. Console, indeed! He thought he had made a tremendous hit; he was more radiant than ever. " I 'm waiting for Colonne to sign this," he said, showing me a bulky document spotted with stamps. That was too much, upon my word; I could not contain myself; I took my courage in both hands and told him bluntly, without stopping for breath, just what I thought : —

" Buisson, we have all made a mistake in trying to make Paris understand the charm of your great drum and the melody of your fife. I made a mistake; Gautier and David made a mistake; and the result is that you are making a mistake. No, you 're no nightingale."

" It came to me — " interposed Buisson.

" Yes, it came to you, I know; but you 're no nightingale. The nightingale sings everywhere, his song is of all countries, and in all countries his song is understood. But you are only a poor cricket, — whose monotonous, shrill refrain is well suited to the pale olive-trees, the pines weeping pitch in golden tears, the deep blue sky, the bright sunlight, the stony hills of Provence, — but an absurd, pitiful cricket under this gray sky, in the wind and rain, with your long wings dripping wet. So go back to Provence, take back your drum, play your serenades, play for the pretty girls to dance the *farandole*, for the triumphal march of the conquerors in the bull-fights. There, you are a poet, an artist; here, you will always be an unappreciated mountebank."

He made no reply; but in his visionary glance, in his mild but stubborn eye, I could read: " The trouble with you is that you 're jealous ! "

A few days later, my man came to me, as proud as Artaban, to inform me that Colonne — another imbecile, like Hostein — had refused to sign a contract; but that another opportunity had presented itself, a marvellous opportunity: an engagement at a café-concert, at 120 francs per evening, signed in advance. He actually had the paper. Ah! a precious paper, truly! I learned the truth afterward.

Some ill-fated manager or other, borne onward, blinded by the muddy current of bankruptcy, had conceived the idea of clinging to that brittle willow-branch, Buisson's drum and fife. Being sure that he could not pay, he signed whatever he was asked to sign. But the Provençal did not look so far ahead; he had a stamped paper, and that stamped paper was enough to gladden his heart. Moreover, as it was a café-concert, he must have a costume. " They have dressed me as a troubadour of ancient times," he said with a condescending smile, " but as I have a very good figure, it does n't look badly on me, as you 'll see ! " I did see, in very truth.

In one of the cafés-chantants in the neighborhood of Porte Saint-Denis, so fashionable in the latter years of the Empire, with the tawdry tinsel of its strange half-Chinese, half-Persian decorations, the daubs and streaks of gold being made more offensive to the eye by the gas-jets and chandeliers; its proscenium boxes, locked and barred, where duchesses and ambassadresses concealed themselves on certain evenings, to applaud the contortions and vocal gymnastics of some eccentric diva; its sea of heads and of beer-glasses, levelled, like the waves on a foggy day, by pipe-smoke and the vapor of many breaths; its waiters running to and fro; its customers calling; its orchestral conductor, in his white cravat, dignified and impassive, arousing or allaying with a gesture *à la Neptune* the hurricane of fifty brass instruments; — between an idiotically sentimental ballad, bleated by a very pretty girl with eyes like a sheep, and a pastoral ditty, cynically roared by a sort of red-armed Theresa, on the stage where some half-dozen damsels in white, very *décolletées*, sat around in a circle awaiting their turn to sing and ogling the audience, there suddenly appeared a personage whom I shall never forget while I live. It was Buisson, with his flute at his mouth, his drum on his left knee, in troubadour costume as he had promised me. But such a troubadour! a doublet (imagine that!) half apple-green and half blue, one leg of his breeches red, the other yellow, and everything so skin-tight that it made one shudder; cap with slashed edges, high-heeled shoes with peaked toes, and with all the rest, moustaches, those superb moustaches, too long and too black, which he could not make up his mind to sacrifice, falling around his chin like a cascade of shoe-blacking!

Fascinated presumably by the exquisite taste displayed in that costume, the audience greeted the musician with a long murmur of approval, and my troubadour smiled affably and was happy, seeing that sympathetic audience before him, and feeling on his back the flaming glances of the lovely ladies seated in a circle and admiring him. Ah! but it was another matter when the music began. The *tu-tus*, the *pan-pans*, could not charm those ears, surfeited as a palate is by alcohol, and burned by the vitriol of the repertory of the resort. And then the company was not, as at the Châtelet, a reserved and distinguished one. — "Enough! enough! Take him away! Have n't you finished, learned pig?" — In vain did Buisson try to open his mouth and say: "It came to me — " the benches rose in their wrath, the curtain had to be lowered, and the green, blue, red, and yellow troubadour disappeared in the tempest of hisses, like a poor macaw stripped of its feathers and whirled away by a gust of wind in the tropics.

Would you believe it? Buisson persisted! An illusion strikes deep and is hard to uproot in a Provençal brain. Fifteen evenings in succession he appeared, always hissed, never paid, until the moment when a bailiff's clerk affixed a certificate of bankruptcy on the openwork doors of the café-concert.

Thereupon the downward course began. From music-hall to music-hall, from brothel to brothel, still believing in his success, still pursuing his chimera of an engagement on stamped paper, the drummer descended to suburban gin-shops — where gambling is carried on in secret — accompanied by a keyless piano for orchestra, to the keenest delight of an audience of tired, tipsy boatmen and dry-goods clerks spending Sunday in the country.

One evening — winter was barely at an end, and spring had not arrived — I was crossing the Champs-Élysées. An open-air concert, being in a greater hurry than others, had suspended its lanterns from the still leafless trees. It was drizzling a little and was dismal enough. I heard a *Tu-tu! Pan-pan!* Buisson again! I saw him through the entrance, drumming a Provençal air before half-a-dozen auditors, sitting under umbrellas, who had entered on complimentary tickets, I doubt not. I dared not go in: after all, it was my fault! It was the fault of my imprudent enthusiasm. Poor Buisson! poor bedraggled cricket!

VII.

HISTORY OF MY BOOKS. — TARTARIN OF TARASCON.

NEARLY fifteen years have passed since I published the *Adventures of Tartarin*, and Tarascon has not yet forgiven me; indeed, travellers worthy of credence inform me that, every morning, at the time when the little Provençal town opens the shutters of its shops and shakes its carpets in the breath of the great Rhone, from every doorway, from every window, there is the same angry shaking of fists; the same flashing of black eyes, the same cry of rage Parisward. "Oh! that Daudet — if he ever comes down here just once!" — as in the story of Bluebeard: "Come down, or I will come up!"

And, joking aside, once Tarascon did come up.

It was in 1878, when the provinces were much in evidence, — in the hotels, on the boulevards, and on the gigantic bridge thrown across the river from the Champ de Mars to the Trocadéro. One morning the sculptor Amy, a native of Tarascon naturalized in Paris, was called upon by a formidable pair of moustaches which had come to Paris by excursion train, ostensibly to see the Universal Exposition, but really to have an explanation with

Daudet on the subject of the gallant commandant Bravida and the *Defence of Tarascon*, a little tale published during the war.

" *Que?* — we 're going to Daudet's !"

Those were the first words spoken by the Tarasconian moustaches on entering the studio; and for a fortnight the sculptor Amy heard nothing but the question: " And, by the way, where can we find that Daudet?" The unfortunate artist exhausted his imagination to spare me that heroi-comic visitation. He took his countryman's moustaches to the Exposition, lost them on the Street of the Nations, in the machinery gallery, watered them with English beer, Hungarian wine, mare's milk, divers outlandish drinks, bewildered them with Moorish music, gypsy music, Japanese music, fatigued them, wore them out, hoisted them — like Tartarin on his minaret — to the towers of the Trocadéro.

But the Provençal's rancor held firm, and as he surveyed Paris from the summit he asked with a frown : —

" Can we see his house from here? "

" Whose house? "

" Why, that Daudet's, *pardi !* "

And it was like that everywhere. Luckily the excursion train got steam up and bore away the Tarasconian's vengeance unwreaked; but when he had gone others might come, and while the Exposition lasted I did not sleep. It is something, I tell you, to feel the hatred of a whole town on your shoulders ! Even to this day, when I travel in the South, I am always ill at ease when I pass through Tarascon. I know that it still bears me a grudge, that my books are banished from its libraries, cannot be found even at the railway station; and from the farthest point at which I can descry the castle of good King Réné from the railway carriage, I am uncomfortable and would like to rush through the station. That is why I avail myself of this new edition to offer to the people of Tarascon, with my most profuse apologies, the explanation which the ex-commander-in-chief of their militia came to demand at my hands.

Tarascon was, so far as I am concerned, simply a pseudonym picked up on the line from Paris to Marseille, because it had a sonorous sound in the Southern accent, and rang out triumphantly, among the names of stations, like the yell of an Apache warrior. In reality, the country of Tartarin and the *helmet-hunters* is a little farther on, some five or six leagues, "on the other hand" of the Rhone. There it was that I, as a child, saw the baobab languishing in the little mignonette pot, the image of my hero in the narrow confines of his little town, where the Rebuffas sang the duet from *Robert le Diable;* and it was from there that Tartarin and I, armed to the teeth and with Algerian sharpshooters' caps on our heads, set out one day in November, 1861, to hunt the lion in Algeria.

To tell the truth, I did not go solely for that purpose, being especially desirous to patch up my somewhat dilapidated lungs in the warm sunshine. But not for nothing, bless my soul! was I born in the country of the *helmet-hunters;* and as soon as I set my foot on the deck of the *Zouave*, upon which our enormous arm-chest was embarked, more Tartarin than Tartarin, I really fancied that I was going to exterminate all the wild beasts in the Atlas Mountains.

O the enchantment of one's first journey! It seems to me as if it were but yesterday that we set sail on that blue sea, blue as a liquid dye, its surface ruffled by the wind, sparkling with grains of salt, while the bowsprit reared and plunged, pricked the waves, then shook itself all white with foam, and rushed on, pointing seaward, always seaward; and all the bells in Marseille striking the noon hour, and my twenty years ringing a resonant peal in my brain.

I see it all again, simply from speaking of it: I am in Algiers, strolling through the bazaars in a half-light that smells of musk and amber, pressed rose-leaves, and warm wool; the *guzlas* give forth their nasal notes on three strings before the little Tunisian wardrobes with mirrors for panels and mother-of-pearl arabesques, while the fountain drips with cool, refreshing note on the porcelain tiles of the *patio*. And here am I snatching a glimpse at Sahel, the orange woods of Blidah, Chiffa, the brook of the Monkeys, Milianah and its green slopes, its orchards of tangled helianthus, fig-trees, and gourd-trees, like our Provençal country-houses.

Here is the immense valley of the Chelif, thickets

of lentils, dwarf palms, dry beds of torrents lined
with rose-laurels; on the horizon the smoke of a
gourbi rising straight in the air from a clump of
cactus, the gray-walled enclosure of a caravansary,
a saint's tomb with its white turban-like cupola, its
ex-votos on the dazzlingly white wall, and here and
there, in the glaring, parched expanse, moving
dark specks which are flocks and herds.

And I still hear, with the sensation in the pit of
my stomach caused by the jolting of my Arab
saddle, the clashing of my great stirrups, the cries
of the shepherds in that wavy, pure atmosphere
where the voice leaps from wave to wave: "Si
Mohame-e-ed-i — ;" the fierce barking of watch-
dogs around the villages, the shooting and
shouting of the horse-races, and the wild music
of the *derboukas*, at night, in front of the open
tents, while the jackals yelp in the fields as persistently as our crickets, and a crescent moon,
Mahomet's crescent, casts its gleam over the
starry velvet of the night. Very distinct in my
memory too is the melancholy of the home-coming,
the sensation of exile and cold on landing at Marseille, and the dark, veiled aspect of the blue sky
of Provence compared with those Algerian landscapes, that palette with its vivid and varied scale
of coloring, dawns of an indescribable green, mineral
green, the green of poison, short evening twilights
with changing shades of purple and amethyst, pink
wells to which pink camels come to drink, where
the well-cord, and the Bedouin's beard, lapping the
very bucket, stream with pink drops; — after the

lapse of twenty years, I am still conscious of that regret, that homesick longing for a light that has disappeared.

There is in Mistral's language a word which defines and summarizes an instinct of the race: *galéja*, to make sport of, to jest. And one can see the flash of irony, the mischievous gleam in the depths of Provençal eyes. *Galéja* recurs on all occasions in conversation, under the form of a verb or a substantive. — " *Vesés-pas? Es uno galéjado.* — Don't you see? It's a joke." — " *Taisote, galéjaïré.* — Hold your tongue, you wretched scoffer." — But the being a *galéjaïré* does not exclude either kindness of heart or affectionate disposition. They are simply amusing themselves, *té!* they say it laughingly; and down yonder laughter goes with all sentiments, the most impassioned, the most tender. In an old, old ballad of our province — the story of little Fleurance — this liking of the Provençaux for laughter appears in an exquisite guise. Fleurance has married, when a mere child, a knight who takes her so young — *la prén tan jouveneto se saup pas courdela* — that she does not know how to clasp her belt. But they are no sooner married than Fleurance's lord and master is obliged to start for Palestine and leave his little wife all alone. Seven years have passed, and the knight has given no sign of life, when a pilgrim with a shell in his hat and a long beard appears at the drawbridge of the castle. He has just returned from among the *Teurs;* he brings news from Fleurance's husband;

and the young lady at once orders that he be ab-
mitted, places him opposite her at table.

What takes place between them thereafter I can
tell you in two ways; for the story of Fleurance,
like all popular ballads, has made the tour of
France in the pedler's pack, and I found it in
Picardie with a significant variation. In the Picard
ballad, the lady begins to weep in the midst of the
repast.

"You weep, lovely Fleurance?" queries the
pilgrim, trembling with emotion.

"I weep, because I recognize you and you are
my dear husband."

The little Provençal Fleurance, on the contrary,
has hardly taken her seat opposite the long-
bearded pilgrim when she begins prettily *to laugh
at him.* "*Hé!* why do you laugh, Fleurance?"
—"*Té!* I laugh because you are my husband."

And, still laughing, she jumps upon his knees,
and the pilgrim laughs too in his wig of tow, for
he, like her, is a *galéjaïré,* which fact does not in-
terfere with their loving each other dearly, in close
embrace, lip to lip, with all the emotion of their
faithful hearts.

And I, too, am a *galéjaïré.* In the mists of Paris,
in the splashing of its mud and its melancholy, I
may perhaps have lost the taste and faculty for
laughter; but on reading Tartarin you will see
that there still remained, in the depths of my being,
a trace of gayety which suddenly developed in the
genial light of the South.

Most assuredly I agree that there was room for

something more to be written concerning French Algeria than the *Adventures of Tartarin ;* for example, a true and pitiless study of its manners and morals, the results of close observation of a new country on the borderland between two races and two civilizations, with their reciprocal action upon each other, the victor vanquished in his turn by the climate, by the enervating mode of life, by Oriental carelessness and rottenness, clubbing and marauding, the Algerian Doineau [1] and the Algerian Bazaine, those two perfect products of the Arab administration. What revelations might be made concerning the vileness of those barrack-room morals, the story of a colonist, the founding of a town amid the rivalries of three powers face to face, — the army, the magistracy, and the government! Instead of all that, I brought back naught save *Tartarin*, a burst of laughter, a *galéjade*.

To be sure, my companion and I looked a fine pair of fools, as we disembarked in red belts and glaring sharpshooters' caps in the good city of Algiers, where there were hardly any Turks except our two selves. With what a meditative, satisfied air did Tartarin remove his enormous hunting-boots at the doors of the mosques and enter the sanctuary of Mahomet, with grave face and tightly

---

[1] Auguste Édouard Doineau, a French officer in Algiers, was in 1852 appointed head of a bureau there. He was sentenced to death for murdering a prominent Arab official and his interpreter. His sentence was commuted to imprisonment for life, and in 1859 Napoléon pardoned him on condition that he should never return to France or Algiers. He was afterwards more or less in the public eye for various unsavory reasons.

closed lips, in colored socks! Ah! that fellow believed in the Orient, the Indian dancing-girls, the muezzins, the lions, the panthers, the dromedaries, — everything that his books had chosen to tell him; and his Southern imagination magnified them all.

I, as faithful as the camel in my tale, followed him through his heroic dream; but at times I was a little doubtful. I remember that one evening, at Oued-Fodda, as we started out to lie in wait for a lion, and passed through an encampment of *Chasseurs d'Afrique* with our whole outfit of leggings, rifles, revolvers, and hunting-knives, I felt keenly the absurdity of the situation as I remarked the silent stupefaction of the honest troopers eating their soup in front of the lines of tents. "Suppose there should n't be any lion!"

And yet, that sensation to the contrary notwithstanding, an hour later, after nightfall, when I was on my knees in a clump of laurel, searching the darkness with my glasses, while cranes flew screaming far overhead, and jackals crept through the grass around me, I felt my rifle tremble on the hilt of the hunting-knife which was stuck in the ground.

I have attributed to Tartarin that shudder of fear and the burlesque reflections which accompanied it; but that is a great injustice. I give you my word that, if the lion had appeared, honest Tartarin would have received him, rifle at rest, and knife in the air; and if his bullet had missed its mark, if his knife had betrayed him in a hand-to-hand struggle, he would have ended the conflict body to body, would have suffocated the monster in his more than muscular arms, torn him with his nails and teeth, without turning a hair; for he was a rough fighter, was that *helmet-hunter*, and furthermore a man of spirit, who was the first to laugh at my *galéjade!*

The history of Tartarin was not written until long after my trip to Algeria. The trip was in 1861–2, the book was written in 1869. I began to publish it as a serial in the *Petit Moniteur Universel*, with amusing sketches by Émile Benassit. It was an absolute failure. The *Petit Moniteur* was a popular newspaper, and the common people have no comprehension of printed sarcasm, which bewilders them, makes them think that you mean to make sport of them. Words fail to describe the disappointment of the subscribers to the one-sou journal, who relish so keenly *Rocambole* and Ponson du Terrail, when they read those first chapters of the life of Tartarin, the ballads and the baobab, — a disappointment which went as far as threats of stopping their subscriptions, and personal insults. Some one wrote to me: " Ah! indeed — and what then? What does that prove? Imbecile!" — and fiercely signed his name. Paul Dalloz was most to be pitied, for he had incurred considerable expense in advertising and illustrations, and he paid dear for an experiment. After some ten or twelve instalments, I took pity on him and carried *Tartarin* to *Figaro*, where it was better understood by the readers, but came in collision with other animosities. The secretary of the editorial staff of *Figaro* at that time was Alexandre Duvernois, brother of Clement Duvernois, former journalist and minister. As ill-luck would have it, nine years before, during my playful Algerian expedition, I had met Alexandre Duvernois, then a modest clerk in the civil service at Milianah, who had always retained a feeling of genuine adoration for the colony. Irritated and disgusted by the light tone in which I spoke of his dear Algeria, although he could not prevent the publication of *Tartarin*, he arranged to divide it up into intermittent fragments, alleging the nauseating, stereotyped excuse of "abundance of matter," so that that poor little novel dragged its slow length along in the newspaper almost as interminably as the *Wandering Jew* or the *Three Musketeers.* "It drags, it drags," rumbled Villemessant's double-bass, and I was terribly afraid that I should be obliged to break off a second time.

Then there were fresh tribulations. The hero of my book was at that time called Barbarin of Tarascon.

Now there was at Tarascon an old family of Barbarins, who threatened me with a lawsuit if I did not instantly remove their name from that insulting buffoonery. Having a holy dread of courts and the law, I consented to substitute Tartarin for Barbarin in the proofs already struck off, which had to be gone over line by line in a careful hunt for *B's.* Some must have escaped in those three hundred pages; and in the first edition there are Barbarins and Tartarins, and even *tonsoir* for *bonsoir*. At last the book appeared, and succeeded very well from the publisher's standpoint, despite the very local flavor which every one does not enjoy. One must be from the South, or know it very well, to realize how common the Tartarin type is among us, and that under the hot Tarascon sun, which warms and magnetizes them, the absurd fancies of men's brains and imaginations are developed into monstrosities as diverse in form and dimensions as the gourds.

Judged impartially, at a distance of some years, Tartarin, running his wild, unbridled course, seems to me to possess the qualities of youth and life and truth, — the truth of the country beyond the Loire, which inflates and exaggerates, never lies, and *tarasconizes* all the time. The grain of the work is neither very fine nor of very close texture. It is what I call " standing literature," spoken and gesticulated with my hero's exuberant enthusiasm. But I must confess that, great as is my love of style, of beautiful prose, melodious and highly colored, in my opinion these should not be the novelist's only care. His real delight should consist in the creation of real persons, in establishing, by virtue of their verisimilitude, types of men and women who will go about thenceforth through the world with the names, the gestures, the grimaces, with which he has endowed them and which make people speak of them — whether they be loved or detested — without reference to their creator and without mentioning his name. For my part, my emotion is always the same, when I hear some one say of a person he has met in his daily life, of one of the innumerable puppets of the political comedy, " He is a Tartarin — a Monpavon — a Delobelle."   At such times a thrill runs over me, the thrill of pride that a father feels, hidden in the crowd while his son is being applauded, and all the time longing to cry out: " That is my boy ! "

VIII.

HISTORY OF MY BOOKS. — LETTERS FROM MY MILL.

ON the right-hand side of the road from Arles to the quarries of Fontvielle, beyond the hill of Corde and Montmajour Abbey, and above a large village, as white and dusty as a stoneyard, rises a little mountain covered with pines, always green amid the parched, brown landscape. The wings of the windmill turn in the wind on the summit; at the foot stands a great white house, the manor of Montauban, an ancient and unique structure which begins as a château — broad stoop, Italian terrace with pillars — and ends with the whitewashed walls of a Provençal farm, with perches for the peacocks, a vine over the door, the well with its iron-work entwined by the branches of a figtree, sheds in which harrows and ploughshares gleam, the enclosure for the sheep, and beyond it a field of slender almond trees with bunches of pink flowers quickly scattered in the March wind. Those are the only flowers at Montauban. There are no flower-beds, no greensward, nothing to remind one of a garden, an enclosed estate; nothing but clumps of pines among the gray rocks, a natural, wild park, with paths through the underbrush, slippery with dry pine needles. Within, there is the same contrast of manor and farm-house; — cool, flagged galleries, furnished with Louis Quatorze couches and easy-chairs, with cane seats and twisted legs, so convenient for siestas in summer; broad staircases, echoing halls where the wind blows at will, whistles under the chamber doors and waves the old-fashioned broad striped curtains. Descend two steps and lo! you are in the rustic living-room, with no floor save the hard-trodden earth, low in the centre, where the hens scratch for the crumbs from the farm breakfast, and with rough-cast walls against which stand walnut side-boards and the roughly made basket and kneading trough.

An old Provençal family lived there twenty years ago, a family no less unique and charming than its dwelling-place. The mother, a country bourgeoise of advanced age, but still perfectly straight in her widow's cap, which she had never laid aside, was the sole manager of that estate, which was of considerable extent and included olive and mulberry plantations, wheat fields and vineyards; her four sons lived with her, four old fellows who were commonly designated by the professions which they severally had practised or were still practising: the Mayor, the Consul, the Notary, the Advocate. Their father being dead and their sister married, they had all four gathered around the old woman, sacrificing their ambitions and their tastes to her, united in a single-hearted love for her whom they called their " dear mamma," with an inflection indicating profound respect and emotion.

Excellent people, blessed house! How often in winter have I gone thither to recuperate in the arms of nature, to cure myself of Paris and its fevers in the healthful emanations of our little Provençal hills. I would appear unheralded, sure of a welcome, my arrival announced by the bugle-call of the peacocks and hunting dogs, Miracle, Miraclet, Tambour, which gambolled around the carriage, while the startled maid-servant's Arlesian head-dress fluttered in the wind as she ran to inform her masters, and " dear mamma " pressed me to her little gray plaid shawl, as if I were one of her own boys. Five minutes of confusion, and then, when the greetings were at an end and my trunk in my room, the whole house became silent and calm once more. I would whistle to old Miracle — a spaniel found on a piece of wreckage at sea by fishermen from Faraman — and I would go up to my mill.

The mill was a ruin ; a crumbling mass of stone, iron and old boards which had not turned in the wind for many years and which lay, with broken limbs, as useless as a poet, while all around on the hillside the miller's trade prospered and ground with all its wings. Strange affinities exist between ourselves and inanimate things. From the first day that cast-off structure was dear to my heart ; I loved it for its desolation, its road overgrown with weeds, those little grayish, fragrant mountain weeds with which Père Gaucher compounded his elixir ; for its little worn platform where it was so pleasant to loiter, sheltered from the wind, while a rabbit hurried by, or a long snake, rustling among the leaves with crafty detours, hunted the field mice with which the ruin swarmed. With the creaking of an old building shaken by the north wind, the flapping of its ragged wings like the rigging of a ship at sea, the mill stirred in my poor, restless, nomadic brain memories of journeys by sea, of landings at lighthouses and far-off islands; and the shivering swell all about completed the illusion. I know not whence I derived this taste for wild and desert places which has characterized me from my childhood, and which seems so inconsistent with the exuberance of my nature, unless it be at the same time the physical need of repairing by a fast of words, by abstinence from outcries and gestures, the terrible waste which the Southerner makes of his whole being. Be that as it may, I owe a great deal to those places of refuge for the mind; and no one of them has been more salutary in its effect upon me than that old mill in Provence. Indeed, I was tempted for a moment to purchase it; and at the office of the notary at Fontvielle may be seen a deed which never went beyond the stage of being drawn, but which I made use of in the preface to my book.

My mill never belonged to me. But that fact did not prevent my passing there long days filled with dreams and memories, until the hour when the winter sun sank between the low, bare hills, filling the valleys as with molten metal, with a smoking stream of gold. Then, at a blast upon a sea-shell, the horn with which M. Séguin called his goat, I returned to partake of the evening meal at the hospitable and unconventional table at Montauban, where every one was served according to his tastes and habits; the Consul's Constance wine beside the water gruel or plate of white chestnuts of which the old mother made her frugal dinner. Having taken our coffee and lighted our pipes, and the four boys having gone down to the village, I remained behind to talk with the excellent woman, an energetic, kindly character, a keen intellect, a memory full of anecdotes which she told with such simple eloquence: incidents of her childhood, people who had disappeared, vanished customs, the gathering of vermilion from the leaves of the kermes-oaks,[1] 1815, the invasion, the heartfelt cry of relief of all mothers at the fall of the First Empire, the dances, the fireworks discharged on all the public squares, and the handsome Cossack officer in a green coat, with whom she had gambolled like a kid, had danced the *farandole* one whole night on the bridge of Beaucaire. And then her marriage, the death of her husband and her oldest daughter, whom, when she was several leagues away, a presentiment, a sudden pulsation of the heart used to reveal to her; and other deaths, and births, and the translation of beloved ashes when the old cemetery was closed. It was as if I were turning over the leaves of one of those old account-books, with worn edges, wherein the moral history of families

---

[1] The *kermes* insect, allied to the cochineal insect, and found on several species of oak near the Mediterranean, has long been used in dyeing.

used to be written down, mingled with the trivial
details of everyday life, and accounts of good crops
of wine and oil side by side with miracles of sacrifice and reisgnation. In that half-rustic bourgeoise
housewife I was conscious of a thoroughly feminine, refined, intuitive mind, the mischievous and
innocent fascination of a little girl. When she was
tired of talking, she would bury herself in her great
easy-chair, at a distance from the lamp; the
shadow of the falling night would close her hollow
eyelids, creep over her aged, deep-lined face, wrinkled, furrowed with crevasses and ravines by the
ploughshare and the harrow; and as she sat there
mute and motionless, I might have believed that
she was dead but for the rattling of her rosary as
her fingers told the beads in the depths of her
pocket. Thereupon I would steal softly from the
room to finish my evening in the kitchen.

Beneath the overhang of a gigantic fireplace
where the copper lamp was hung, a numerous
company would have assembled in front of a bright
fire of olive-tree stumps, its intermittent flashes
casting a curious light upon the pointed caps and
jackets of yellow *caddis*. In the place of honor,
on the hearthstone, sat the shepherd in a crouch-
ing attitude, with his closely shaven chin, his skin
like tanned leather, and his *cachimbau* (short pipe)
in the corner of his finely-cut mouth; he spoke but
little, having acquired the habit of contemplative
silence in the long summer months when he kept
his flocks on the mountains of Dauphiné, beneath
the stars, all of which he knew by name, from *Jen*

de Milan to the *Char des Âmes*. Between two whiffs of his pipe he would utter in his sonorous patois fragmentary sentences, incomplete parables, mysterious proverbs, a few of which I remember.

"The ballad of Paris, the most pitiful thing on earth. — [You can tell] man by his speech and the ox by his horns. — A monkey's job, mean and hard. — Pale moon, 't will rain soon. — With a red moon, you know, the wind will blow. —.When the moon is white, the day will be bright." — And every evening the same quotation, with which he closed the session: "The older she grew, the more she knew, and so did n't want to die."

Next him was the keeper Mitifio, called Pistolet, with the merry eyes and the little white spaniel, who entertained the company with a multitude of tales and legends which his mocking, mischievous, thoroughly Provençal wit made ever new. Sometimes, amid the laughter aroused by one of Pistolet's anecdotes, the shepherd would remark with the utmost gravity: "If to have a white beard entitles one to be considered wise, goats ought to be." — There was old Siblet too, Dominique the coachman, and a little hunchback nicknamed *lou Roudéirou* (*Le Rôdeur*),[1] a sort of hobgoblin, a village spy, with keen eyes that could pierce the darkness and stone walls, a quick-tempered creature, consumed by religious and political animosities.

You should have heard him describe and imitate old Jean Coste, a Red of '93, recently dead and

[1] The Prowler.

loyal to his beliefs to the end. There was Jean
Coste's journey, twenty leagues on foot, to see the
curé and the two *secondaries* (vicars) of his village
guillotined. — " I tell you, my children, when I
saw them stick their heads through the little
window — and they didn't like to put their heads
through the little window — but God bless me! I
enjoyed it all the same (*taben aguéré dé plesi*)."
And Jean Coste, shivering with cold, warming his
old carcass against some wall in the blazing sun.
and saying to the boys about him: " Young men,
have you read Volney? —*Jouven auès legi Voulney?*
— He proves mathematically that there's no God
but the sun! — *Gès dé Diou, doum dé Liou! rèn
qué lou souleù!* " — And his opinions concerning
the men of the Revolution: " Marat, good man;
Saint-Just, good man; Danton, also a good man.
But, toward the end, he ruined himself, he fell
into the snare of moderatism — *dins lou mouderan-
tismo!* " — And Jean Coste's death-agony when he
sat up like a spectre in his bed and spoke French
for once in his life, to roar in the priest's face:
" Out with you, crow — the carrion is n't dead
yet! " — The little hunchback would utter that
last outcry in such a tone that the women would
exclaim: " Ah! holy mother! " and the sleeping
dogs would wake and plunge growling at the door
where the night wind wailed through the cracks,
until a shrill, fresh female voice would strike up,
to do away with the painful impression, one of
Saboli's Christmas chants: " I saw in the air — an
angel clothed in green — who wore great wings —

above his shoulders." Or the arrival of the Magi at Bethlehem: " Behold the Moorish king — with his eyes all red with weeping — the Child Jesus weeps — the king dares not enter; " — a simple, lively air for the flute, which I noted down with all the local metaphors, expressions and traditions collected among the ashes on that venerable hearth.

Often too, my fancy indulged in little excursions around the mill. I went hunting or fishing in Camargue, in the direction of the pond of Vacarès, among the cattle and wild horses running at will in that region of desolate plains. Another day I would go to visit my friends the Provençal poets, the Félibres.[1] At that time the Félibrige had not become a dignified academical institution. Those were the early days of the *Church*, the fervent, ingenuous hours, without schisms or rivalries. Five or six good fellows, laughing like children in apostles' beards, met by appointment, sometimes at Maillane, in Frédéric Mistral's little village, separated from me by the lace-like heights of the Alpilles; sometimes at Arles, in the forum, amid a swarm of drovers and shepherds come thither to hire themselves out to the farmers. Sometimes we

[1] The movement which resulted in the " Provençal Renaissance " was founded by Roumanille, when, it is not possible to say definitely, but probably between 1840 and 1850. It is said by Larousse to have been due to the fact that his mother was unable to understand some verses which he wrote for her when he left college, because she had forgotten her school French. He thereupon determined to write and to encourage others to write poetry for the common people of Provence in their language. Frédéric Mistral acquired the greatest fame of those who supported him in his undertaking.

went to Aliscamps, to listen, lying in the grass
among the sarcophagi of gray stone, to one of
Théodore Aubanel's beautiful dramas, while the
air vibrated with grasshoppers and the hammers
in the machine-shops of the P. L. M. rang out
ironically behind a curtain of pale trees. After
the reading, a turn on the Lice to see the haughty
and coquettish Arlesian girl for love of whom
poor Jan killed himself pass by in her white neck-
erchief and little cap. At other times our rendezvous was at Ville des Baux, that crumbling heap
of ruins, of wild cliffs, of ancient escutcheoned
palaces, crumbling away, swaying in the wind like
an eagle's nest on the height, whence one descries
beyond vast plains and plains, a line of deeper,
sparkling blue, which is the sea. We would sup
at Corneille's inn; and wander all the evening,
singing poetry, through narrow jagged lanes,
among crumbling walls, remains of stairways, of
uncrowned capitals, in a ghostly light which
touched the grasses and stones as with a light
snow. "Poets, *anén!*" said Master Corneille.
"Those who love to look at ruins by moonlight."

The Félibrige still met among the reeds of the
island of Barthelasse, opposite the ramparts of
Avignon and the papal palace, which witnessed the
scheming and adventures of little Vedène. Then,
after a breakfast in some sailor's wine-shop, we
went up to the poet Anselm Mathieu's at Château-
neuf-des-Papes, famous for its vineyards, which
were for a long time the most renowned in Provence. Oh! the wine of the popes, the golden,

royal, imperial, pontifical wine! we drank it there on the shore, singing Mistral's verses the while, new fragments of the *Îles d'Or:* —

"En Arles, au temps des fades — florissait la reine Ponsirade — un rosier;" [1] or the beautiful ballad of the sea: "Le bâtiment vient de Mayorque — avec un chargement d'oranges." [2]

And one could readily fancy oneself at Majorca, looking at that blazing sky, those vine-clad slopes, terraced with walls of loose stones, and the olive-trees, pomegranates and myrtles. Through the open windows flew the rhymes, humming like bees; and we flew behind them, for days and days, through the smiling landscapes of the Comtat, attending elections and brandings, making brief halts in the villages, under the plane-trees of the Cours and the Place and, from the *char-à-bancs* that bore us, distributing orvietan to the assembled populace with much shouting and gesticulation. Our orvietan consisted of Provençal poems, beautiful poems in the language of those peasants who understood and applauded the strophes of *Mirèille*, Aubanel's *Vénus d'Arles*, a legend of Anselm Mathieu or Roumanille, and joined with us in singing the song of the sun: "Grand Soleil de Provence — gai compère du mistral — toi qui siffles la Durance — comme un coup de vin de Crau." [3] The

---

[1] At Arles, in the days of the *fades*, flourished Queen Ponsirade — a rose bush.

[2] The ship hails from Majorca — with a cargo of oranges.

[3] Bright sunshine of Provence — the minstrel's merry comrade — thou who dost drink the Durance dry — like a draught of Crau wine.

whole celebration would end in an improvised ball, a *farandole*, boys and girls in their working clothes, and corks popping over the little tables; and if any old mumbler of prayers attempted to criticise our unconventional gayety, the handsome Mistral, proud as King David, would say to her from the eminence of his grandeur: " Let be, mother, let be — poets are allowed full liberty."   And he would add confidentially, winking at the old woman as she bowed in respectful bewilderment: " *Es nautré qué fasen li saumé.*   We are the ones who wrote the psalms."

And how pleasant it was after one of these lyric escapades to return to the mill, stretch myself out on the grass-grown platform, and think of the book I would write later, describing it all, a book in which I would put the ringing I could still hear in my ears of those songs, that bright laughter, those mystic legends, and a reflection of that pulsing sunshine, the perfume of those parched hills, and which I would date from my ruin with the dead wings.

The first *Letters from my Mill* appeared about 1866 in a Parisian newspaper in which those Provençal chronicles, signed at first with a double pseudonym borrowed from Balzac, " Marie-Gaston," struck a jarring note by their strange flavor. Gaston was my comrade Paul Arène, who, when he was a mere boy, had had a play produced at the Odéon, a little one-act affair sparkling with wit and bright color, and who lived very near me on the outskirts of the forest of Meudon.   But although that finished writer had not yet to his credit *Jean des Figues* nor *Paris Ingénu* nor many other refined and solid pages, he had too much genuine talent, a too real individuality to be long content with that position of miller's assistant. I was left alone therefore to grind my little stories, at the caprice of the wind and the hour, in a terribly agitated life. There were intermissions and breaks; then I married and took my wife to Provence to show her my mill. Nothing had changed, neither the landscape nor the welcome. The old mother pressed us both affectionately against her little plaid shawl, and they made a little place for the new-comer at the boys' table. She sat beside me on the platform of the mill, where the north wind, remarking the presence of this Parisian, a foe to wind and sun, amused himself by buffeting her, by snatching her up and carrying her away in a whirlwind like Chénier's young Tarentine. And it was on our return from that journey that, being taken captive once more by my Provence, I began in *Figaro* a new series of *Letters from my Mill,*— *The Old People, The Pope's Mule, Pere Gaucher's Elixir*, etc. — written at Champrosay, in Eugène Delacroix's studio, which I have mentioned heretofore in *Jack* and *Robert Helmont.* The volume was published by Hetzel in 1869; two thousand copies were sold with difficulty, awaiting, like my other earlier works, the times when the popularity of the novels should result in increasing their sale and their circulation. Be it so! that is still my favorite book, not from a literary standpoint, but because it reminds me of the pleasantest hours of my youth, wild laughter, intoxication without remorse, beloved faces and sights which I shall never see again.

To-day Montauban is abandoned. "Dear mamma" is dead, the boys scattered, the wine of Château-neuf exhausted to the juice of the last grape. Where are Miracle and Miraclet, Siblet, Mitifio, the Prowler? If I should go there, I should find no one. But the pines, they tell me, have grown much taller; and over their gleaming green swell, my mill, fitted with new spars and canvas, like a corvette afloat, turns in the sunshine, a poet once more exposed to the breeze of inspiration, a dreamer returned to life.

IX.

MY FIRST PLAY.

OH! how long ago it was! I was far, very far from Paris, in the midst of gayety and light, at the farthest extremity of Algeria, in the valley of the Chélif, one fine day in February, 1862. A plain thirty leagues in extent, bordered on the right hand and the left by a double line of mountains, transparent in the golden mist and purple as amethyst. Lentils, dwarf palms, dry torrents whose stony beds are overgrown with rose laurel; at intervals a caravansery, an Arabian village, or, on the height, a marabout, whitewashed and dazzling, like a great die capped with half an orange; and here and there, in the white expanse of sunlight, moving spots, which are flocks, and which one would take, were not the sky of a deep and immaculate blue, for shadows cast by great clouds passing over. We had hunted all the morning; then, the afternoon heat being too intense, my friend the *bachaga* Boualem had pitched the tent. One of the sides being raised and held up by stakes formed a sort of marquee; the whole horizon entered the tent that way. In front the hobbled horses stood motionless, hanging their heads; the great greyhounds lay curled up in circles fast

asleep; lying on his stomach in the sand, among
his little kettles, our coffee-maker prepared the
mocha over a small fire of dry twigs, the slender
thread of smoke rising straight into the air; and
we rolled stout cigarettes without speaking,—
Boualem-Ben-Cherifa, his friends Si-Sliman and
Sid' Omar, the aga of the Atafs, and myself,—lying at full length on the couches in the shadow
of the white tent, to which the sun outside gave a
yellowish tinge, outlining on the canvas the sym-
bolic crescent and the print of the bloody hand,
compulsory decorations of all Arabian dwellings.

A delicious afternoon which ought never to
have come to an end! One of those golden
hours which still stand forth after twenty years, as
luminous as on the first day, against the grayish
background of life. And observe the illogical-
ness and perversity of our pitiful human nature.
To-day I cannot think of that siesta under the
tent without regret and homesickness; but candor
compels me to confess that at the time I regretted
Paris.

Yes, I regretted Paris, which my health, seriously
endangered by a literary novitiate of five years,
had compelled me to leave abruptly; I regretted
Paris because of the beloved objects I had left
there, its fogs and its gas-lights, its newspapers,
its new books, the discussions, in the evening, at
the café or under the porch of the theatres; because of that fine artistic fever, that never-failing
enthusiasm, which I saw then only on their sincere
sides; I regretted it especially because of my play

— my first play! — which, I was informed on the very day of my departure, had been accepted at the Odéon. Beyond question the landscape upon which I was gazing was beautiful, and its frame had a singularly poetic charm; but I would gladly have exchanged Algiers and the Atlas, Boualem and his friends, the blue of the sky, the white of the marabouts and the pink of the rose-laurels, for the gray colonnade of the Odéon and the little passage-way by which the artists entered, and Constant's office — Constant, the concierge and man of taste — its walls covered with autographs of actors and photographs of actresses in costume. But there I was, suddenly transported into Algeria, leading the life of a *grand seigneur* of the heroic times, when I might have been walking triumphantly, with the hypocritically modest mien of the new author whose play is about to be acted, through those unamiable corridors which had seen me shy and trembling! I was trifling away my time in the society of those Arab chiefs, picturesque doubtless, but unsatisfying in the matter of conversation, when the prompter, the scene-shifters, the stage-manager and the acting-manager, and the whole innumerable tribe of over-painted actresses and blue-chinned actors were intent upon my work! I was inhaling the pungent and refreshing aroma of the orange-trees kissed by the breeze, when it was within my power to regale my nostrils with the close and damp, but peculiarly seductive odor exhaled by the walls of a theatre! And the ceremony of reading the play to the actors, the carafe and glass of water, the manuscript glistening under the lamp! And the rehearsals, at first in the green-room around the high fireplace, then on the stage, the mysterious stage with its unfathomable depths, all encumbered with scaffoldings and scenery, facing the empty auditorium, resonant as a cellar and freezing to look upon, with its great chandelier covered with gauze, with its boxes and its proscenium, its stalls covered with gray drugget covers! Later would come the first performance, the façade of the theatre shedding upon the square the cheerful brilliancy of its rows of gas-jets, the carriages arriving, the crowd at the box-office, the anxious waiting in suspense at a café opposite, all alone save for one faithful friend, and the great throb of emotion, striking the heart as if it were a bell, at the moment when black-coated shadows, outlined against the transparent mirror in the greenroom, announce with much animation, that the curtain is falling, and that amid the applause and shouting the author's name has been proclaimed.

"Come!" says the friend, "courage; now we must go and see how it went off, thank the actors and shake hands with the fellows who are waiting impatiently in the private dining-room at Café Tabourey."

Such was the dream I dreamed wide-awake, under the tent, in the benumbing heat of a lovely African winter month, while in the distance, amid the oblique rays of the setting sun, a well — white but a moment before — assumed a pinkish hue, and in the profound silence of the plain no sound could be heard save the tinkling of a bell and the melancholy calls of the shepherds.

Nor did aught happen to disturb my reverie. My four guests collectively knew perhaps twenty words of French; I, barely ten words of Arabic. My companion, who had been my guide and ordinarily served as my interpreter — a Spanish grain merchant, whose acquaintance I had made at Milianah — was not there, having persisted in prolonging the hunt; so that we smoked our fat cigarettes in silence, sipping black Moorish coffee from microscopic little cups resting in egg-cups of silver filigree.

Suddenly there was a great uproar: the dogs barked, the servants ran hither and thither, and a long-legged devil of a Spahi in a red burnous stopped his horse short in front of the tent: — " Sidi Daoudi?"

It was a despatch from Paris, which had followed my trail from village to village, all the way from Milianah. It contained these simple words: " Play produced yesterday; great success; Rousseil and Tisserant magnificent."

I read and reread that blessed despatch, twenty times, a hundred times, as one reads a love-letter. Think of it! my first play! Seeing my hands tremble with excitement and happiness gleaming in my eyes, the agas surrounded me and talked to one another in Arabic. The most learned resorted to all his learning to say to me: " France — news — family?" Well, no, it was not news from my family that made my heart beat with such a delicious

sensation.   And being unable to accustom myself
to the idea of having no one to whom to divulge
my joy, I took it into my head to explain, to the
aga of the Atafs, to Sid' Omar, to Si-Sliman and
to Boualem-Ben-Cherifa, with the four words of
Arabic which I knew and the twenty words of
French which I supposed them to know, what a
theatre is, and the importance of a first performance in Paris.   An arduous task, as you can
imagine!   I cudgelled my brains for comparisons,
I gesticulated freely, I waved the blue cover of the
despatch, exclaiming: *Karaguez! Karaguez!* as
if my affecting little play, intended to touch men's
hearts and to compel virtuous tears, had any possible connection with the ghastly farces in which
the abnormal Turkish Mr. Punch finds his enjoy-·
ment; as if one could without blasphemy compare
the classic Odéon with the secret dens of the
Moorish city, to which the good Mussulmans
resort in the evening, despite the prohibition of the
police, to enjoy the spectacle of their favorite
hero's prurient prowess!

Those were the mirages of the African atmosphere.   Disillusionment awaited me in Paris.   For
I returned to Paris; I returned forthwith, sooner
than prudence and the faculty would have had me.
But what cared I for the fog and snow toward which
I hastened, what cared I for the balmy azure which
I left behind?   To see my play, that was my sole
object in life.   Embarked!   disembarked!   I rushed
through Marseille, and behold me on the railway,
shivering with excitement.   I arrived at Paris about

six o'clock in the afternoon ; it was dark. I did not
dine. "To the Odéon, driver!" O youth!

The curtain was just about to rise when I took
my place in my stall. The theatre had a strange
look; it was Mardi-Gras, there would be dancing
all night at Bullier, and not a few students of both
sexes had come in their masquerade costumes, to
while away a couple of hours at the theatre. There
were buffoons, Follies, Polichinellos, Pierrettes and
Pierrots. "It is hard, very hard," I thought, "to
make a Polichinello weep!" But they did weep,
they wept so profusely that the spangles on their
humps where the light struck them seemed like so
many glistening tears. I had on my right a Folly
whose emotion kept her cap and bells constantly
quivering, and at my left a Pierrette, a buxom
tender-hearted wench, comical to see in her
emotion, with two great springs gushing from her
great eyes and ploughing a double furrow through
the flour on her cheeks. Decidedly the despatch
had told the truth; my little curtain-raiser was a
tremendous success. Meanwhile, I, the author,
would have liked to be a hundred feet underground.
The play which those good people applauded
seemed to me disgraceful, odious. O misery! was
that what I had dreamed of, that vulgar creature
who had made himself up after the style of Béranger,
in order to appear paternal and virtuous? I was
unjust, be it understood; Tisserant and Rousseil,
both artists of great talent, acted as well as men
can act, and to their talent my triumph was due in
no small measure. But the disillusionment was too

complete, the difference too great between what I had thought I was writing and what appeared before me now, with all its wrinkles visible, all its holes lighted up by the pitiless glare of the footlights; and I really suffered to see that my ideal was stuffed with straw. Despite the emotion of the audience, despite the bravos, I was conscious of a feeling of unspeakable shame and embarrassment. Hot waves, burning flushes, rose to my cheeks. It seemed to me that all that carnival audience must know me and was laughing at me. Perspiring, suffering acutely, losing my head, I repeated the gestures of the actors. I would have liked to make them walk faster, talk faster, rush madly through the dialogue and across the stage so that my torture might be the sooner ended. What a relief when the curtain had fallen, and how quickly I fled, keeping close to the walls, with my collar turned up, as furtive and shamefaced as a thief!

X.

HENRI ROCHEFORT.

ABOUT 1859 I became acquainted with a most excellent fellow, an under-clerk in one of the departments at the Hôtel de Ville. His name was Henri Rochefort, but that name meant nothing then. Rochefort was leading a modest and very orderly life, living with his parents on the ancient Rue des Deux-Boules, close at hand to his place of employment in that swarming Saint-Denis Quartier, now invaded by commerce and by the petty industries of Paris, with their house-shops, plastered with signs from top to bottom, samples displayed and frames hung on the door-posts: " Feathers and Flowers — False Jewelry — Paper Toys and Silver Thread — Hollow Pearls; " — trades on every floor, a continuous roar of toil passing out through the windows into the street; drays loading, packages being corded, clerks running about with pens behind their ears; a work-girl passing in a smock-frock, with gold-filings clinging to her hair; and at intervals some sumptuous mansion transformed into warerooms, its escutcheon and carvings carrying your thoughts back two centuries and causing you to muse upon servants grown rich, bankers stuffed with gold, the Count of Horn, the Regent, Law and the Mississippi, the System,

in a word, upon the time when, in those streets now
given over to commerce and the bourgeoisie, the
most fabulous fortunes waxed and waned from
hour to hour, with the ebb and flow of fever and
of gold, as impassive as the tide, to and from that
narrow reeking rift, close at hand, which is still
called Rue Quincampoix! My friend Rochefort
was a little like his street, and held his past very
cheap. He was known to be of noble birth, the
son of a count; he seemed not to know it himself,
allowing people to call him plain Rochefort; and
that American simplicity did not fail to make an
impression on me, who had just landed in Paris
from our vain, legitimist South.

Monsieur de Rochefort, the father, belonged to
that generation of young men to whose future the
Revolution of July, 1830, interposed an insurmount-
able obstacle, and whose careers it interrupted.
An especially attractive and clever generation,
preserving a sort of perfume of the old régime in
the atmosphere of Louis-Philippe's reign, turning
its back upon the new dynasty, but not upon France,
attached to the elder branch, but knowing so well
that any restoration was out of the question for a
long while that its sceptical loyalty never displayed
the sombre humor of the fanatic or sectary. While
some protested against the dull monotony of bourgeois manners by descending the legendary pavement of La Courtille [1] with a great uproar, amid

---

[1] La Courtille, "a portion of the faubourgs on the northern
side of Paris where there are many wineshops." The " descent
of La Courtille " means the return of the maskers to Paris after
celebrating Mardi Gras at La Courtille. — LITTRÉ.

the shouts of masked figures and the jangling of bells, or amused themselves by bombarding the Tuileries with volleys of champagne corks, others, less scatterbrained or less wealthy, tried to provide themselves by labor with resources for which they could no longer rely on the favor of the sovereign. Thus did M. de Lauzanne, whom we have seen very recently, still fresh and smiling, still erect despite his great age, still a gentleman despite his trade of vaudevillist and the sobriquet of Père Lauzanne bestowed upon him by the affectionate familiarity of his confrères; thus must M. de Rochefort's father have done, who was in his time a prominent figure among the ardent royalist youth and a particular friend of the ex-body-guard *Choca*. Having a fondness for strolling through the wings, the elder Rochefort, like Lauzanne, remembered the road to the theatre as soon as the cold weather arrived, and betook himself thither; but it was to seek his livelihood. Every lover of the theatre has an author under his skin, and it is an easy transition from applauding plays to trying to write them. M. de Rochefort-Luçay, then, wrote plays and became a vaudevillist.

These details were not unnecessary, because they may serve to give us an idea of Rochefort's childhood. A curious, characteristic, thoroughly Parisian childhood, passed wholly between the school and the theatrical world — which is more patriarchal than is generally supposed — the actors' and authors' cafés to which his father took him on Sunday, and where one heard, instead of the drunken orgies dreamed of by provincials, the sharp sound of the dice thrown on the backgammon board, or of the dominoes as they were moved over the table. Thus Rochefort was the schoolboy, son of an artist or man of letters, of whom we have all known the type, initiated in his childhood into the secrets of the wings, calling famous actors by their names, familiar with the new plays, giving theatre tickets to his tutor on the sly, and acquiring thus the privilege of composing with impunity in the secrecy of his desk, between a tame lizard and a pipe, a heap of masterpieces, dramatic or other, which he will carry, on holidays, with his cap pulled over his eyes and his heart beating as if it would burst the buttons off his jacket, to drop them in the never-opened boxes of newspapers, or leave them with cunning theatre concierges. The destiny of such boys is all prearranged : at twenty they enter some department of the civil service, national or municipal, and continue to write secretly behind their desks, hiding from their superiors as they hid from their teachers. Rochefort did not escape the common fate. After having tried his hand at serious literature and sent I know not how many sonnets and odes to all the poetic competitions in France, always without success, when I first knew him he was using the pens and paper of the Parisian municipality to write petty theatrical reviews for *Charivari*, which was then changing its editorial management and trying to secure an infusion of younger blood.

Although I could not divine what Rochefort

would one day grow to be, his face interested me from the outset. It was evidently not the face of a man likely to be long content with that clerk's life, regulated by the coming and going of office hours as by the exasperating tic-tac of a cuckoo in the Black Forest. You are familiar with that unusual face, which was the same then that it has been ever since, that hair of the color of blazing punch over a too-expansive brow, a box for sick-headaches and a reservoir of enthusiasm, those black deep-set eyes gleaming in the shadow, that straight thin nose, that sneering mouth, in a word that whole face, lengthened by a beard trimmed to a point like a boy's top, which inevitably makes me think of a sceptical Don Quixote, or a Mephistopheles of a mild type. He was very thin, wore a villainous black coat that was too small for him, and had a habit of always keeping both hands buried in the pockets of his trousers. A deplorable habit, which made him appear even thinner than he really was, emphasizing wofully the sharpness of his elbows and the narrowness of his shoulders. He was of a generous disposition and a good friend, capable of the greatest sacrifices, and nervous and easily irritated beneath an appearance of coldness.

One day he had an affair with the manager of the *Gaulois*, growing out of some article or other, I do not now remember what it was. The *Gaulois* of that day — for the title of a newspaper in France has more incarnations than Buddha and passes through more hands than the King of Garbe's betrothed — the *Gaulois* of that day was one of

those ephemeral cabbage-leaves which spring up
between the pavements in the neighborhood of
theatre cafés and literary breweries. Its manager,
a jovial, clever little fellow, chubby and pink-
cheeked, was named Delvaille, if I remember
aright, and signed Delbrecht, doubtless considering
that the prettier name. Delvaille or Delbrecht, as
you please, had challenged Rochefort. Rochefort
would have preferred pistols, not that he was a very
deadly shot, but he had sometimes won a prize at
fairs; as for the sword, he did not remember that
he had ever seen one, at a distance or close at hand.
Delvaille, being the person insulted, had the choice
of weapons and chose the sword. "Very good,"
said Rochefort, " I will fight with the sword."   The
duel was rehearsed in Pierre Véron's rooms. Rochefort was willing to be killed, but he did not wish to
seem ridiculous. So Véron had sent for a tall
devil of a sergeant-major of Zouaves, afterward cut
in two at Solferino, who was very expert in the
way of salutes, attitudes and good manners, as
understood in the fencing-rooms in barracks: —
" After you."   " By no means."   " I insist."   " Go
on, monsieur."   After ten minutes' practice,
Rochefort had attained, so far as grace was concerned, the level of any moustachioed La Ramée.
The two champions met the next day, between
Paris and Versailles, in those lovely Chaville woods
which we knew well, as we often went there on
Sundays intent upon less warlike pastimes. On
that day a fine, chilly rain was falling, which made
bubbles on the pond and veiled with a light mist

the green circle of the hills, a ploughed field on the slope and the reddish excavations of a gravel-pit. The combatants removed their shirts, notwithstanding the rain, and, except for the gravity of the occasion, one would have been tempted to laugh at the spectacle of those two standing face to face — that short, stout man, fair of skin, in a flannel undershirt stitched with blue about the hips, standing on guard as correctly as if on the fencing-room floor, and Rochefort, tall, thin, yellow, gaunt, and so cuirassed with bones as to make one doubt whether there was a crevice in his body for a sword to enter. Unluckily he had forgotten all the sergeant-major's valuable lessons over night, held his weapon like a candle, thrust like a deaf man and laid himself open. In the first exchange he received a straight thrust which slid along his ribs. The sword had drawn blood, but so little! That was his first duel.

I shall astonish no one when I say that at that time Rochefort possessed wit; but it was a sort of interior wit, a peculiar essence, consisting especially in stinging remarks long meditated, in unexpected combinations of astounding ideas, in monumental absurdities, in cold, savage jests, which he would utter between clenched teeth, in the voice of Cham and with the silent laughter of Leatherstocking. Unfortunately that wit remained congealed, useless. There were occasional good things to repeat, to laugh over a little between friends; but to write them, to print them, to rush through literature with such frantic capers — that

was what seemed impossible. Rochefort did not
know himself; as almost always happens, it was a
mere chance, an accident, that revealed him to
himself. He had for a friend, for an inseparable
companion, a most extraordinary puppet, whose
name will certainly bring a smile to those of my
own age who remember having known him. His
name was Léon Rossignol. A perfect type of the
son of a septuagenarian; one might say that he
was born old. As thin and pale as a blade of
grass growing in a cave, at eighteen he was an inveterate snuff-taker, coughed and spit and leaned
with a dignified air on grandpapa's canes. Compounded of most incongruous elements, or rather
having a screw loose somewhere in his brain, that
excellent creature, strange to say! had a horror of
blows and a great liking for quarrels. As imper-
tinent and cowardly as Panurge, he was quite capable of insulting a carabineer in the street, reserving
the right — if the carabineer took the jest in bad
part — to fall upon his knees and implore forgiveness with such exaggerated humility that the
insulted individual really did not know whether he
ought to laugh or be angry. A great child, in
short, weak and sickly, whom Rochefort loved for
his vulgar chatter, witty after the style of the faubourgs, and whom he saved more than once from
the consequences which certain too venturesome
sallies might have brought upon his back. Rossignol, like Rochefort, was employed at the Hôtel
de Ville. He had a perch there on the upper floor,
under the eaves, in an out-of-the-way office at the

end of a labyrinth of narrow staircases and corridors, and there, in the capacity of superintendent
of stationery, he gravely distributed, upon requisi-
tion, paper, pens, pencils, erasers, paper-cutters,
paper-weights, pieces of rubber, jars of powdered
pumice, blue ink, red ink, yellow sand, illustrated
calendars, and heaven knows what — the innumerable useless articles with which the idle quill-drivers
in the government departments love to surround
themselves, and which are, as it were, the flowers
of bureaucracy. Naturally, Rossignol too had his
literary ambitions. To put his name upon something printed was his dream, and we, that is to say
Pierre Véron, Rochefort and I, used to amuse ourselves by scratching off bits of articles for him or
improvising quatrains, with which he would hurry
off, as proud as Lucifer, to the *Tintamarre.* How
strange are the effects of irresponsibility! Rochefort, who was always hampered by a tendency to
imitate and to stick to the conventional lines when
he wrote for himself, developed originality and individuality as soon as he began to write over the
signature of Rossignol. He was free then, he no
longer felt the irritated eye of the Institute following on the paper the by no means academic contortions of his thought and his style. And it was
a pleasure to witness the untrammelled working of
that mind, very cold, very nervous, astounding in
its audacity and familiarity, with a fashion entirely
its own of *feeling* the details of Parisian life and of
making them the text for all sorts of buffooneries,
planned with great patience and without pity,

wherein the words maintain the seriousness of a clown between two grimaces, contenting itself with a sly wink when the paragraph is finished.

" Why, this is charming, novel, original, it is like you; why don't you write thus on your own account?"

" Perhaps you are right; I must try."

Rochefort's style was found; now let the Empire look to itself.

Some one has said that it was de l'Arnal reduced to writing, and that Rochefort had simply arranged the dialogues of Duvert and Lauzanne in paragraphs. We do not deny the influence. Evidently certain ways of looking at things and certain tricks of speech, a certain habit — which had become a rule — of using the dialogue form and of making the thought perform strange antics, which, during the endless games of dominoes on Boulevard du Temple, had made an impression on his schoolboy's brain, were of some use to him later. But they are the unconscious imitations which nobody avoids altogether. There is no law, in literature, against picking up a rusty weapon; the important thing is to be able to sharpen the blade and to reforge the hilt to fit one's hand.

Rochefort made his first appearance in the *Nain Jaune*,[1] edited by Aurélien Scholl. Who does not know Scholl? If you have, no matter how infrequently, trodden the Parisian boulevard during the last thirty years, or visited its appurtenances, you certainly have noticed, it may be in front of Tor-

______
[1] Yellow Dwarf.

toni's pavilion, or under the lindens of Baden-Baden or the palms of Monte-Carlo, that eminently Parisian and boulevardist physiognomy. Scholl, by virtue of his always cheerful tone, his clear and concise workmanship, and the keen and slashing brilliancy of his style, when Paris was overrun by the patois of parliamentary scribes and the idiotic scribbling of reporters, was one of the last, one might almost say the very last, *petit* journalist. The *petit* journalist in the accepted meaning of the phrase, is a journalist who considers himself called upon to be at the same time a writer; the *grand* journalist dispenses with it. Like many others, in these later troublous times, Scholl, without intending any harm, gradually became involved in the political hurly-burly. He is in the thick of the fight now, and it is a pleasure to see that grandson of Rivarol, turned republican, directing against the enemies of the Republic the golden arrows, with a little curare rubbed on the point, borrowed from the reactionary arsenal of the *Acts of the Apostles*. But in the days of the *Nain Jaune* politics were stagnant and Scholl was hardly looking forward to a republic, any more than Rochefort. He was content to be one of the most good-natured sceptics and cleverest scoffers in Paris. Being very much in love with the *paroistre*, as a native of Bordeaux, he maintained — and in those days of the canonization of Bohemia the doctrine could not fail to savor slightly of paradox — he maintained that it is the duty of a man of letters to pay his bootmaker, and that one may be clever with fresh gloves and clean linen.

In conformity with his principles, he indulged in all the refinements of the period, even the monocle set into the eye, to which he still clings; he breakfasted at Bignon's and afforded the Parisians the truly novel spectacle of a simple news-writer partaking daily of egg in the shell and cutlets with the Duc de Grammont-Caderousse, the king of swelldom for the moment. The *Nain Jaune* was the only serious rival Villemessant ever encountered. Admirably seconded by his social connections, Scholl succeeded in a few months in making his paper the official sheet of high life and the clubs, the arbiter of Parisian fashion; but, after a year, he became disgusted with it, he was fitted for something better than that; he was too much of a writer, too much of a newspaper man to remain long a manager.

Rochefort's success in the *Nain Jaune* was rapid; in *Figaro*, which made haste to enlist him, it was even more brilliant. The Parisians, always inclined to grumble and for a long while unaccustomed to independence, enjoyed those pamphlets, which introduced the fashion of addressing themselves in familiar language, in a tone of good-humored mockery, to all sorts of solemn and official matters which hitherto even the boldest had hardly dared to make fun of beneath their breath. Rochefort is fairly launched, he fights duels — with better fortune than the one on the shore of the pond at Chaville; he plays a bold game, lives freely, fills Paris with the echoes of his name, and remains in spite of everything, in spite of the triumph of an evening or of a single hour, the same Rochefort whom I had known at the Hôtel de Ville, still of a kindly and obliging disposition, still modest, always anxious concerning the next article, always afraid that he has emptied his bag, exhausted the lode and that he will be unable to go on.

Villemessant, naturally despotic with his editors, had a sort of awestruck admiration for him. That impassive, scoffing mask, that self-willed and capricious temperament astonished him. It is a fact that Rochefort was extraordinarily obstinate and had strange whims. I have described elsewhere the effect of his article concerning M. de Saint-Rémy's theatrical works, and the mischievous familiarity with which he dealt the *coup de grâce* to that ill-fated presidential and ducal volume, which all the Dangeaus, all the Jules Lecomtes of journalism crowned with the most flattering periods. Paris was delighted with his audacity; Morny was touched to the quick by it and appealed from it.[1] With the candor of an irritated author, well adapted to cause wonder when displayed by a man of intellect, he sent his dramatic works to Jouvin, confident that Jouvin would have more taste than Rochefort and would publish a compensatory article in *Figaro*.

Jouvin accepted the volume, did not write the article, and the unhappy duke was compelled to

---

[1] The Duc de Morny, died 1865, President of the Council (introduced by Daudet as the Duc de Mora in the *Nabob*), wrote plays under the nom de plume of M. de Saint-Rémy. — *Vide ante*, p. 24.

keep in his heart the bitter prose that Rochefort
had forced him to swallow. Thereupon an extraordinary thing took place, improbable at first
glance, but in spite of everything profoundly
human. Morny, the flattered and fawned upon,
the omnipotent, suddenly conceived for the man
who was not afraid to poke fun at him, a sort of
timid, spiteful affection. He desired to see him, to
know him, to have an explanation with him, as
between two friends, in a corner. His adherents
exerted all their ingenuity to prove that Rochefort
possessed neither wit nor style, and that his judgment was entitled to no weight. Sycophants (a
vice-emperor never lacks them!) went about upon
the quays collecting little vaudevilles, youthful sins
of Rochefort's, analyzed them, plucked them to
pieces, and maintained by dint of a thousand conclusive arguments that M. de Saint-Rémy's were
far superior to them. Imaginary crimes were im-
puted to Rochefort. A fanatical saint came running in one day, red with virtuous indignation, his
eyes starting from his head; "You know Rochefort, that famous Rochefort who makes himself out
such a paragon? Well, what do you suppose we've
discovered about him? He was a *boursier* of the
Empire!"[1] What a black-hearted wretch he must
be, after having been a *boursier* of the Empire at
the age of eight, to consider Monsieur le Duc's
plays vile trash at the age of thirty! A little more,
and they would have held Rochefort responsible

---

[1] That is to say, he had pecuniary assistance from the government while he was at the public school.

for his nurse's political opinions! Vain efforts;
fruitless revelations. Morny, like a rejected lover,
became more and more persistent in his fixed idea
of winning Rochefort's regard. The whim became
a mania, a mania the more besetting because
Rochefort, being advised as to what was in the
wind, displayed a sort of comical coquetry in
avoiding the duke's acquaintance. I can see
Morny stopping Villemessant in the corridor at
the first performance of *La Belle Hélène* — " You
really must introduce me to Rochefort this time!"
— " Monsieur le Duc! Yes, Monsieur le Duc!
We were talking about that very thing not a
second ago." — And Villemessant ran after Rochefort, but Rochefort had disappeared. Thereupon
it occurred to some one to resort to stratagem,
to form a sort of conspiracy to bring the duke and
Rochefort together. The latter was known to be a
great authority on curios — did he not publish the
Little Mysteries of the Public Auction Room? — and
a zealous collector of pictures. The duke had an
interesting gallery. They would bring Rochefort
to see the gallery, the duke would happen to be
there at the time, and the introduction would
naturally follow. The day is appointed, a friend
undertakes to bring Rochefort, the duke is waiting
in his gallery; he waits one hour, two hours, tête-
à-tête with his Rembrandts and his Hobbemas,
and again the longed-for monster does not appear.

So long as the duke lived — by the merest
chance, doubtless, for I do not think that that
friendship at long range and so inadequately **re-**

quited can have extended so far as to protect the ungrateful pamphleteer against the thunderbolts of the law — so long as the duke lived, Rochefort was hounded comparatively little. But when Morny had disappeared the persecutions began. Rochefort, spurred on by them, redoubled his insolence and audacity. Fines poured down upon him like hail, imprisonment succeeded fines. Ere long the censorship took a hand. The censorship with its sensitive palate as a taster of principles concluded that everything that Rochefort wrote had a political after-taste. *Figaro's* very existence was threatened, and Rochefort had to leave the paper. Thereupon he founded *La Lanterne*, unmasked his batteries and boldly hoisted the pirate's flag. Once more it was Villemessant, Villemessant the conservative, the Villemessant of the rascals assembled around the green table, who freighted that fireship. The censorship and Villemessant on that occasion rendered a peculiar service to conservatism and the Empire. Everyone knows the history of *La Lanterne*, its bewildering success, the little flame-colored paper in every hand, sidewalks, cabs, railway-carriages all gleaming with red sparks, the government beside itself, the scandal, the prosecution, the suppression and — the expected and inevitable result — Rochefort Deputy for Paris.

Even there Rochefort remained the same; he carried to the benches of the Chamber, to the tribune, the insulting familiarity of his pamphlets, and refused, to the very end, to treat the Empire as a serious adversary. Do you remember the sensation? A ministerial orator, adopting a lofty tone, with the disdain with which a stiff, precise parliamentarian may look upon a simple journalist, had made use of the word ridiculous in reference to him. Rochefort rose from his bench, pale and with clenched teeth, and, lashing the sovereign across the face over the heads of his ministers, exclaimed: "I may have been ridiculous sometimes, but no one ever met me in the costume of a tooth-extractor, with an eagle on my shoulder and a piece of bacon in my hat!" — M. Schneider was presiding that day. Well do I remember the terror depicted on his fat, good-natured countenance. And, imagining in its place the Duc de Morny's refined, impassive, sneering face, with its silky moustaches, I said to myself: "What a pity he is not here! he would have gratified his whim at last and made Rochefort's acquaintance."

I have seen Rochefort but twice since then: the first time was at the burial of Victor Noir,[1] riding in a cab, fainting, exhausted by a two hours' struggle beside Delescluze against a frantic crowd, two hundred thousand unarmed men with women and children, who insisted with all their might upon taking the body to Paris where the cannon awaited them, upon marching to certain slaughter. And I saw him once more during the war, in the chaos of the battle of Buzenval, amid the crackling of musketry, the dull roar of the heavy guns of

---

[1] Victor Noir was a journalist who was shot near Paris in January, 1870, by Prince Pierre Bonaparte, in an altercation over a newspaper article published by the prince.

the forts, the rumbling of ambulance wagons, amid
the feverish excitement and the smoke, bishops
riding about on horseback in masquerade costumes
and gallant bourgeois going forth to be killed, full
of confidence in the Trochu plan; amid the heroic
and the grotesque, amid that never-to-be-forgotten
drama, moulded, like Shakespeare's, from the
sublime and the comical, which is known to history
as the siege of Paris. It was on the road to Mont
Valérien; it was cold and muddy, the leafless trees
shivering sadly against the lowering sky. My friend
passed in a carriage, still pale and gaunt as I saw
him through the glass, still tightly buttoned in a
scanty black coat, as in the far-off days at the Hôtel
de Ville. I cried out to him through the storm:
"How are you, Rochefort?" I have never seen
him since.[1]

[1] This portrait of Rochefort appeared in Russia, in the *New
Times* (*Novoë Vremya*) in 1879.

XI.

HENRY MONNIER.

I SEE myself in my youthful garret, in winter, with frost on the window-panes and a hearth à la Prussienne, with no fire. Sitting in front of a small, unpainted wooden table, I am at work scribbling verses, my legs enveloped in a travelling rug. Some one knocks. "Come in!" And a decidedly fantastic spectacle appears in the doorway. Imagine a protruding stomach, a false collar, a ruddy, clean-shaven bourgeois face, and a Roman nose surmounted by spectacles. The individual bows ceremoniously and says: "I am Henry Monnier."

Henry Monnier, a celebrity of that period! Actor, author, designer, all in one; people pointed him out on the street, and M. de Balzac, a keen observer, esteemed him highly for his powers of observation. Observation of a strange sort, it must be said, which in no wise resembles the observation of most people. Many writers have acquired wealth and renown by making sport of the faults and infirmities of others. But Monnier did not go far in search of his model: he planted himself before his mirror, listened to himself think and speak, and, deeming himself prodigiously ridiculous, he conceived that pitiless incarnation, that tremendous satire of the French citizen of the middle class, known as Joseph Prudhomme.[1] For Monnier is Joseph Prudhomme and Joseph Prudhomme is Monnier. They have everything in common, from the white gaiters to the cravat with thirty-six turns. The same swelling turkey's frill, the same burlesque air of solemnity, the same commanding glance through the golden circle of the spectacles, the same unmeaning apothegms pronounced in the voice of an old vulture with the influenza. "If I could only come out of my skin for an hour or two," says Fantasio to his friend Spark, "if I could be that gentleman who is passing!" Monnier, who bore only a distant resemblance to Fantasio, never desired to be the gentleman who was passing; as he possessed in a higher degree than any other person the curious faculty of bipartition, he came out of his skin sometimes to laugh at himself and his own make-up; but he very soon resumed the cherished skin, the precious envelope, and that pitiless satirist, that cruel scoffer, that Attila of bourgeois idiocy, became once more, in private life, the most artlessly idiotic of bourgeois.

Among other preoccupations, really worthy of Joseph Prudhomme, Henry Monnier was possessed of a fixed idea, common, by the way, among all

[1] The salient feature of Monnier's creation of Prudhomme is his custom of making the most trivial, often the most idiotic remarks with the utmost solemnity of manner. He was the outcome of his sketches of popular types made in M. Girodet's studio and combined with comical (written) sketches. The character was developed more carefully in his later works.

provincial magistrates who write wretched im-
promptu verses, and among all the ex-colonels
who employ their leisure hours on half-pay trans-
lating Horace: he wished to bestride Pegasus, to
don Thalia's buskins, to stoop, at the risk of bursting his braces, and scoop up a little of the pure
stream of Hippocrene in the hollow of his hand;
he dreamed of laurel wreaths, of academic triumphs, of a play accepted at the Théâtre-Français.
Already — does any one remember it to-day — a
play of his had been produced on the Odéon stage
— a play in three acts and in verse, by your leave!
as the posters say: *Peintres et Bourgeois*, written
in collaboration with a young man, a travelling
salesman, I believe, and very expert in the art of
turning rhymes. The Odéon is very well; but the
Français, Molière's play-house! And for twenty
years Henry Monnier prowled about the famous
temple, haunted the Café de la Régence, the Café
Minerve, every place patronized by the members
of the company, always dignified and well-dressed,
clean-shaven like a noble father, and with the knowing, self-satisfied air of the typical argumentative
personage of the old plays.

The worthy man had read my poems, he relied
upon me to assist him to realize his dream, and it
was to propose to me that we should work together
that he had climbed the numerous and steep flights
of stairs to my lodging on Rue de Tournon, puffing
slightly with the exertion. You can imagine
whether I felt flattered and whether I accepted the
offer joyfully!

The next morning I was at his house; he lived on Rue Ventadour, in an old house of bourgeois exterior, where he occupied a small apartment of very characteristic aspect, which smelt of the economical, careful actor of virtuous habits as well as of the old bachelor. Everything, furniture and floor, glistened with cleanliness. In front of each chair was a small round mat with a border of red cloth carefully pinked. Four cuspidores, one in each corner. On the mantel were two saucers, each containing a few pinches of very dry snuff. Monnier took a pinch occasionally, but offered me none.

That apartment produced an impression of avarice on me at first. I have learned since that that parsimonious exterior concealed a very hard life. Monnier was without means; from time to time only, a performance of one of his plays, a newspaper article, the sale of a few sketches augmented, but to no considerable extent, his slender revenues, So he had gradually adopted the habit of dining out every day. People were glad to invite him. He paid for his dinner by telling, by acting rather — for there was nothing extemporaneous in his performance — salacious stories at dessert. Perhaps it was particularly indecent dialogue, with imitations of both voices; or else his favorite hero, Monsieur Prudhomme, carrying his paunch and his imperturbable solemnity through the most *risqué* adventures. And all without a smile, for the bourgeois element in Henry Monnier's character rebelled secretly against that rôle of buffoon. And furthermore he was despotically exacting in certain respects: he must have a quarter of an hour's nap, for instance, after the repast, however exalted the place; and there were fits of jealousy and sulkiness, the angry outbursts of an old parrot at any one who steals his cutlet bone, if by chance it happened that some other than he took the floor and seemed likely to eclipse him. At one time there was a plan to obtain a pension for him: it would have been wealth to him; but at that juncture his after-dinner pleasantry served the poor man a bad turn. Malassis had published a collection of his anecdotes in Belgium, a copy crossed the frontier, ministerial prudery declared itself insulted thereby, and the promised pension vanished on the spot. Do not confuse them with the *Basfonds de Paris*, which might seem, in comparison with them, to have been written for young girls, although the publication was authorized only by special favor, and of such a limited number of copies and at a price so high that the volume could not in any event exert its baneful influence beyond the excommunicate frontiers of the world of bibliophiles.

Such was the twofold man — *homo duplex* — who did me the honor to wish to associate his literary labors with mine. Slave of my imagination as I was at twenty, I might perhaps have come to terms with the buffoon; but, unfortunately, it was the bourgeois Prudhomme, and the bourgeois Prudhomme alone, who suggested collaboration with me. After a few sessions I went no more. Doubtless Henry Monnier felt little regret, and naught remains of my first dream of glory save the memory of that comical old man, in his poor, neat home, smoking little pipes with little puffs in the leather arm-chair, in which he was found dead one morning fifteen years ago !

XII.

THE END OF A MOUNTEBANK AND OF MURGER'S BOHEMIA.

WHEN I was about eighteen years old, I met a most extraordinary character, who appears to my mind, at a distance, as the living incarnation of a world apart, with a language and strange manners of its own, a world to-day vanished and almost forgotten, but which filled a great space at that time in the Paris of the Empire. I refer to that gypsy band, irregular troops of art, rebellious subjects of philosophy and letters, capricious followers of all caprices, audaciously camped in front of the Louvre and the Institute, which Henri Murger, not without embellishing and idealizing the picture a little, has commemorated under the name of Bohemia. We will call this personage Desroches. I had met him at a ball in the Latin Quarter, with some friends, one summer evening. Having returned home very late — to my little room on Rue de Tournon — I was sleeping soundly the next morning, when there appeared at the foot of my bed a gentleman in a black coat, a scanty coat of that curious shade of black which only police officers and undertakers' men have the art of obtaining.

" I come from Monsieur Desroches."

" Monsieur Desroches?   Who is Monsieur Desroches? "   I exclaimed, rubbing my eyes, for my
memory persisted in waking much later than my
body that morning.

" Monsieur Desroches, of *Figaro;* you passed
last evening together; he is at the police station
and refers to you."

" Monsieur Desroches — why, yes — of course
— he refers to me; very well, let him go ! "

" I beg your pardon, it will be thirty sous ! "

" Thirty sous !   Why? "

" That's the custom."

I produced the thirty sous. The black coat
departed, and I remained seated on my bed, half
dreaming and with no very clear comprehension
of the strange adventures which had resulted in
my being called upon — a newly enlisted Brother
of Mercy — to ransom an editor of *Figaro* from the
claws, not of the Turks but of the police, at a cost
of one franc fifty.

My reflections were not of long duration. Five
minutes later Desroches, freed from his fetters,
entered my apartment smiling.

" A thousand pardons, my dear confrère, this is
all the fault of the *Raisins Muscats* [1] — yes, the
Raisins Muscats, my first article, which appeared
yesterday in *Figaro*. Accursed Muscat grapes !
I had received the money, you understand — my
first money — and it went to my head. We wandered all over the quarter after leaving you, and —
my memory is a little confused, but I have a vague

---

[1] Muscat grapes.

sensation of receiving a kick somewhere. Then I found myself in the station; a charming night! First they put me down below, you know — the black hole; how it stunk! but I made the fellows laugh, they were glad enough to take me with them into the guardhouse; we talked and played cards — I had to read them the *Raisins Muscats,* a great success! Wonderful, what good taste policemen have!"

Imagine my stupefaction and the effect produced upon an ingenuous provincial youth like myself by the revelation of such disorderly morals in literary men! And my confrère who thus described his adventures was a plump little man, well brushed and shaved, with an affectation of polished manners, whose white gaiters and frock-coat of bourgeois cut formed a most perfect contrast to his frantic gestures and the contortions of his mountebank's face. He surprised and alarmed me, he realized that fact and evidently took pleasure in exaggerating for my benefit the cynicism of his paradoxes.

" I like you," he said, as he left me; " pray come and see me next Sunday afternoon. I live in a fascinating nook, near the Château des Brouillards, on the hills, the side overlooking Saint-Ouen, — you know where I mean — Gérard de Nerval's vineyard! I will introduce you to my wife; she is well worth the journey. I have just received a fresh cask of wine; we will drink it by the goblet, as they do at the wholesale wineshops at Bercy, and we will sleep in the cellar. And then a friend of mine, a Dominican unfrocked day before yesterday, is to come and read me a drama in five acts. You shall hear him! a superb subject; full of ravishing and that sort of thing — that is understood. Gérard de Nerval's vineyard, don't forget the address!"

All of Desroches' promises were fulfilled. We drank the new wine, and in the evening the alleged Dominican read us his drama. Dominican or not, he was a tall, magnificent Breton, with broad shoulders modelled for the gown, and with something of the preacher in the fulness of his voice and his gestures. He afterwards made a name for himself in the world of letters. His drama did not surprise me. It is true that, after an afternoon at Gérard de Nerval's vineyard, in what Desroches called his interior, surprise was not easily aroused.

Before climbing the hills, it had occurred to me to read once more the exquisite pages which Gérard, the lover of *Sylvie*, in his *Promenades et Souvenirs*, devotes to a description of that northern slope of Montmartre, a corner of the fields enclosed within the walls of Paris, and all the dearer and more precious to us on that account: — "We still have a number of hills girdled with dense green hedges which the barberry adorns with its violet flowers and later with its purplish berries. There are windmills, wineshops and arbors, rustic elysiums and silent lanes; there is even one vineyard there, the last of the famous vintage of Montmartre, which, in Roman times, rivalled Argenteuil and Suresnes. Each year that humble hill loses one row of its stunted vines, which fall into a quarry. Ten years ago I might have bought it for ten thousand francs; I would have built such a light and airy house in that vineyard! a little villa in the Pompeiian style, with an *impluvium* and a *cella.*"

In that Greek poet's dream my friend Desroches dwelt. There it was — oh! shocking antithesis! — that, on a lovely, bright summer's day, beneath an arbor of flowering elder-bushes in which swarms of bees were buzzing, he presented to me an androgynous monster in a wagoner's costume: blue blouse, velvet waistcoat, a cap with red stripes tipped over her ear, and a whip over her shoulder.

" Monsieur Alphonse Daudet — Madame Desroches ! "

For that monster was really his wife, his lawful wife, always dressed in that costume, which pleased her and which, to be sure, harmonized as well as possible with her masculine face and voice. Smoking, spitting, swearing, with all the vices of the other sex, she managed the household with loud cracks of the whip; first of all her husband, who was thoroughly tamed, and then two thin daughters — her daughters! — of a curious, boy-like build, whose thirteen and fifteen years, ripened prematurely and gone to seed, gave promise of all that their mother's forty years displayed. It was indeed well worth the journey, as he had said, to make the acquaintance of that household.

And yet Desroches was the son of a wealthy Parisian tradesman in good standing, a manufacturer of jewelry, I believe. His father had cursed

him several times and paid him a small allowance.
It is not an uncommon experience in France to
find these wild creatures, a sort of scourge sent by
God, appearing suddenly in families to disturb
their tranquillity and put the hoarded gold pieces
in circulation; in short, to punish the bourgeoisie
in those of its sentiments which are too egotisti-
cally bourgeois. And I have known more than
one of these ducklings, hatched by hens, who, as
soon as they have burst their shells, have waddled
away to the pond. The pond is art, letters, the
trade that is open to all without licence or diploma.
Desroches, then, on leaving school, had paddled
about in art, in all the arts. He had begun with
painting, and that cynic's passage through the
studios, cold-blooded, punctual in his attendance,
close-mouthed, and retaining, amid the wildest
flights of his imagination, the stigma, the indelible
brand of his borgeois origin, had become a sort of
legend. As painting would have none of him,
Desroches fell upon literature. He had just written the *Raisins Muscats* — inspired by his vineyard
perhaps — a hundred lines, an article! He tried in
vain afterward to write another; he never could
strike the vein again and reached the age of forty
with the *Raisins Muscats* for his complete works!

The conversation, the sky-rockets of friend Desroches amused me; but his home was by no
means attractive to me. I went no more to Montmartre, but I sometimes crossed the river in the
evening to meet him at the brewery on Rue des
Martyrs. The *Brasserie des Martyrs*, now such a

peaceful resort, where the drapers on the street go for their game of checkers, was at that time a power in literature. The brewery issued decrees, reputations were made by the brewery; and in the profound silence of the Empire, Paris turned to listen to the noise made there every evening by eighty or a hundred good fellows as they smoked their pipes and emptied the beer-glasses. They were called Bohemians and they did not resent it. The *Figaro* of those days, which was non-political and appeared only once a week, was generally their tribune.

You should have seen the brewery — we used to call it the Brewery, just as the Romans said the City when speaking of Rome — you should have seen the brewery about eleven o'clock when all the voices were talking at once and all the pipes lighted.

Murger was enthroned at the table in the centre; Murger, the Homer of that world by him discovered, to which his fancy has imparted a somewhat roseate hue. Although he was then decorated and famous, publishing his novels in the *Revue des Deux Mondes*, he still came to the brewery none the less, to retemper himself, he said, and also to receive the homage of the honest fellows he had described. He was pointed out to me: a fat, melancholy face, red eyes and a scanty beard, indications of second-rate Parisian blood. He lived at Marlotte, near the forest of Fontainebleau; he always had a rifle on his shoulder, pretending to hunt, but pursuing health rather than partridges or hares.   His residence in the village had attracted thither a whole Parisian colony, men and women, flowers of the asphalt and the brewery, who produced a curious effect under the great oaks; Marlotte still feels it.   Ten years after Murger's death — he died, as every one knows, at the Hôpital Dubois. — I happened to be there with a few friends one day, at Mère Antony's, a famous wineshop!   An old peasant was drinking near where we sat, a peasant *à la* Balzac, with a tanned, earthcolored face.   An old woman came to fetch him, dressed in rags, with a red handkerchief about her head.   She called him glutton, drunkard; and he tried to make her drink.

"Your wife is n't very mild in her manners!" said some one, when she had gone.

"She ain't my wife, she's my mistress!" retorted the old peasant.

You should have heard the tone in which he said it!   The goodman evidently had known Murger and his friends, and was leading the bohemian life after his fashion.

Let us return to the brewery.   As my eyes became accustomed to the stinging of the smoke, I saw famous faces emerge through the mist, on the right hand and the left, from every corner.

Each great man had his table, which became the kernel, the centre of a whole clan of admirers.

Pierre Dupont, old at forty-five, stout and bent, his beautiful eye, like that of an ox, hardly visible beneath its drooping lid, would sit with his elbows on the table, trying to sing some of the political or rustic ballads with the golden rhythm, quivering with the splendid dreams of '48, resonant with the sounds of the thousand trades of the Croix-Rousse, fragrant with the thousand perfumes of the Lyonnese valleys. The voice was no longer there, it had been burned by alcohol and resembled a death-rattle.

"You need the fields, my poor Pierre!" said Gustave Mathieu, the singer of *Bons Vins*, the *Coq Gaulois*, and *Les Hirondelles*. Mathieu, born of excellent bourgeois stock in the Nivernais, had travelled in his youth, and retained from his travels a most intense fondness for fresh air and the open country. He found them both in the neighborhood of his little house at Bois-le-Roi, and seldom visited the brewery except to walk through, erect and smiling, with the air of a Henri IV., and a bunch of wild flowers in his buttonhole at all seasons.

Dupont died, wretchedly enough, at Lyon, in the smoky manufacturing city. He was as sound and as thin as a vine-shoot. Mathieu outlived him a long while. It was only a few years ago, after a brief illness, that his friends escorted his body to the little cemetery at Bois-le-Roi, separated only by a slender hedge from the open fields; a fitting cemetery for a poet, where he sleeps under the roses in the shade of the oaks.

The first evening that I saw Gustave Mathieu, a tall, thin, red-haired devil, with the swaggering airs of a bully, was seated beside him, mimicking his voice, copying his gestures: Fernand Desnoyers, an original creature who wrote *Bras-Noir*, a pantomime in verse! On the other side of the table, some one was arguing with Dupont; it was Reyer, shrunken and excitable, who was jotting down the airs composed without musical talent by the poet; Reyer, the future author of the *Statue*, of *Sigurd*, and of so many other beautiful works.

How many memories that mere name, the Brewery, evokes within me! how many faces that I first saw there in the reflection of the beer mugs, through the dense smoke!

Let me mention at random a few names of those who still survive, while the great majority have vanished. Here is Monselet, refined prose-writer, refined poet; M. de Cupidon, plump and curled and smiling, resembles a gallant abbé of the old *régime ;* one looks for the little cloak on his back, the little cloak as buoyant as a pair of wings. Champfleury, too, at that time the leader of a school, the father of realism, who confounded in the same frantic passion Wagner's music, old porcelain and pantomime. Porcelain finally won the day: Champfleury, his dearest ambition satisfied, is to-day superintendent of the ceramic museum at Sèvres.

Here is Castagnary, in a waistcoat with broad lapels, *à la* Robespierre, cut from the velvet cover of an old easy-chair. He is chief clerk to a solicitor, but has escaped from the office to come and recite Victor Hugo's *Châtiments*, with all their flavor of forbidden fruit. He is surrounded and acclaimed; but he is off again to find Courbet; he must see Courbet, he must talk with Courbet about his *Philosophy of Art in the Salon of* 1857. Without renouncing art, and continuing to write with graceful pen more than one noteworthy page upon our annual Salons, the sly Saintongeois,[1] always smiling a cunning smile behind his drooping moustaches, has allowed himself to glide by slow degrees into politics. Municipal Councillor, then manager of the *Siècle*, and to-day a member of the Council of State, he no longer declaims poetry and no longer wears a red waistcoat.

Here is Charles Baudelaire, a great poet beset by a passion for the unexplored in art, in philosophy by fear of the unknown. Victor Hugo said of him that he invented a new shiver. In truth, no one else has succeeded as he has done in making the souls of things speak; no one has brought from a greater distance those flowers of evil, brilliant and strange as tropical flowers, which grow apace, swollen with poison, in the mysterious depths of the human soul. A patient, sensitive artist, devoting much thought to the turn of the phrase and the choice of words, Baudelaire, by a cruel sarcasm of fate, lost the power of speech before he died, retaining his intelligence intact, as was made painfully clear by the plaint of his black eye, but unable to translate his thoughts except by the same indistinct oath, mechanically repeated again and again. Correct and cold in bearing, endowed with a wit as cutting as English steel, and with a courtesy that seemed paradoxical, he astonished the habitués of the brewery by drinking liqueurs from across the Chan-

---

[1] Native of Saintonge.

nel, in company with Constantin Guys, the designer, or Malassis, the publisher.

Such a publisher as we seldom see was that same Malassis; a clever fellow, with a curious taste for letters, he devoured a handsome provincial fortune in royal fashion by printing the works of people whom he liked. He too is dead, he died smiling, far from rich, but without a complaint. And I never think without emotion of that jovial, pale face, made longer by the two points of a reddish beard, a Mephistopheles of the days of the Valois.

Alphonse Duchesne and Delvan, two more who have gone, I used also to see in a corner at the brewery. A strange destiny, that of that generation, so soon mowed down, in which no one passes his fortieth year! Delvan, a Parisian interested in Paris, who admired her in her beauties, loved her in her blemishes, the descendant of Mercier and Rétif de la Bretonne, whose little books, very carefully written, filled with trivial facts and picturesque observations, have become a feast for gourmands and the joy of bibliophiles. Alphonse Duchesne, at that time heated by his quarrel with Francisque Sarcey who, planting the banner of the Normal School in front of the banner of the Bohemians, had just made his début in literature with a bellicose article: *Les Mélancoliques de Brasserie.*[1]

It was at the brewery that Alphonse Duchesne and Delvan wrote those *Letters of Junius*, which a

[1] As these pages were passing through the press the news came of Francisque Sarcey's death (May, 1899).

mysterious messenger delivered every week at the office of *Figaro*, and which turned Paris topsy-turvy. Villemessant swore by the mysterious Junius. He was evidently some great personage. Everything indicated it: the style of the letters, their insolent, aristocratic tone, a flavor of nobility and of the old faubourg. Imagine his rage, therefore, on the day when the mask fell to the ground, and he learned that those aristocratic pages were written by two needy Bohemians on a wine-shop table, to eke out their living! Poor Delvan! poor Duchesne! Villemessant never forgave them.

I pass on, for it would require a whole volume to describe the whole brewery, table by table. Here is the thinkers' table: these fellows say nothing, they do not write; they think. We admire them on trust, we say that they are as deep as wells, and indeed one can readily believe it to watch them swallow beer. Bald heads, dishevelled beards, an odor of cheap tobacco, cabbage soup and philosophy.

Farther on, blouses, skull-caps, cries of animals, thrusts and parries, puns; those are artists, sculptors, painters. In their midst a sweet, refined face, Alexandre Leclerc, whose fanciful frescoes covering the walls of the Moulin-de-Pierre tavern at Châtillon the Prussians destroyed.

They found him dead one day; he had hanged himself, sitting down and pulling himself up by a rope, in the midst of a multitude of graves in the highest part of Père-Lachaise, where Balzac stands calling Rastignac's attention to the immensity of

Paris. In my memories of the brewery Alexandre Leclerc is always in high spirits, singing Picardie ballads; and those provincial airs, those rustic verses diffused about his table, in the tobacco-reeking atmosphere, an indefinable perfume, poetic and pervading, of the country and of waving fields of grain.

And then the women, whom I had forgotten, for there are women there, ex-models, lovely creatures if slightly faded. Unusual faces and strange names, sobriquets which smell of bad places, pretentious *des:* Titine *de* Barancy and Louise Coup-de-Couteau. Abnormal types, strangely refined, for, having passed from hand to hand, they have retained a sort of smearing of artistic erudition from each of their innumerable liaisons. They have opinions on every subject, and declare themselves, according to the views of the lover for the time being, realist or idealist, Catholic or atheist. It is affecting and laughable.

Some new ones there are, quite young, just admitted by the awe-inspiring areopagus; but most of them have grown old there and have acquired by prescription a species of uncontested authority. And then there are the widows, the ancient flames of famous authors or artists, engaged in superintending the education of some débutant recently arrived from his province. And all of them sprawling about, smoking cigarettes which contribute their tiny bluish spirals to the gray fog of pipe-smoke and breath.

The beer flows freely, the waiters run to and fro,

the discussions wax warmer; there are excited exclamations, arms raised in air, manes shaken threateningly, and in the thick of it, shouting for two, gesticulating for four, standing on a table and apparently swimming in an ocean of heads, Desroches guides and dominates with his mountebank's voice the deafening uproar of the fair. He looks well so, with an inspired air, his shirt open, his cravat untied and floating in the wind, a true natural son of Rameau's nephew!

He comes here every evening to stupefy himself, to fuddle himself with talk and beer, to arrange collaborations, to tell of his projects in the way of writing books, to lie to himself and to forget that his home has become hateful to him, sedentary work impossible, and that he would not even be capable of writing the *Raisins Muscats* again.

Doubtless there were noble minds at the brewery, intent upon serious subjects; and sometimes a beautiful poem, an eloquent paradox freshened the atmosphere like a current of pure air, and scattered the pipe-smoke. But for every man of talent, how many Desroches! For a few moments of elevating excitement, how many unhealthy, wasted hours!

And then what dejection on the morrow, what bitter awakenings with the depression caused by nausea, what disgust with such a life without the moral strength to change it! Look at Desroches; he no longer laughs, his grimace vanishes, he is thinking of the children who are growing up, of the wife who is growing older and becoming more and more degraded, of the whip and the cap and the smock-frock, of the wagoner's costume, which was amusing one evening long ago, when she wore it for the first time at a ball, but is sickening to-day.

When those black thoughts seized him Desroches would disappear, go away into the provinces, dragging his strange family after him.

Dealer in watches, actor at Odessa, bailiff's follower at Brussels, juggler's assistant — what extraordinary trades had he not followed? Then he would return, speedily tired out and disgusted, even with that.

One day, in the Bois de Boulogne, he tried to hang himself, but some keepers cut him down. They made fun of him at the brewery and he himself talked about his adventure with an affected little laugh. Some time after, having determined to make an end of it, he threw himself into one of those horrible quarries, abysses of limestone and clay, which are numerous about the fortifications of Paris. He passed the night there with his ribs crushed, his wrists and thighs broken. He was still alive when they took him out.

"Deuce take it!" he said, "they will call me the man who always misses fire."

Those were his last words. He lived in agony for sixty days, then died. I shall never forget him.

XIII.

HISTORY OF MY BOOKS. — JACK.

I HAVE before me, on the table on which I am writing these lines, a photograph by Madar, the portrait of a boy of some eighteen or twenty years, a sweet, sickly face with undecided features, the eyes of a child, playful and clear, whose animation contrasts sharply with a weak mouth, flabby and drooping as if the muscles had lost their elasticity, the mouth of a poor man who has suffered much. It is a portrait of Raoul D—, the Jack of my book, as he was when I knew him in the latter part of 1868, as he was when I welcomed him at the little house I was then occupying at Champrosay — shivering with cold, round-shouldered, his arms drawing his thin coat tight over a narrow chest in which the cough rang like a funeral knell.

We were neighbors in the forest of Sénart. Already ill, worn to a shadow by the terribly laborious life forced upon him by the whim of a lover of his mother's, he had come to seek rest in the country, in a large solitary house, much out of repair, where he lived like Robinson Crusoe, with a bag of potatoes and credit for a daily loaf at the baker's at Soisy. Not a sou had he, not even enough to pay his passage to Paris. When he was homesick for a sight of his mother, he did six good leagues on foot, and returned exhausted but overjoyed; for he adored his mother, spoke of her with affectionate admiring enthusiasm, the respect of a half-breed for his white wife, the superior being. " Mamma is a canoness! " he said to me one day, and in such a tone of conviction that I had not the heart to ask him of what chapter. But a few remarks of that sort enabled me to judge what manner of woman that foolish creature was, ambitious of titles, of noble connections, who consented to make her child a mechanic. Why, at one time she told him that he was the son of the Marquis de P——, a name well known under the Empire! And the idea of being a nobleman's son amused the poor boy, seasoned his distress and the usual melancholy of the old dairy farm with a spice of vanity. Later, forgetting that first confession, she gave him for a father an officer of high rank in the artillery; and it was impossible to say which time she lied, or whether she spoke with honest intention, at the will of her capricious vanity and of a heavily laden memory. In my book this characteristic detail offended certain readers; although taken from real life, it seemed an exaggeration of the psychologist, who most assuredly would never have invented it.

But Raoul forgave his mother even that; and I have never seen any other indication of rancor on his part than a sad smile which implored pardon for the mad creature. " What would you have? she is made that way."— It should be said, too, that the common people know nothing of many moral refinements and delicate shades of feeling; and Raoul was of the common people, among whom he had been thrown at the age of eleven, after a few months passed at a fashionable boarding school at Anteuil. From that experiment in bourgeois education, he had retained some vague notions, names of authors, titles of books, and a great love for study which he had never been able to satisfy. Now that the doctor forbade him to do any manual labor, and I threw the doors of my library wide open to him, he turned his attention to reading, and read ravenously, like a famished man making up for lost time. He would leave me, laden with old books for his evenings, his nights, his long nights of fever and coughing, when he lay shivering in his cold, poorly lighted house, with all his wretched clothes piled on his bed. But he liked above all things to read at my house, sitting in the window-recess of the room where I was working, with the window open on the fields and the Seine.

" I can understand better here," he used to say. Sometimes I assisted him to understand, for, in obedience to a sort of superstition, an ambition of his mind, he selected deep reading, Montaigne, La Bruyère. One of Balzac's or Dickens's novels amused him too much, nor did it make him so proud as the slow deciphering of some classic work. In his intervals of repose I led him to talk about his life, about the condition of the working class, of which he had a very clear perception, far above his years and his occupation. He was quick to see the painful or comical side of things, the grandeur of certain incidents in factory life. For instance, the first trial of the machine which I describe in *Jack* is one of his reminiscences as an apprentice. The thing that interested me above all else was the awakening, the rounding out of that intellect, like a far-off memory which came back to his mind more and more vividly under the spur of books and our pleasant chats. A change took place even in the physical being, invigorated by the intellectual effort. Unfortunately, life was soon to part us. And while I returned to Paris for the winter, Raoul, resuming his tools, obtained employment in the shops of the Lyon railway. I saw him two or three times in six months; each time thinner and more changed, in despair at the feeling that he was much too weak for his trade. " Very well — leave it. Let us look for something else." But he chose to struggle on, fearing to distress his mother and touched in his manly pride. And I dared not insist, not realizing how deep-seated his disease was, and dreading above all things to take that poor mechanic out of his proper station, to make a *raté*[1] of him, in the name of romance.

Time passed. One day I received a pitiful little note in a trembling hand : " Ill, at La Charité, hall of Saint-Jean de Dieu." And there I found him, lying on a litter, because the winter which was just closing had been very severe and there was no unoccupied bed in that hall, which was set aside for consumptives. Raoul would have one

1 Literally, one who has missed fire.

when death made the first vacancy. He seemed to me very ill, his eyes were so hollow and his voice so hoarse, and, more than all else, his imagination was so impressed by his sad surroundings, the groans, the racking coughs, the prayer of the nun in attendance at nightfall, and the chaplain, in red slippers, attending those patients whose lives were despaired of. He was afraid that he should die there. I did my utmost to encourage him, but was greatly surprised that his mother had not taken him home to nurse him. " I was the one who objected," said the poor victim. " They are getting on in the world; they are building a new house; I should have been in their way." And, as if in reply to the reproach in my eyes, he added: "Oh! mamma is very good. She writes to me and comes to see me." I am convinced that he was lying; his evident destitution, the plain hospital accommodations, without the slightest delicacy, not even an orange, savored of friendlessness. It occurred to me, when I found him so lonely and unhappy, to induce him to write down what he saw, what he underwent there, convinced that in that way it would make a deeper impression on his mind. And then, who could say? Perhaps it might become a source of income to that proud creature, whom it was so hard to induce to accept a little money. At my first word, the sick man sat up, clinging with both hands to the wooden handles hanging at the head of the bed.

" Really, do you really mean it? do you think that I could write? "

" I am sure of it."

As it turned out I did not find ten words to change in the four articles Raoul sent me from the hospital.   Their tone was simple and sincere, with a painful air of reality well suited to their title : LIFE IN THE HOSPITAL.   Those persons who happened to read those brief pages in an ephemeral medical sheet, the *Journal d'Enghien*, never could have suspected that they were written on a hospital cot, and with such a painful effort, such feverish excitement.   And how delighted he was, the fine fellow, when I carried him the few louis produced by his writings !   He would not believe in his good fortune, he turned them over and over on the counterpane in front of him, while curious faces from the neighboring beds leaned forward toward that unfamiliar chink of gold.   From that day the hospital was beautiful in his eyes, because he made it his study.   He left it soon after, in a burst of youthful vigor ; but the interns who attended him did not conceal from me the gravity of his condition.   The wound still existed, ready to reopen, incurable, especially if the poor fellow should resume the hard trade of iron-worker and machinist. Thereupon I remembered that when I was of the same age, and my health seriously impaired, a stay of a few months in Algiers was of the greatest benefit to me.   I applied to the prefect of Algiers, whom I knew slightly, asking him to give Raoul employment.   M. Le Myre de Vilers, now the representative of France at Madagascar, probably has forgotten the incident long ago, but I have not forgotten with what promptness and good will, which doubled the value of the service, he answered my letter and offered me for my friend a fifteen-hundred-franc clerkship in the land-registry office; five hours' work a day, work that was not fatiguing, in the loveliest country on earth, with a stage-setting of green trees and blue water before his eyes.

That departure, that long journey, were genuine enchantment to Raoul, coupled with the thought that he need never return to the workshop, that he would have black hands no more and could earn his daily bread without killing himself. In the family in which I live I am surrounded by kindly creatures with great, noble hearts whom that boy's misfortunes had conquered; and they clubbed together to provide for his comfort. "I will pay for the journey," said the old grandmamma. Another undertook to provide the linen, another the clothes, for he must leave the blue blouse and overalls at the factory. Raoul accepted everything, now that he had a place, and the certainty of paying his debts. Think of it! Fifteen hundred francs a year? And then he would write, he would send me articles. He planned many other joys beside, of which he talked to me on the evening that we bade each other adieu: he meant to send for his mother, to have her come and lead a happy respectable life with him. Others had had her long enough; now it was his turn. In his new clothes, which became him well, his eyes sparkling and his face intelligent and handsome once more, while he talked to me in that strain he was no longer the poor, disinherited wretch, but a comrade, one of my comrades who was about to leave me — and whom I was never to see again.

He wrote to me often from Algiers. — "I am dreaming, I am dreaming. It seems to me that I am in heaven." — He lived in a suburb, separated from the sea by a forest of orange trees, near the house of a painter, a friend of mine, to whom I had given him letters, as well as to Charles Jourdan, who lost no time in throwing open his house at Montriant, with unreserved hospitality, to the poor exile. His office work took but little of his time and gave him leisure to continue his education by a course of reading which I had marked out for him. But we had taken hold too late to rescue him from his miserable fate. He had suffered so much and so early in life: the wounds of infancy grew with the man. "I have just had a good shaking-up," Raoul wrote me on June 18, 1870, "but thanks to energetic treatment I am on my feet again, weak, very weak, to be sure, and obliged to count my steps when I walk. During the fortnight of convalescence I have just passed through, without leaving the house, my imagination took many walks with you in the forest, and we talked a deal together in the great studio. My head was too weak for reading and I was lying and dreaming, a little lonely and depressed, when Charles Jourdan, the kind-hearted giant, came in a *bourricot* to fetch me, and took me away to a house which would be very dear to me if there were no such place as

Champrosay. The air at Montriant is so pure, the view so lovely, the silence so profound that I feel as if I were born again. And what a charming fellow Jourdan is, so full of heartiness and youthful vigor! His study is provided with a great library, and I pass my days turning over the leaves here and there as I used to do with you. He also dictates to me his articles for the *Siècle* and the *Histoire*. To-day we have been scoring the general councils." His tone was cheerful enough, but one could detect genuine fatigue, and toward the end the long, straight handwriting wavers, and the ink changes color; he was obliged to stop and rest several times before finishing it.

Then came the war and the siege. I heard nothing more from him and I forgot him. Who among us, during those five months, thought of anything save the country? As soon as the gates of Paris were opened, in the flood of letters which overflowed my table there was one from a physician in Algiers, informing me that Raoul was very ill and asking for information as to his mother; it would be charitable to him to let him know something about her. Why did the mother, after she was told of his condition, still refrain from giving any sign of life so far as her child was concerned? I have never known. But, on February 9th, she received from Charles Jourdan these indignant lines; "Madame, your son is at the hospital. He is dying. In pity's name send a word in your handwriting to the child whom you will never see again."

A short time after, the sad news reached me:

"Raoul died at the civil hospital in Algiers on the 13th of February last, after a long and painful death agony. Until the last he begged for the caress which his mother refused him. 'I am suffering terribly,' he said to me, 'A word from my mother would allay my suffering, I am sure.'— That word did not come, was not sent. I tell you, that woman has treated her son cruelly, pitilessly. Raoul adored his mother; and yet, on his death-bed, he pronounced a terrible sentence upon her: 'I can no longer esteem her either as mother or woman; but my whole heart, on the point of ceasing to beat, is filled with her; I forgive her the wrong she has done me.' — Raoul talked to me a long while about you before he died. In the midst of his melancholy life of suffering and privations, he was surprised to find one pleasant, cheerful memory. — 'Say to him that, as I am leaving this world, I most regret losing him and his dear wife.' — I had become very intimate with the unhappy invalid whom you sent to us. I live in a great expanse of open country, inundated with flowers and sunlight; I wished Raoul to look upon it as his usual place of resort, but the sweet-natured, excellent youth was always afraid of being a trouble. Toward the last I begged him to come to my house to be taken care of. He refused and entered the hospital, on the pretext that he would receive better care there. The truth is that the poor fellow felt that his end was near and did not wish to subject a friend to the sad spectacle of his death."

So much of my material real life furnished me. For a long time I saw in this story nothing more than one of the innumerable external afflictions which alternate with our own afflictions. It had taken place too near me for my novelist's glance; the study of humanity was lost sight of in my personal sorrow. One day at Champrosay, as I sat with Gustave Droz on a fallen tree, in the melancholy atmosphere of the woods in autumn, I described Raoul's wretched existence to him, only a few steps from the red-brick hovel in which his hours of illness and friendlessness had worn themselves away.

"What a fine subject for a book!" said Droz, deeply moved.

That very day, laying aside the *Nabob*, upon which I was at work, I started off on this new scent with feverish haste, with that quivering at the ends of my fingers which seizes me at the beginning and the end of all my books. On comparing Raoul's story and the novel of *Jack*, it is easy to distinguish what is true from what is invented, or at least — for I invent but little — from what came to me from other sources. Raoul did not live at Indret, he was not a stoker. He has often told me, however, that, during his apprenticeship at Havre, the neighborhood of the sea, the air of travel, with the shouts of the sailors and the ringing of hammers in the refitting dock, sometimes made him long to go to sea, to accompany in its journey around the world one of the mighty machines made by the firm of Mazeline.

The whole episode of Indret is imaginary. I
needed a great centre of the iron-working industry;
I hesitated between Creuzot and Indret. I finally
decided in favor of the latter because of the river
life, the Loire and the Port of Saint-Nazaire. It
occasioned a journey and many short trips during
the summer of 1874. Taking my little Jack thither,
I set about becoming familiar with the atmosphere,
the class of people among whom his life was to be
passed. I spent many long hours on the island
of Indret, walked through the enormous shops
during working hours and in the more impressive
periods of repose. I saw the Roudics' house with
its little garden; I went up and down the Loire,
from Saint-Nazaire to Nantes, on a boat which
rolled and seemed tipsy like its old rower, who
was much surprised that I had not preferred to
take the Basse-Indre railway, or the Paimbœuf
steamer. And the harbor, the transatlantic liners,
the engine-rooms, which I inspected in detail, furnished me with the real notes for my study.

In these excursions I was almost always accompanied by my wife and my little boy — I had but
one at that time, a pretty little urchin with tawny
curls, displaying his ingenuous wonder amid these
varied surroundings. When the trip was too rough
for them, the mother and child waited for me in a
little inn at Piriac, a genuine Breton inn, square
and white like a die on the shore of the vast ocean,
with its great chamber with rustic beds, one of
which shut up like a wardrobe in the roughly
whitewashed wall, the mantel adorned with sponges

and sea-horses as at the Roudics', two little windows secured by the transverse bar familiar in the
coast provinces, one looking on the jetty and the
infinite expanse of the sea, the other revealing
orchards, a corner of the church and cemetery,
with the black crosses, crowded together and toppling over, as if the rolling of the waves near by
and the wind from the offing shook even the graves
of the coast population. Below us was the com-
mon-room, a little noisy on Sunday evenings, where
they sung old provincial airs whose echo can be
found in my book. Sometimes, when the handsome brigadier Mangin was there — yes, brigadier
Mangin, I have changed neither his name nor his
rank — our host allowed them to move the benches
out of the way and to dance "to mouth music."
Thither came, with their wives, fishermen and
sailors who were friends of ours and took us in
their skiffs to breakfast on Île Dumet, or on some
rock out at sea. They knew that the big waves no
longer had any terrors for my little Parisian or his
mamma; and one of them, an old whaler, told us
that, seeing monsieur, madame, and the little boy
always travelling together reminded him — with
due respect — of three "spouters" in the North
Sea who always swam in company, father, mother,
and child.

On all our excursions we talked of nothing but
Jack. He was so completely a part of our lives
that to-day, when I think of that corner of Bretagne,
it seems to me that my poor Raoul was with us
there. On my return to Paris I went to work at

once. I had no notes as to the life of Parisian workingmen. I knew naught of it beyond what the street has to tell of misery, debauchery and fighting; but what of the factory, the wine-shops, the low taverns on the shore of the lake at Saint-Mandé, where I photographed Bélisaire's wedding-party, the dust of the Buttes-Chaumont, where I idled away divers Sunday afternoons, drinking thin beer and watching the kites ascend? As for the hospital, which occupies so large and so sad a place in the life of the common people, with that I was familiar; I had made long visits there during Raoul's illness, to say nothing of the information in his articles. But as the Goncourts had described La Charité exhaustively and definitively in *Sœur Philomène,* I could not go over the same ground. So I have barely touched upon it, and only in short passages.

But what served me best in depicting the people of the faubourgs, in the third part of *Jack,* were my memories of the siege and of the National Guard, the battalion of workmen with whom I patrolled Paris and the suburbs for four months, sleeping on the damp floors of the barracks, on the straw in ox-wagons, and who taught me to love the common people even in their vices, born of poverty and ignorance. The Bélisaire of my book — his true name was Offehmer — was with me in the *Sixth* of the *Eighty-Seventh;* and I can see him now, with his huge, deformed feet, breaking the rank by his limping, always the last man in the battalion on the interminable Rue de Charenton.

Denis Poulet's book, *Le Sublime*, which Zola's fine novel has since made popular, was also of great assistance to me, being full of typical expressions, of a slang peculiar to certain trades, just as I found in Turgan's *Manuel Roret* and *Les Grandes Usines* the technical details of the interior of the work-shops, all new to me. Such are the foundations of a novel, the preparation, as gradual as possible, but compact and thorough, which are to furnish the author with the plot, the style, the real prestige of the work. And to think that some people insist upon asking you two months after you have published a new book: "When may we look for the next book? — Come, lazybones!"

The *ratés* and their environment cost me much less labor and investigation. I had only to look behind me through my twenty-five years in Paris. The prosy Dargenton exists as I have described him, with his vast forehead, his imaginary par-oxysms, his egotism, the blind and savage egotisim of a powerless Buddha. Not one of his "cruel remarks" was invented; I culled them from his fruitful lips as they blossomed there; and his faith in his genius is so profound that, if he has seen himself painted at full length in my book, as black and solemn and dismal as a country bailiff, he must have smiled disdainfully and said: "That's envy!" — Ten copies of Labassindre can be seen in a well known café on the boulevard, during the summer, when the mullets are idle. — Hirsch is a more specialized type; twenty years ago I used every day to see that *raté* of medicine, slovenly in his person, cracked-brained, with a phial of ammonia protruding from the pocket of his ample nankeen waistcoat, perfectly possessed to attend and dose the sick without a diploma. He always had some victim in hand, studying the effect upon him of strange and dangerous drugs; then, in default of patients, he doctored himself and died, at the hospital at Bordeaux, as the result of taking his own remedies. Moronval the mulatto is also a real person; he had a share in the management of the *Revue Coloniale*, and was in the Chamber of Deputies for some time after 1870. When I knew him, he occupied a little house with a garden at Batignolles and lived with some half-dozen little negroes forwarded to him from Port-au-Prince and Tahiti, who had been brought up together and acted as his servants, going to market and blacking boots while explaining the *Epitome.*

I have retained, practically intact, the principal character of the real living drama, the main features of his life and his cruel death. The mother, whom I never knew, I have represented as I made her out to be from what her child told me. Also true and closely resembling the truth is worthy Doctor Rivals, a hero, a saint, who has been travelling for thirty years the paths familiar to Jack and his biographer. For fear of distressing him, of causing embarassment to his great modesty, I refrain from giving here his name, which a whole population of peasants has blessed for two generations; I beg his forgiveness for having, in the moral of my story, mingled a gloomy drama, drawn from other sources,

with his noble, straightforward, upright existence.[1]
I had almost forgotten two other witnesses of
Raoul's great destitution: the wife of the keeper
who still occupies the humble house in the forest,
where the poor little fellow more than once found
a place at table and by the fire, and old Salé, to
whom I have left her true name, the hooked-nose
peasant, the terror of the abandoned child, who
used to dream of her at night in the hospital. I
have a weakness for sometimes retaining the real
names of my models, imagining that a change of
name impairs the completeness of creations which
are almost always reminiscences of life, of exhaust-
ing, haunting visions, not to be appeased until I
place them in my work, as like as possible.

All these foundation stones firmly in place, my
characters ready for action, my chapters outlined,
I set to work.   It was in the spacious study, lighted
by two broad, high windows, of the Palais Lamoi-
gnon.   Read the first pages of the chapter entitled
Jack en Ménage, and you will obtain the general
view of workingmen's houses, of zinc roofs, of tall
factory chimneys supported by long iron cables,
which my eyes, when they looked up from the paper,
saw through the streaming window-panes and the
haze of Parisian days.   At night, all the windows
crowded closely together on every floor of those
towering façades were brightly lighted, outlining the

---

[1] He is dead to-day; his name was Doctor Rivals, and his bust
still adorns the pretty green square of the village of Draveil. —
AUTHOR'S NOTE.

figures of brave-hearted toilers, leaning over their work far into the night, especially about the first of the year, when that toy-makers' quarter supplies material for the street booths and shop-windows. But the best pages were written at Champrosay, where we arrived with the first lilacs for a sojourn in the country often prolonged till the snow flew.

Our most carefully closed and guarded houses in Paris are open to too many distractions and unexpected incidents. There is the friend who brings you his cares or his joys, the morning newspaper with exciting news, the unblushing bore who forces his way by the servants, and the burdens of society, the dinners, the first nights, from which the observer, the painter of modern manners, has no right to absent himself. In the country there is plenty of space, the air is pure, the days long, and being able to dispose of his person and his time as he pleases, one has, above all else, the sense of security due to that independent life, the comforting consciousness of being quite alone with one's idea. There is a sort of intoxication of thought and of work. I never felt it more clearly than when I was writing *Jack*. Those days of frenzied production left delightful memories behind. Long before daylight I was installed at my unpainted table, two steps from my bed, in the dressing-room. I wrote by lamp-light, under a window in the sloping-roof, still cold and wet with dew, which reminded me of the misery of my early years. Beasts of night crept over the roof, scratching the tiles, an owl shrieked, cattle lowed in the straw of a shed close by; and without glancing at the clock which ticked in front of my pen, without raising my eyes to look at the pale rays of dawn, I knew the time by the crowing of the cocks, by the bustle in a neighboring farmhouse, the tramping of wooden shoes, the jangling of the iron hoops on pails that were being filled with water for the cattle, hoarse voices calling to one another in the keen air of daybreak, with shouts and screaming and the heavy flapping of wings. Then the sleepy tramp of bands of workmen passing on the road; and a little later a swarm of children hurrying toward the school a league away, with the whirring noise of a covey of partridges.

The fact that spurred me on and gave intense interest to that terrible, breathless task was this: in the month of June, and long before I had finished my book, the *Moniteur*, conducted by Paul Dalloz, began to publish it. I have the habit, which may seem at variance with my slow and conscientious method of working, of turning over the chapters to the newspapers as fast as they are finished. I am the gainer by it, in that I am obliged to part from my work, without yielding to that tyrannical craving for perfection which leads authors to go back and remodel the same page ten, yes, twenty times. I know some who wear themselves out in that way, consume their strength to no purpose for years on a single work, paralyze their real faculties, and finally produce what I call "deaf men's literature," whose beauties and refinements are appreciated by none but themselves.

I am also the gainer in that I put the spurs to my natural indolence, that inherited capacity for idling which makes long-continued attention and reflection distasteful, its effect being doubled in my case by a disgusting faculty of analysis and criticism.   Once in the water, one must swim; and that is why I resolutely throw myself in.   But what feverish excitement, what panics; and the fear of falling ill, and the agony of feeling that that serial with its giant strides is always close upon one's heels !

Jack was finished late in October.   I had taken nearly a year to write it; it is by far the longest and the most rapidly done of all my books.   So it was that it left me in such a state of exhaustion that I went with my two dear travelling companions to recuperate in the genial sunshine of the Mediterranean, among the violets of Bordighera.   There I passed long days of genuine cerebral convalescence, with the silences, the absorbed contemplations of nature, the blissful inspiration of pure, life-giving air which follow a serious illness.   On my return *Jack* appeared with the imprint of Dentu, in two thick volumes, but did not have so large a sale as *Fromont*.   A story in two volumes is long and dear according to our French ideas. — "A little too much paper, my son," said my great Flaubert, to whom the book is dedicated, with his kindly smile. I was also blamed for having dwelt too much on the poor martyr's sufferings.   George Sand wrote me that her heart was so oppressed by reading the book, that "for three days she was unable to work." The impression must have been profound indeed to interrupt that noble toil, always undaunted and imperturbable.

Well, yes! it is a cruel book, a bitter book, a dismal book. But what is it compared with the *real existence* I have described?

XIV.

ÎLE DES MOINEAUX. — A MEETING ON THE SEINE.

IN those days I had no rheumatism, and, six months in the year, I worked in my boat. Ten leagues above Paris there is a pretty bit of the Seine, of the true provincial Seine, limpid and rustic, invaded by reeds, irises, water-lilies, freighted with tufts of grass and roots on which the wagtails, tired of flying, float downward with the current. On the slopes on either bank are fields of grain and vineyards; here and there a green island, the Île des Paveurs, and the Île des Moineaux, a tiny affair, a veritable bouquet of brambles and riotous branches, which was my favorite port. I would pull my yawl in among the reeds, and when the silky rustling of the long stalks had ceased and my wall had closed in behind me, a little round harbor with water as clear as crystal, in the shadow of an old willow, became my study, and two oars, crossed, my desk![1] I loved that odor of the river, the buzzing of insects among the reeds, the murmur of the long leaves quivering in the wind, all that mysterious, infinite movement which the silence of man arouses in nature. What happiness that

[1] This spot is described in *The Little Parish Church.*

silence causes! how many living things it reassures!
My island was more thickly peopled than Paris.
I heard creatures ferreting in the underbrush, birds
chasing one another, the whirring of wet wings.
No one stood on ceremony with me, they took me
for an old willow. The black spiders spun their
webs under my very nose, the fish spattered me as
they leaped flashing into the water; the swallows
came to drink under the very oar.

One day, on pushing my way in to my island, I
found my solitude invaded by a light beard and a
straw hat. At first I saw nothing but that, a light
beard under a straw hat. The intruder was not
fishing; he was stretched out in his boat, his oars
crossed like mine. He was actually writing, writing on my premises! At first sight we both made
the same wry face. However, we bowed. There
was no escape; the shadow of the willow was
limited in extent and our two boats touched. As
he did not seem disposed to go away, I settled
myself without speaking; but that hat and beard
so near me upset my work. I evidently embarrassed
him too. Inaction forced us to speak. My yawl
was named the *Arlésienne*, and the name of
Georges Bizet put us on friendly terms at once.[1]

"You know Bizet? Do you happen to be an
artist?"

The beard smiled and answered modestly:

"I am interested in music, monsieur."

Literary men as a general rule abhor music.

[1] Bizet wrote the incidental music for Daudet's play,
L'Arlésienne.

Every one knows Gautier's opinion concerning " the most disagreeable of all noises." Leconte de Lisle and Banville shared it. As soon as a piano is opened Goncourt turns up his nose. Zola has a vague remembrance of having played something in his youth; he has no idea now what it was. The good Flaubert, to be sure, claimed to be a great lover of music, but he did it to please Tourgueneff, who, in reality, never cared for any other music than that which he heard at the Viardots. For my part I love all kinds to distraction, the scientific and the simple, Beethoven, Glück and Chopin, Saint-Saëns, the *bamboula*, Gounod's *Faust* and Berlioz', popular ballads, street-organs, the tambourine, even the church-bells. Music that dances and music that dreams, all kinds appeal to me and move me. The melodies of Wagner lay hold of me, subdue me, hypnotize me like the sea, and the zigzag movements of the Hungarians' fiddle-bows kept me from seeing the Exposition. Whenever those infernal violins seized me as I passed, it was impossible for me to go on. I must needs sit until evening in front of a glass of Hungarian wine, with a tight feeling at my throat, my eyes beyond my control, my whole body shaken by the nervous thrumming of the dulcimer.

That musician suddenly appearing on my island finished me. His name was Léon Pillaut. He had a mind and ideas of his own, a very pretty wit; we took to each other at once. As we had both renounced almost the same notions, our paradoxes made common cause. From that day my island was as much his as mine; and as his boat, a flat-bottomed Norwegian, rolled horribly, he fell into the habit of coming into mine to talk music. His book: *Instruments et Musiciens*, which procured his appointment as professor at the Conservatoire, was already buzzing in his head and he told me about it. He and I lived that book together.

I find between his lines the echo of our unreserved chats, just as I used to watch the Seine sparkle between the reeds. Pillaut told me some absolutely novel things concerning his art. Endowed with musical talent, and brought up in the country, his delicate ear has retained and noted all the sounds of nature; he hears as a landscape painter sees. In his ears every sound of wings has its peculiar note. The confused buzzings of insects, the rustling of autumn leaves, the rippling of streams over pebbles, the wind, the rain, the sound of voices in the distance, the rumbling of trains, wheels creaking in the ruts — all these details of life in the country you will find in his book. And many other things beside, ingenious criticisms, an attractive display of the erudition of a man with a hobby, the poetical biography of the orchestra and all its instruments, from the *viole d'amour* to the Saxe trumpet, told by him for the first time. We talked about it under our willow, or in a waterside inn, drinking muddy white wine of the new vintage, dissecting a herring on the corner of a broken plate, among quarrymen and boatmen; we talked about it as we rowed on the Seine and explored the little streams that flow into it.

Oh! our rows upon the Orge, a pretty, changing stream, all black with shadow and edged with fragrant lianes, like a brook in Oceanica! We rowed on and on, not knowing whither. At times we passed between worldly lawns, where a white peacock flaunted his tail amid a bouquet of light dresses. A picture by Nittis. In the background the château, gayly decked out with its old-fashioned flower-beds, retreated beneath the high, luxuriant foliage, embellished by melodious trills, by the warbling of rich men's birds. Farther on we found the wild flowers of an island, the tangled branches, the grizzly, gnarled willows, or perhaps an old mill, tall as a fortress, with its moss-grown bridge, its high walls irregularly pierced with holes, and on the roof, covered with pigeons and Guinea fowl, a constant whirring of wings which the bulky machine seemed to set in motion. And then the floating down with the current, singing the simple old melodies of nature! The screams of the peacocks echoed over the bare lawns; in the middle of a pasture we could see the shepherd with his little wagon, collecting his sheep to drive them to the fold. We started up the kingfisher, the blue bird of the small streams; we stooped at the mouth of the Orge, to pass under the arch of the bridge, and the Seine, as it suddenly appeared in the twilight haze, gave us the impression of the open sea.

Among all our delightful vagabond rambles, one remains especially clear in my memory, a luncheon one autumn day at a waterside tavern. I can see now that chilly morning, the Seine sluggish and melancholy, the countryside lovely in its silence, the ruddy folds of a penetrating mist which made us turn up our coat-collars. The tavern was a little below the Coudray dam, a former posting-station, to which the good people of Corbeil go to make merry on Sundays, but which is frequented in winter only by the dam-keepers and the crews of barges and tugs. At that moment the kettle was steaming for the passage of the *chaîne*. God! what a pleasant puff of warmth as we entered! " And with the beef, messieurs? — How would you like a tench *à la casserole ?* " — It was perfectly delicious, that tench served on a common earthenware plate, in a small room hung with a paper which offered pleasant suggestions of a bourgeois merry-making. The repast at an end and our pipes lighted, we began to talk of Mozart. It was a typical autumn conversation. Outside, on the inn terrace, I could see through the leafless arbors a swing painted green, a game of *tonneau*, the targets of a shooting gallery, all shivering in the cold wind from the Seine, in the touching melancholy of deserted places of amusement. — " Ah! — a spinet! " said my companion, raising the dusty cover of a long table covered with plates. He tried the instrument, produced some cracked, quavering notes, and until nightfall we drank ourselves blissfully drunk with Mozart.

XV.

HISTORY OF MY BOOKS. — FROMONT AND RISLER.[1]

THE first idea of *Fromont* came into my mind during a general rehearsal of the *Arlésienne* at the Vaudeville theatre. With a magnificent bit of Camarguese scenery for stage-setting, which the gas-jets, arranged in triangles, lighted brightly even to the curtain at the rear, the pastoral unfolded its slow, rhythmic scenes, to the accompaniment of Bizet's charming music, with refrains of old Christmas ballads and old-fashioned marches. Contemplating that impassioned fairy-like spectacle, which fascinated me, Southerner that I am, but which I felt to be too local, too simple in its action, I said to myself that the good people of Paris would soon weary of hearing the talk about grasshoppers, the girls of Arles, the mistral and my mill, that it was time to interest them in a work upon some subject closer to them, a work dealing with their every-day life, its action taking place in their atmosphere; and as I was then living in the Marais, it naturally occurred to me to locate my drama in the midst of the active working life of that business quarter. The partnership idea tempted me; being the son

---

[1] *Fromont and Risler* was published in 1874; the *Arlésienne* was produced in 1872.

of a manufacturer, I knew the vexations of that com-
mercial collaboration, in which common interests
associate in the performance of a never-com-
pleted task, sometimes for years, men who differ
widely in temperament and education. I was
familiar with the jealousies between families, the
bitter rivalry of the women, in whom the spirit of
caste retains its vigor better and fights more fiercely
than in man, and all the tribulations of life under
the same roof. At Nîmes, at Lyon, at Paris, I had
ten models at hand, all in my own family, and I
began to meditate upon a work in which the plot
should turn upon the honor of the firm's signature,
of the firm itself. Unfortunately, one must introduce an element of passion even on the stage.
Adultery engrosses attention with its falsehoods,
its excitements, its risks ; and it was for that reason
that the interest of my study was lessened, diverted,
concentrated on Sidonie and her adventures, when
the partnership was intended to be its leading
theme ; but I propose to return to it some day.

The *Arlésienne*, as we know, did not succeed.
It was insane to think that, at the heart of the
boulevard, in that coquettish corner of the Chaussée
d'Antin, right in the path of the fashions and
whims of the day, of the changing, bewildering
eddy of all Paris, people would be interested in
that love-drama, the action of which takes place
in a farm-yard, in a Camargue plain, exhaling the
fragrance of well-stocked granaries and flowering
lavender. It was a gorgeous failure, with the
sweetest music imaginable, and silk and velvet

costumes amid opera-comique scenery. I went away discouraged, sick at heart, with the idiotic laughter called forth by the emotional scenes still ringing in my ears; and, without attempting to defend myself in the newspapers, where every one assailed that play with its lack of unexpected incident, that picture, in three tableaux, of manners and adventure of which I alone could know the absolute fidelity to nature, I determined to write no more plays, and I piled up the hostile reviews as a rampart to my determination. *Fromont,* which was all thought out and prepared, almost done to a turn, seemed to me capable of being transformed into a novel. I was obliged thereupon to change the framework of the plot, to rearrange the order and sequence of the sentiments; but nothing is so difficult as this demolition of a work whose pieces fit together, supplement one another and form a perfect mosaic; nothing is so cruel as this voluntary miscarriage of our conceptions when the mind has borne them for a long time, intensely alive and painful. And as the elements of the drama — I mean the drama as I had shaped it in my mind, and not as it was acted later — did duty for the novel, that is how it happens that the plot of *Fromont and Risler* is slightly conventional and romantic, with types of character and environments strictly true to life, copied from nature.

From nature!

I have never had any other system of work. As painters carefully preserve sketch-books in which they jot down silhouettes, poses, an effect of perspective, a movement of the arm, taken on the wing, so I have been collecting for thirty years a multitude of little note-books, containing observations and thoughts, sometimes comprised in one closely written line, with which to recall a gesture or a tone, to be developed and magnified later as one of the harmonious elements of an important work. In Paris, in the country, travelling, these sheets become black unconsciously, without a thought of the future work that is heaping up there; I sometimes find proper names jotted down which I cannot make up my mind to change, finding in the names a characteristic physiognomy, a striking likeness of the persons who bear them. Some of my books have given rise to a great hue and cry, to much talk about *novels with keys;* the keys have even been published, with lists of illustrious personages, without regard to the fact that, in my other books as well real persons had figured, but unknown persons, lost in the crowd where no one would dream of looking for them.

Is not that the true method of writing novels, that is to say, the story of people who will never have a story? All the characters in *Fromont* have lived or are still living. With old Gardinois I caused pain to a man of whom I am very fond, but I could not suppress that type, the selfish, redoubtable old man, the implacable parvenu, who sometimes said to his assembled children, as he stood on the terrace of his park, embracing with his miser's glance the great buildings of the farm and château: "The thing that consoles me for having to die is the thought that after I am gone no one of you will be rich enough to keep up the estate." — Planus the cashier was really named Schérer. I knew him in a banking-house on Rue de Londres, where he would stand in front of his well-filled safe, shaking his head and murmuring in his German accent with tragi-comic distress: " Ja, ja, money, much money; put I haf no gonfidence." — Sidonie too exists, and her parents' humble home, and Mère Chèbe's little box set with diamonds in a corner of the Empire commode, the only luxury the poor Chèbe household had seen for a long time. But the true Sidonie is not so black as I have painted her. Scheming, ambitious, dazzled by her new fortune, drunk with dissipation and extravagant toilets, but incapable of adultery in her own home, a detail invented with a special view to effective scenes. — Madame Fromont still polishes her rings with the same conscientious care, down in the provinces; but she will never read the book, for she does not read at all, her fingers are too busy. — Risler is a memory of my childhood. That tall fair-haired factory draughtsman worked for my father. I transformed him from an Alsatian to a Swiss, in order not to introduce into my book sentimental patriotism, the declamation which wins applause so easily. — Delobelle lived near me, and has said to me ten times: " I have no right to abandon the stage." In him, to perfect the type, I summed up all that I knew about actors, their manias, the difficulty they find in recovering their footing in life when they go off the stage, in maintaining an individuality under so many varying masks. I find among some old notes which I have been looking over to assist me in writing these lines, a "Benediction of the Sea," narrated by an actor, which is really the most extraordinary thing you can imagine. I do not transcribe it, despairing of my ability to do justice to the rolling of eyes and voice, the emotion at an angle of sixty-seven and a half degrees, the puffing, the pose quivering with intense feeling, which accompanied that strange tale, heard in the greenroom of the old Vaudeville. And, here again, in a sketch-book, the amazing attitude of another Delobelle, standing in front of his house which the Prussians had burned, and expressing a genuine feeling of regret by the aid of artificial gestures of the most comical sort; for it is the special privilege of that race, whose study it is to interpret life, to understand everything wrong, and to retain in their eyes the conventional, unshaded perspective of the stage. Thus Delobelle was firmly planted in my mind, but I had not yet rounded him out by his family when I attended, about that time, the funeral of a great actor's daughter; there I saw, in a courtyard on Rue de Bondy, the theatrical world in its entirety, and all the details that I introduced later at the death of little Désirée: the typical *entrées* of the guests, their pump-like action in shaking hands, varied according to the practices of their respective rôles, the tear caught in the corner of the eye and looked at on the end of the glove. I instantly conceived the idea of giving Delobelle a daughter, and I determined to represent the child as having inherited a trace of her father's extravagance and as having transformed the artistic frenzy into the gentle sentimentality of a woman and a cripple. In view of her infirmity, and by way of contrast, I gave her a fanciful, ornamental trade. At first I made her a doll's dressmaker, so that that humble, disfigured creature might at least be able to satisfy her taste for refinement and elegance, to clothe her dreams, if not herself, in scraps of silk and gold lace. The trade was characteristic of that noisy, humming Marais, whose smoke-begrimed five-story houses, whose venerable escutcheoned mansions shelter the amusement of Paris in course of preparation, scattering bits of fine gold and valuable woods in the dust of their garrets and their iron-bound staircases. Enter those narrow halls, climb those dismal flights of stairs; through the open doors on each landing you will see in the light of the stone lamp, around a meagre fire, women and children working. A bit of wire, a bit of glue, a scrap of gilt paper, of velvet, that is all they need to fashion with their finger-tips, almost without tools, by dexterity and ingenuity alone, in spite of cold and hunger, those trivial articles, " pretty and well made," as the hucksters say when they offer them to you: clowns, dancers, butterflies that flap their wings, marvels for four sous, the toys of the poor made by the poor, wherein the shrewd, kindly taste of that amazing Parisian populace is clearly discernible.

Following my mania for talking about my book aloud when I am constructing it mentally, I spoke one day to André Gill, the painter and designer, who was every inch an artist, of the little Delobelle as I intended to create her; he informed me that in one of Dickens's novels with which I was not familiar, *Our Mutual Friend*, there was precisely the same conception of a young cripple who was a doll's dressmaker, rendered with all the great English novelist's profound tenderness for the lowly, with his magic art of depicting low life. It was a pretext for me to recall how many times I had been compared to Dickens, even long, long before, when I had not read him, before the time when a friend, returning from a trip to England, told me of the resemblance between *David Copperfield* and *Little What's-His-Name*. An author who writes according to his eyes and his conscience has no answer to make to that, unless it be that there are certain mental relationships for which one is not oneself responsible, and that on the day of the grand kneading of men and novelists, nature, in a moment of distraction, may have mixed the dough. I feel in my heart Dickens's love for the deformed and the poor, for the child-life steeped in misery of great cities; like him I had a heart-rending introduction to life, being obliged to earn my living before I was sixteen; therein, I imagine, consists our greatest resemblance. In spite of everything I was disheartened by that conversation with Gill, and, abandoning my doll's dressmaker, I tried to find another trade

for little Delobelle.   But such things are not to be
invented ; and how was I to find a trade so poeti-
cally chimerical as that of doll's dressmaker,
making possible what I wished to depict: exquisite grace in poverty, smiling dreams within dismal
walls, the fingers giving shape to the fanciful flights
of longing.   Ah! I searched many dark houses
that year, climbed many cold stairways with a rail
of rope, seeking my ideal environment among the
innumerable petty industries.   One day, on Rue du
Temple, on a leather sign in one of the frames in
which, for the convenience of customers, all the
industries carried on in a house are inscribed and
advertised, I read these words in faded gold letters,
which fairly blinded me :

BIRDS AND INSECTS FOR ORNAMENT.

The habit, which I mentioned a moment ago, of
talking aloud about my books, is with me one
method of working.   While explaining my work
to others, I make my subject clearer to myself, I
saturate myself with it, I experiment upon my
auditors to see what passages will make a hit, and
the conversation results in surprises and discover-
ies which I do not forget, thanks to an excellent
memory.   Woe to the visitor who interrupts me in
my fever of creation.   I continue pitilessly in his
presence, talking instead of writing, tacking together as well as I can, so that they may be intel-
ligible to him, the different portions of my novel,
and, heedless of the ennui, the evident wandering
of glances which try to avoid a copious improvisa-

tion, I construct my chapter, I develop it in words. In my study at Paris, in the country, in my excursions through the fields or on the river, I have bored in this way many of my friends who had no suspicion of their mute collaboration. But my wife has had more to endure than any other of these repetitions of my work, of this turning and re-turning a subject twenty times in succession: "What do you think of killing Sidonie off? — Suppose I should let Risler live? What would Delobelle say or Frantz or Claire under such circumstances?" — That sort of thing from morning till night, every minute in the day, at table, in cabs, on the way to the theatre, on returning home at night, during those long cab drives through silent, sleeping Paris. Ah! ye poor wives of artists! It is true that mine is a consummate artist herself and has taken the deepest interest in everything I have written! Not a page which she has not looked over and retouched, on which she has not sprinkled a little of her lovely gold and azure powder. And so modest, so simple, so little of a literary woman! I had given expression to all these thoughts one day and testified to her untiring, loving collaboration, in the dedication of the *Nabob ;* my wife would not allow that dedication to appear, and I printed it in only some ten or twelve copies for my friends, which are very rare now and which I commend to collectors.[1]

[1] "To my devoted, judicious and unwearying collaborator, to my beloved Julia Daudet, I offer, with all the thanks of a grateful and loving heart, this book, which owes so much to her."

My method of work is well known. When all
my notes are made, the chapters arranged in order
and separated, the characters well defined and living in my mind, I begin to write rapidly, in a round
hand. I dash off ideas and incidents, without taking time to revise or even to correct, because the
subject hurries me on, overflows upon me, both
details and characters. When one page is covered
I pass it to my collaborator; then I look it over
again and finally recopy it, with such delight! The
delight of a schoolboy who has finished his task,
retouching certain passages, perfecting, polishing:
that is the most enjoyable stage of the work.
Fromont was written thus in one of the oldest mansions in the Marais, where my study, with its enormous windows, looked out upon the foliage, the
blackened trellises of the garden. But outside of
that zone of tranquillity and of chirping birds was
the busy life of the faubourgs, the columns of
smoke from the factories, the rumbling of the vans;
and I can still hear on the pavement of a neighboring courtyard the jolting of a wheelbarrow which,
when the time for New Year's gifts approached,
went about delivering toy drums from seven o'clock
in the evening far into the night. There is nothing
so healthy, so inspiring as to work in the very atmosphere of your subject, in the environment in
which you can feel your characters moving. The
going to and from the workshops, the factory-bells
passed across my pages at stated hours. Not the
slightest effort was required to find the local color,
the ambient atmosphere, for I was invaded by it.

The whole quarter assisted me, carried me along, worked for me. At the two ends of the enormous room were my long table and my wife's little desk, and, running with the sheets from one to the other, my oldest boy, now a medical student, then a little urchin with thick flaxen curls falling over his little pinafore, black with the ink of his first scrawl. It is one of the pleasantest memories of my life as an author.

Sometimes I found it necessary to go to some special locality for greater precision of detail. Thereupon the whole family would set out in search of the required impression. Risler and Sigismond's dinner after the crash I myself ate, with my wife and son, at the Palais Royal, at the hour when the band was playing, when the straw chairs arranged in a circle, the bored attitudes of the people listening, even the dripping of the fountain in the dust at the close of a hot day, exhale a peculiar atmosphere of melancholy: the emptiness, the provincialism of Paris in summer. I felt permeated with that atmosphere; and, full of my subject, I was suddenly profoundly affected by that commonplace military music and fancied it playing a subdued accompaniment to the melancholy conversation of my two worthy friends. Risler's death necessitated another longer expedition; I remembered Poulet-Malassis the publisher's little house near the fortifications, and I had installed Planus there, facing the green slopes with yellow flowers, trodden and stripped by the Sunday promenaders. I must needs inspect the region once more, follow

Risler's trail from the house door to the dark arch-
way where he was to hang himself, near those barracks from which the view of Paris resembles the
view of it from the suburbs — a smoky, compact
mass of cupolas, steeples and roofs, with suggestions of a vast harbor where chimneys represent
the masts. After that I had frames for all my
chapters. I had nothing more to do but write, and
under those circumstances, the drama being figured,
so to speak, illustrated by my memories and my
walks, the work was half done.

Fromont and Risler appeared as a serial in
the *Bien Public*, and during its publication I was
conscious for the first time of the serious interest
of the multitude in my work. Claire and Désirée
had friends; I was blamed for Risler's death; I
received letters interceding for the little deformed
girl. Life contains nothing more charming than
that upspringing of popularity, that first communication between the author and the reader.

The book was published by Charpentier, who
was then just establishing himself on Quai du
Louvre, in cheerful quarters flooded with sunlight,
in that delightful, hospitable shop which has become a veritable rendezvous for literary folk. Upon
leaving there one autumn-like evening late in April,
as I stood among the rows of plants arranged for
the following day's market, gazing at the Seine
streaked with bands of light from lanterns, I had a
very distinct vision of Désirée Delobelle's death.

The large sale of my book surprised me greatly.
I had theretofore been admitted to fellowship in a

small artistic group, but had never dreamed of great popularity, and I remember my happy surprise on being informed that a second edition was necessary, when, a few days after my book appeared, I went in fear and trembling to make inquiries as to its fortune.

Soon fresh impressions began to succeed one another rapidly, then there were orders for translations for Italy, Germany, Spain, Sweden and Denmark; England also joined the ranks, but less promptly. That is the country where I have found it most difficult to gain a footing, with all my taste for homely things, which, it would seem, should prove more attractive there than elsewhere.

One more detail, in conclusion.

In those days we used to have, at Gustave Flaubert's, Sunday reunions, which gradually made of a small group of writers, united in their respect and passionate love for letters, a group of warm friends. It was on Rue Murillo, in a suite of small rooms overlooking the carefully-tended shrubbery, the artificial ruins of Parc Monceau. Within, there was the silence of a private house looking on a park, and an unconstrained artistic conversation which afforded me the keenest enjoyment. We four, or five when Tourgueneff had not the gout, always dined together once a month — the dinner was jocosely called " the dinner of authors who have been hissed " — and roundly cursed the prevailing indifference to literature and the alarm of the public at every new revelation. The fact is that

not one of us had the good luck to please that
terrible public.

Flaubert was tormented by the melancholy of
past triumphs, drained to the very dregs, even to
the reproaches of the critics and the common herd
who are forever throwing your first book in your
face, and who held up *Madame Bovary* as a glorious obstacle to the success of *Salammbô* and the
Éducation Sentimentale. Goncourt seemed fatigued,
sick at heart, as the result of a great mental effort
of which a whole new generation of novelists would
reap the advantage, and which would, at all events
he so believed, leave him, the originator, almost
unknown. Suddenly I found myself the only one
in the party who felt popularity coming his way to
the tune of several thousand copies, and I was
embarrassed, almost ashamed, in presence of
authors of such talent. Every Sunday, when I
arrived, they questioned me: " How about new
editions? what's the number now?" Every time
I had to own up to new impressions; really I no
longer knew what to do with myself and my success. "We others shall never sell," said Zola,
without envy but with a touch of sadness.

That was twelve years ago. To-day his novels
sell by hundreds of editions. Goncourt's are in
every hand, and I smile when I remember that
heart-rending resigned lament: " We others shall
never sell !"

Copyright 1899, by Lane, Brown & Co.   Goupil & Cie Paris

XVI.

TURGÉNIEFF.

IT was ten or twelve years ago at Gustave Flaubert's on Rue Murillo. Small, daintily furnished rooms, upholstered in Algerian stuffs, and looking on Parc Monceau, the prim, aristocratic garden which hung blinds of verdure at the windows. We met there every Sunday, five or six of us, always the same, upon a most delightfully intimate footing. No admittance for mutes and bores.

One Sunday, when I went as usual to join the old Master and our friends, Flaubert waylaid me at the door.

"You don't know Turgénieff? He is here."

And without awaiting my reply, he pushed me into the salon. A tall old man with snow-white beard rose, as I entered, from the couch on which he was stretched out, uncurling on the pile of cushions the rings of his boa constrictor's body with its immense, astonished eyes.

We Frenchmen live in extraordinary ignorance of all foreign literature. Our minds are as domestic as our limbs, and, because of our horror of travelling, we read no more than we establish colonies when we are exiled. It so happened that I knew Turgénieff's work through and through. I had read with great emotion the *Memoirs of a*

Russian Nobleman, and that book, which fell into my hands by chance, had led me on to an acquaintance with the others. We were bound together, without knowing each other, by our mutual love for grain-fields, for underbrush, for nature generally —a twin-like comprehension of its development.

In general, descriptive writers have only eyes and content themselves with painting. Turgénieff has the sense of smell and hearing. All his senses have doors opening into one another. He is full of the fragrance of the country, of the sound of rippling water, of cloudless skies, and allows his nerves to be soothed by the orchestra of his sensations without becoming a partisan of any school.

Does not such music reach every ear? Those who live in cities, whose ears are deafened in childhood by the great city's roar, will never detect it; they will not hear the voices that speak in the silence, that is no silence, of the woods, when nature deems itself alone, and man, by holding his peace, has caused his presence to be forgotten. Do you remember the fall of an oar on the bottom of a boat, which you heard on one of Fenimore Cooper's lakes? The boat is miles away, you cannot see it; but the size of the forest is magnified by that far-off noise echoing over the sleeping water, and you feel the thrill of solitude.

It was the Russian steppes that brought Turgénieff's senses and heart to maturity. Man becomes kind-hearted by dint of listening to nature, and they who love it do not lose their interest in mankind. Hence that sympathetic gentleness, sad as one of the Russian peasants' ballads, which sob through the Slav novelist's books. It is the human sigh of which the Creole song speaks, the safety-valve that prevents the world from bursting: " Si pas té gagné, soupi n'en mouné, mouné t'a touffé." And that sigh, repeated again and again, makes the *Memoirs of a Russian Nobleman* another *Uncle Tom's Cabin*, minus the declamation and the shrieks.

I knew all this when I met Turgénieff. For a long time he had been enthroned in my Olympus, on an ivory chair, among my gods. But, far from having a suspicion of his presence in Paris, I had never asked whether he was dead or alive. Imagine my amazement, therefore, when I suddenly found myself face to face with him, in a Parisian salon, on the third floor of a house on Parc Monceau.

I laughingly told him the truth and expressed my admiration for him. I told him that I had read him in the forest of Sénart. There I had found his soul, and the pleasant memories of the scenery and of his books were so completely blended in my mind that such an one of his novels had retained in my thoughts the coloring of a little field of pink heather, already withered by the approach of autumn.

Turgénieff was greatly surprised.

"What! you have read me?"

And he gave me some details concerning the small sale of his books and the obscurity of his name in France. Hetzel published for him as an act of charity. His popularity had not crossed the frontier. It was distressing to him to pass his life unknown to a country of which he was very fond, and he confessed his disappointment, a little sadly, but without bitterness. On the other hand, our disasters in 1870 had drawn him nearer to France, he could not make up his mind to leave it. Before the war he had passed his summers at Baden, now he no longer went thither but was content with Bougival and the banks of the Seine.

As it happened there was no one else at Flaubert's that Sunday, and our tête-à-tête was prolonged. I questioned him as to his method of work and was surprised to find that he did not make his own translations, for he spoke very pure French, possibly a little slowly because of the subtlety of his mind.

He confessed to me that the Academy and its dictionary froze the blood in his veins. He turned the leaves of that formidable dictionary with fear and trembling, as if it were a codification of the laws governing the use of words, and of the penalties for audacious violations thereof. He came away from his investigations with his conscience stuffed with literary scruples which destroyed his vein and disgusted him with the venture of writing French. I remember that in a novel he was then writing he thought that he could not risk "*ses yeux pâles*," for fear of the Forty and of their definition of the phrase.

It was not the first time that I had come in contact with this same anxiety; I had found it in my friend Mistral, who likewise was fascinated by the dome of the Institute, the burlesque monument which adorns in the shape of a circular medallion the cover of the Didot publications.

On that subject I said to Turgénieff what I felt in my heart, that the French language is not a dead language, to be written with a dictionary of defini tive expressions, classified as in a *Gradus.* For my own part I felt that it was quivering with life and energy, a noble river flowing full between its banks. The river gathers up much rubbish on the way for everything is tossed into it; but let it roll on, it will do its own filtering.

Thereupon, as the day was advancing, Turgénieff said that he was going to meet " the ladies " at the Concert Pasdeloup, and I left the house with him. I was overjoyed to learn that he was fond of music. In France literary men as a rule hold it in horror; painting has invaded everything. Théophile Gautier, Saint-Victor, Hugo, Banville, Goncourt, Zola, Leconte de l'Isle, all are music-haters. So far as my knowledge goes, I am the first who ever confessed aloud his ignorance of colors and his fondness for notes; this peculiarity is due doubtless to my Southern temperament and to my near-sightedness; one sense is highly developed at the expense of another. In Turgénieff's case the taste for music was a part of his Parisian education. He had acquired it in the environment in which he lived.

That environment was an intimate friendship of thirty years' standing with Madame Viardot,[1]

[1] M. Louis Viardot (1800–1883) who married in 1838 Mlle. Pauline Garcia, sister of the famous Malibran, and herself an

Viardot the great singer, Viardot-Garcia, Malibran's sister. A bachelor and without kindred, Turgénieff had lived for years at the family mansion, 50 Rue de Douai. "The ladies" of whom he spoke to me at Flaubert's were Madame Viardot and her daughters, whom he loved as his own children. It was at that hospitable abode that I called upon him.

The house was furnished with refined sumptuousness, with much care for artistic effect and for physical comfort. As I passed through the hall on the ground floor, I saw through an open door a gallery of paintings. Fresh voices, the voices of young girls, reached my ears through the hangings; they alternated with the impassioned contralto of *Orphée*, which filled the hall and went upstairs with me.

On the third floor was a small suite, as luxurious and snug and crowded as a boudoir. Turgénieff had borrowed from his friends their artistic tastes: music from the wife, painting from the husband.

He was lying on a sofa.

I sat beside him, and we at once resumed the conversation begun the other day.

artiste of great merit, was a versatile and accomplished character. He began life as a lawyer, then adopted the profession of journalism. He wrote for many periodicals, *Revue des Deux Mondes*, *Revue de Paris*, etc., and in 1841 founded with George Sand the *Revue Indépendante*. He was for a time joint director with M. Robert and afterward sole director of the Théâtre des Italiens. He visited many countries with his wife on her tours, wrote interestingly of them and helped to spread knowledge of their literature in France. Translated Cervantes, Nikolai, Gogal, Pouchkine, Turgénieff, etc.

He had been impressed by my remarks and promised to bring to Flaubert's on the following Sunday a novel that was being translated under his eyes. Then he mentioned a book that he proposed to write, *Virgin Soil*, a picture in sombre colors of the new strata rumbling in the depths of Russia, the story of those poor " simplified," whom a pitiful misunderstanding is forcing into the arms of the people. The people do not understand them, mock at them and reject them. And while he was speaking, I reflected that Russia is in truth virgin soil, soil still soft, where the lightest step leaves its mark, a land where everything is new, to be explored and worked. With us on the contrary there is not a deserted road, not a path which the crowd has not trodden hard; and, to mention the field of novel-writing only, Balzac's shadow stands at the end of every avenue.

After that interview we met frequently. Among all the moments that we passed together, there is one Sunday afternoon in spring on Rue Murillo which has remained fixed in my memory, unique and luminous. We had been talking about Goethe, and Turgénieff had said to us: " You do not know him." The following Sunday he brought us *Prometheus*, and the *Satyr*, that Voltairean tale, rebellious and impious, expanded into a dramatic poem. Parc Monceau sent up to us its shouts of children playing, its bright sunshine, the cool air from its freshly watered shrubbery, and we four, Goncourt, Zola, Flaubert and I, deeply moved by that impressive improvisation, listened to the render-

ing of genius by genius.   That man, who trembled
when his pen was in his hand, had, when he was on
his feet, all the audacity of the poet; it was not the
lying translation which coagulates and petrifies;
Goethe lived and spoke to us.

Often too Turgénieff hunted me out in the
depths of the Marais, in the old Henri II. mansion
where I lived at that time.   He was entertained by
the strange spectacle of that court of honor, of that
royal abode with its gables and *moucharabies*, overflowing with the petty branches of Parisian commerce, with manufacturers of tops, seltzer water and
sugar-plums.   One day when he came in, a colossal
figure, leaning on Flaubert's arm, my little boy
whispered to me: "Why, they're giants!"   Giants
in very truth, kindly giants, great brains and great
hearts in proportion to their chests and shoulders.
There was a bond between those two genial natures,
the affinity of ingenuous kindliness.   It was George
Sand who brought them together.   Flaubert, hyper-
bolical, grumbling, Quixotic, with his voice like a
bugle-blast, the powerful irony of his observation,
the bearing of a Norman of the Conquest, was the
virile half of that marriage of minds; but who
could have divined in that other colossus, with his
eyebrows like bunches of tow and his enormous
frame, the woman, the keenly sensitive woman
whom Turgénieff has depicted in his books, that
nervous, languid, passionate Russian, slothful as an
Oriental, tragic as a latent force in revolt?   So true
is it that in the confusion of the great human manu-
factory, souls often mistake their proper envelopes,

and we find men's souls in feminine bodies, women's souls in Cyclopean frames.

It was about that time that the suggestion was made of a monthly meeting around a bountifully spread table; it was called the " Flaubert dinner," or the "dinner of authors who have been hissed." Flaubert was admitted by virtue of the failure of his *Candidat*, Zola with *Bouton de Rose*, Goncourt with *Henriette Maréchal*, I with my *Arlésienne*. Girardin tried to insinuate himself into our circle; he was not a literary man, so we rejected him. As for Turgénieff, he gave us his word that he had been hissed in Russia; and as it was a long distance away we did not go there to see.

There could be nothing more delightful than those dinner-parties of friends, where we talked without restraint, with minds alert and elbows on the table-cloth. Like men of experience, we were all gourmands. There were as many different varieties of gluttony as there were temperaments; as many tastes as provinces represented. Flaubert must have Normandy butter and Rouen ducks *à l'étouffade ;* Edmond de Goncourt, with his delicate, exotic appetite, ordered sweetmeats flavored with ginger; Zola, shell-fish; Turgénieff smacked his lips over his caviare.

Ah! we were not easily fed, and the Parisian restaurants must remember us. We often changed. At one time we dined at Adolphe and Pelé's, behind the Opéra, at another time on Place de l'Opéra-Comique; then at Voisin's, where the cellar satisfied all our demands and won the favor of our appetites.

We sat down at seven o'clock, and at two we had not finished. Flaubert and Zola dined in their shirt-sleeves, Turgénieff reclined on the couch; we turned the waiters out of the room — an entirely useless precaution, for Flaubert's roar could be heard from top to bottom of the house. And we talked literature. We always had one of our own books which had just appeared. Flaubert brought his *Tentation de Saint-Antoine* and *Trois Contes*, Goncourt his *Fille Élisa*, Turgénieff the *Living Relics* and *Virgin Soil*, I *Fromont* and *Jack*. We talked with perfect freedom, without flattery, without any agreement for mutual admiration.

I have before me a letter from Turgénieff, in a coarse, foreign, old-fashioned hand, a manuscript hand, which I transcribe at length, for it gives an excellent idea of the tone of sincerity that characterized our relations.

Monday, May 24, '77.

" My dear friend, —

" My reason for not having spoken to you about your book before this was that I wished to do so at length and not to content myself with a few trite phrases. I postpone all that to our next interview, which will take place soon, I trust, for Flaubert is coming back and our dinners will begin anew.

" I confine myself to saying one thing: the *Nabob* is the most remarkable and the most uneven book that you have written. If *Fromont and Risler* be represented by

a straight line, thus ——, the *Nabob* should be represented thus ∧∨∨∧, and the highest points of the zigzags
cannot be reached by any save a *talent of the first order.*

" I ask your pardon for explaining myself so geometri-
cally.

" I have had a very long and very violent attack of the
gout. I went out for the first time only yesterday, and I
have the legs and knees of a man of ninety. I very much
fear that I have become what the English call a *con-
firmed invalid.*

" A thousand regards to Madame Daudet; I press
your hand most cordially.

" Yours,

" IVAN TURGÉNIEFF."

When we had done with books and the interesting topics of the day, our chat assumed a broader
range, we recurred to subjects and ideas that were
ever present; we talked of love and of death.

The Russian on his divan held his peace.

" And you, Turgénieff? "

" Oh, as for death, I never think of it. With us,
no one has a clear conception of it, it remains in the
distance, shrouded in the Slavic mist."

That remark was very eloquent concerning the
nature of his race and his own genius. The Slavic
mist hovers over all his work, clouds it, makes it
quiver, and his conversation too was drowned in it
as it were. What he said to us always began painfully, hesitatingly; then suddenly the clouds,
traversed by a shaft of light, an incisive word,
would vanish. He described his Russia to us, not
the historical, familiar Russia of the Beresina, but

a Russia of summer sunshine, of fields of grain, of flowers hatched under the snow; Little Russia, alive with budding plants and the humming of bees. And so, as we must give some habitation to the exotic stories that are told us and frame them in a familiar landscape, Russian life appeared to me, as the result of his descriptions, like the existence of a châtelaine on an Algerian estate surrounded by native villages.

Turgénieff told us of the Russian peasant, of his ingrained taste for alcohol, of the torpid state of his conscience, of his ignorance of liberty. Or else it was some fresher page, a fragment of an idyll, the memory of a miller's daughter, whom he had met in the hunting-field, and with whom he had been in love for some time.

"What shall I give you?" he always asked her.

And the lovely girl would reply with a blush:

"Bring me some soap from the city so that I may perfume my hands, and then you can kiss them as you do to the ladies."

After life and death we talked of diseases, of the slavery of the body dragged along like a ball. What melancholy confessions we hear from men who have passed the fortieth mark! For my part, as rheumatism had not yet begun to devour me, I laughed at my friends, at that poor Turgénieff who suffered tortures with the gout and came limping to our dinners. Later, I lowered my tone.

Alas! the death of which we used always to talk came at last. It took Flaubert from us. He was the soul, the bond that united us. When he vanished, our lives changed, we met only at long intervals, as no one felt brave enough to resume the meetings interrupted by mourning.

After many months Turgénieff tried to bring us together once more. Flaubert's place was always reserved at our table, but we missed his loud voice and hearty laugh too much; they were not like the old dinners. I met the Russian novelist afterward at a reception at Madame Adam's. He had brought the Grand Duke Constantine, who, as he was passing through Paris, wished to see some of the celebrities of the day, a Madame Tussaud collection, alive and feasting. Turgénieff was depressed and ill. The cruel gout! It laid him flat for weeks, and he asked his friends to call upon him.

Two months ago I saw him for the last time. The house was still full of flowers, the same fresh young voices at the foot of the stairs, the same friend upstairs on his couch: but how changed and enfeebled! He was in the clutches of angina pectoris, and was still suffering with a ghastly wound, caused by the removal of a cyst. As he did not take chloroform, he described the operation to me with a perfectly clear memory. At first there was the sensation of a circular movement of the knife as when one peels an apple, then the excruciating pain of the cutting into the living flesh. And he added:

"I have analyzed my sensations for you to describe at one of your dinners, thinking that they would interest you."

As he could still walk a little, he went downstairs to escort me to the door. We went into the picture gallery on the ground floor and he showed me some of the works of his fellow-countrymen: a halt of Cossacks, billowy fields of grain, landscapes of hot Russia, the Russia he has described.

Old Viardot was there, slightly indisposed. In an adjoining room Garcia was singing, and Turgénieff, encompassed by the arts he loved, smiled as he bade me adieu.

A month later I learned that Viardot was dead and Turgénieff in the agony of death. I cannot believe in that agony. There must be a reprieve for noble and sovereign intellects so long as they have not said all that they have to say. The weather and the mild air of Bougival will give Turgénieff back to us, but there will be for him no more of those intimate meetings which he was so delighted to attend.

Ah! the "Flaubert dinners!" We began them again the other day: there were only three of us.[1]

While I am correcting the proofs of this article, which first appeared several years ago, a book of *Souvenirs* is handed me, wherein Turgénieff, from the grave,[2] excoriates me in the most approved style. As a writer, I am at the foot of the list; as a man, the lowest of men. And my friends are well aware of it, and they tell some fine stories about me! To what friends does Turgénieff

---

[1] Written in 1880, for the *Century Magazine*, New York.

[2] Turgénieff died near Paris, September 3, 1883.

refer? and how have they continued to be my friends since they know me so well? Indeed, who compelled the excellent Slav himself to wear that mask of friendliness? I can see him now in my house, at my table, gentle, affectionate, embracing my children. I have cordial, delightful letters from him. And this is what there was beneath that kindly smile. My God, how strange a thing life is, and how pretty that pretty Greek word: EIRONEIA ! [1]

[1] Dissimulation.

ULTIMA.

ULTIMA.

FOR Edmond de Goncourt's friends, and for them alone — for to others these pages, like everything which has no other merit than that it is inspired by affection, would seem childish — I describe the illustrious author's last visit to Champrosay, in other words the last moments of his life. That visit was so brief — from Saturday evening to an early hour on Thursday — that I have been able, supplementing my own memory by that of the members of my household, to clothe my narrative in the familiar, vivid form of a journal, which he preferred above any other because of its warm atmosphere of intimacy, its flexibility, and because it more nearly approaches actual verity, fits it more closely; the form to which he resorted to describe the death of his brother, an imperishable masterpiece of sympathy and clearness of vision. Not that I assume the power to write anything so thrilling, so profoundly touching as those leaves of the *Journal des Goncourt* of June, 1870, but my affection, as a friend and as one who witnessed his last moments, moves me to try to do for him what he did for his brother Jules.

Saturday evening, July 11.

EDMOND DE GONCOURT arrived at six o'clock this evening. I went to meet him at the Ris-Orangis station — ten minutes from Champrosay on the other bank of the Seine — in the two-horse landau which I have kept in the country during the summer, ever since my legs became indolent. The approaching fêtes of the 14th of July, the extraordinary number of cars and the multiplication of stations have delayed the train half an hour. At last the gate opens, people flow through in waves upon waves, but not my *Grand.* What has happened? I am beginning to worry, aware of the weariness, the intense weariness which "his cursed *Journal*" has caused him of late. If only he is not ill; that threatened attack of his liver trouble he mentioned in his last letter. But no. The coachman has turned on his seat with an air of delight: "There's Monsieur de Goncourt!" He is so cordial and open-handed — all my servants adore him.

My son Lucien, who has met him at the Lyon station in Paris, appears first, carrying a red leather bag which I know well, and the sight of which makes me smile affectionately. Outside of, aside from the actual flesh and blood, and fraught perhaps with even deeper meaning, we all have what I will call our little effigies, the impression of ourselves, of our ways, of our gestures, which we leave upon all the objects which we constantly use. If some one whom we love dearly disappears, leaves us forever, a garden hat hanging on a nail, a broken eye-glass in a drawer, often brings him before us more vividly than a portrait, affects us far more deeply. In my eyes that little red bag, which I have seen so many times on the Champrosay road, is Goncourt travelling, Goncourt astray in railway stations, his horror of the crowds and the jostling, the feverish unrest of his hands, the long, supple hands of a born artist. On the instant I see his poor dear hands, empty and quivering with impatience, waving in the distance.

"Pray what has happened to you, my Goncourt?"

He shouts at me from afar:

"They have lost my trunk, little one — there are times when one has no luck."

And while he continues his altercation with the railway people, I contemplate admiringly the dauntless virility, the slender grace of his seventy-four years, which seem no more than fifty. Sturdy and erect, in his gray suit and little hat of brown straw, he has never seemed to me younger than to-day.

Luckily the trunk is not lost, it is simply delayed until the evening train, when the coachman will come and fetch it. Goncourt, reassured, enters the carriage; we embrace and the landau starts. At closer quarters our friend does not look so well. His eye seems restless and preoccupied, his skin is burning. He speaks nervously.

"Ah! I tell you I have had trouble enough,

and of a superior quality. Godfrey told you, did n't he? — a line omitted in my text, and the botheration it caused — all the excellent people whom I wounded unintentionally. And threats of law-suits, volumes to be withdrawn from circulation; and that Fasquelle with his tranquil air. For my part, I passed two nights without sleep, tossing and turning, till my shirt was twisted like a well-rope. I thought I was surely going to have an attack. But, no, I think I shall avoid it."

Already, the cool air of the river as we drive across, the fresh breeze from the avenue of poplars, as from a huge fan, the prevailing peacefulness of the atmosphere relax his nerves and soften him.

"And how is everybody here, little one? Léon is still at the sea-shore, so Lucien tells me; he also told me of your old Tim's death; you must have felt very badly."

"Very, Goncourt; we have been closely attached to each other for thirty-five years. Now I have no friend left in the south but Mistral; in the north I have only you."

The carriage has stopped, we are at home.

Mademoiselle Edmée, aged ten, tall and slender in her English frock, with her red-gold hair falling in bunches over her shoulders, leaps on her godfather's neck.

"*Bonjour*, godfather. How do you do? — you know, the gardener's cat has a kitten — oh! such a pretty one, with blue eyes. And the little donkeys have had their hair cut; and we have a new cow that gives good milk, but she 's very naughty."

Although deeply interested in this local chronicle, Goncourt is obliged to interrupt it in order to salute the mistress of the house and her mother, Madame A., who come to greet him. Before going up to his room he gazes longingly through my study at the background of verdure sloping to the bank of the Seine.

" I say, Madame Daudet " — *Mon Dieu!* it seems to me that I hear him now — " suppose we take a turn in the garden? Come, master, take my arm."

And we wander, all three, among the paths, where the daylight still lingers, halting by flower-beds whose fragrance evaporates in the warmth of the declining day. Madame Daudet shows him her roses, he tells us about his own, his *espaliero*, the trellised porches of his house at Auteuil, where he has workmen even now, repairing the roof. Luckily Pélagie is at hand, keeping watch and ward, sternly forbidden to leave the premises on any pretext. And suddenly, as if his anxiety concerning his unroofed house has reminded him of other causes of anxiety, he returns to the annoying mischance he told me about a moment ago. I feel that he feels some embarrassment about telling us of the fresh irritation his journal is causing him. Doubtless he foresees one of the friendly discussions which we have had heretofore on the same subject, and which can all be summarized thus:

I. — You are not careful enough, my Goncourt; you take for good money whatever any one chooses to hand you.

GONCOURT. — Oh! if I took your advice I should never believe anything.

And then, after an exchange of feints, he would deal me this home thrust, to close the discussion:

"After all, little one, whose fault is it? Who but you persuaded me to publish my journal?"

"Very good, but according to my idea you should not have gone beyond the year '71, Jules' death, the siege and the Commune. That year makes a sort of fissure in contemporary history, or a high cemetery wall riddled with bullets, at which everything stops. The other side of the wall is a hundred leagues away from us; on this side everything is within reach of our hand, there is no recoil, no perspective. I had a feeling that as to anything of later date you would be accused of writing nothing but gossip and small talk."

"Might not the same thing be said of Saint-Simon?"

This discussion, almost always the same, shall not be repeated to-day. Our friend seems too depressed, disturbed above all by the enmities, the indignation which his journal has kindled against him; they have gone so far as to threaten him with an action for defamation of character.

"And yet I publish nothing but the truth or what I believe to be the truth; I tell the truth about those whom I love most dearly, myself as well as others."

And the sincere, the ingenuous tone, the straightforward glance, the glance of an honest man, which accompany these words, would suffice to absolve him in the eyes of his most determined enemies.

But the dinner-gong sounded a long while ago.

"What luck to be all by ourselves!" says Goncourt as we take our seats.

And when he learns that we had thought of inviting two or three literary friends to make the house more lively, he protests, declares his preference for a family party; to have company on Thursday will be quite enough.

Nevertheless no one is more fond than he of literary chat, those games of intellectual tennis in which the players are enlivened by the smiles of a gallery, and words and ideas fly back and forth as if from rackets. This latest experience with his journal must have changed him, depressed him strangely, to give him this inclination for solitude and a small dinner-table. I should be greatly surprised if such savagery is of long duration with this thrice-refined devotee of art, this model of super-exquisite civilization. The dinner speedily enlivens him and he eats heartily, something that he has not done for a long while. Every day, he tells us, he is thirsty only, his tongue is dry, there is a bitter taste in his mouth, and he has been living at a restaurant on a slice of melon and a plate of soup, with a glass of good champagne to wash it down.

"Oh! Monsieur de Goncourt," the grandmother

interrupts him, moved to indignation. "For a man subject to liver complaint!"

"That makes no difference, Madame. These doctors are knaves. As soon as you 're ill, they ask you confidentially what you like best and then proceed to deprive you of it, like cowards. That 's what they call dieting."

The dispute waxes warm, is carried to other subjects. We recognize once more the Goncourt of the good old days, him whom none but his intimate friends ever knew, artless and loving, entirely free from moodiness and distrust, and yet endowed with a disconcerting keenness of vision, an armed candor which I have never observed in any other mortal. Divers facts concerning Auteuil and his villa, Fasquelle the publisher's banquet, an afternoon in the country, at his dear Mirabeau's, in company with the poet Robert de Montesquiou, his meeting with the very learned author of *Aphrodite*, at Jean Lorrain's table — on such varied themes his mind played until the end of the meal, which seemed to us very short. It was quite dark when we went out on the terrace and stood there a few moments. The air was very heavy. Silent lightning flashes laid bare the lowest depths of the sky. On the shores of the ponds the frogs emitted their crystal notes. We had been talking of a literary friend whose disposition, morals and talent had undergone a curious modification, quite without warning, and from that subject we passed to the transformations which life imposes upon certain beings through contact with different types and through the underhand strokes of destiny, and Goncourt exclaimed, putting his head out of the sheltered bay in which he had shiveringly taken refuge, despite the sultriness of the air:

"Aha! my boy, in that case what becomes of your theory that we *are all put in type very early in life*, and that, after thirty, the impressions that life leaves with us are simply reprints?"

MADAME DAUDET. — That theory of his is sickening, abominable; you should see how I slashed at it in his little note-book!

GONCOURT. — And you were quite justified, Madame, because it is not true. I believe, on the other hand, that man changes constantly to the last day of his life, that we change our skins an infinite number of times, like snakes.

I. — You are probably right, Goncourt, and it only proves what dangerous things to handle formulæ are. Our best ideas perish because of their formulæ, which wither before the ideas themselves. Opportunism, naturalism, in themselves are not evil things; but the label is no longer of any value. Don't you remember our telling Zola that one evening?

GONCOURT. — At a dinner with Flaubert, on Place de l'Opéra-Comique, was n't it? That was a devilish long while ago!

The flashes became more frequent, great drops of rain pattered on the veranda. We returned to the salon for tea, served by Mademoiselle Edmée; a spacious country-house salon, hung with Genoese linen, where Goncourt found his easy-chair in the same place as in other years, between the fireplace and the divan. At times, when an idea makes an impression upon him, he rises, walks back and forth two or three times, says what is in his mind or meditates on it, then resumes his seat, always in the same corner. Although very talkative, he has no chance to work himself up, for we have no dispute. A volume of verses recently published displays its flower-bedecked cover on the table. Goncourt makes a wry face as he spies it. We know that he has almost as intense a horror of poetry as of music. My wife, to punish him, compels him to listen to two or three pieces taken at random; and, when we unanimously expressed our admiration —

"It would be much finer in prose," says our friend, in whose eyes the most beautiful poetry in the world is not worth a page of the *Mémoires d'Outre-Tombe*, of Victor Hugo's *Choses Vues*, or ten lines of Joubert, Labruyère, Veuillot, or Vallès.

This name of Vallès, being casually mentioned in conversation, suggests the name of a collaborator on *La Rue*, a poor devil who disappeared a long while ago and from whom I received this very morning a heart-rending letter that would have brought tears to Inspector Javert's eyes.

"My brother and I knew him at Vichy, in the last days of the Empire," muses Goncourt aloud. "It was Vallès who introduced him to us. Later I undertook to write a preface for a book Char-

pentier was to publish for him, when we learned
of the charming profession he was practising in
addition to that of man of letters."

After a pause, he adds:

"All the same he had a fine touch, the brute!
If you do anything for him, count me in."

When old friends like us begin to fan the flame
of reminiscence, they never know when to stop.
The clock on the little parish church near by
strikes ten. Mademoiselle Edmée has left the
salon long ago; now it is the grandmother's turn,
then Lucien's, who takes the first train every
morning because of his studio. Goncourt, as he
says good-night to the tall youth whom he has
known from his birth, asks him what they are
doing at the studio, if they have a model at the
moment.

"Yes, monsieur, a female model till the end of
the week."

We glance at each other with a smile. Why,
it was only yesterday that Goncourt, to amuse a
little fellow of five years, mad over bright colors
and daubing, drew up a commission on parchment,
as in the days of Louis XV., the Well-Beloved,
sealed with huge red seals, and countersigned
Blanche Denis, daughter of Pélagie Denis, the
excellent maid-servant at Auteuil — a commission constituting Lucien Daudet his little pastel
artist! And now, the female model! What a
magic lantern, this life! There are only three of
us left in the salon. Another hour of intimate
conversation, of reviving old memories. Men-

tioned Georges Brandès' visit to Champrosay, his keen comments upon Ibsen, Tolstoï, Turgénieff.

I. — You know that Brandès insists that the unkind allusions to you and me attributed to Turgénieff are pure invention.

GONCOURT. — He did not care for us, my boy. I have always felt certain of it, despite his Slavic cajolery.

MADAME DAUDET. — I had my suspicions too.

GONCOURT. — Turgénieff's antipathy was due to the fact that he was never able to understand your irony, nor my brother's. You disconcerted him. All foreigners are the same. French irony frightens them, they think people are making fun of them.

I. — Like working men and women and children. But what can be the matter with this Goncourt to-night, that he keeps us sitting up so late? Are we never going to bed, pray?

The lighted candles await us at the foot of the stairs. There is a shaking and kissing of hands, and we go up to our respective bedrooms. Goncourt's is above ours and of exactly the same size and shape, with a window looking on the orchard and the little church, another on the park, and two, in a large dressing-room, on the courtyard. As he walks about I can hear his footstep, the only thing which shows his age, because it does not realize that we are listening to it. I have told him that we can hear nothing. It is a heavy, tired step, as of one who has completed a hard day's work.

Sunday, July 12.

AT my study table an hour when Goncourt comes down from his room and takes me out for a turn in the garden. He has slept well enough for the first night in a strange bed, but complains of the heat, of a constant thirst which he attributes to the stormy weather, to this infernal month of July which brings on his liver complaint. The odor of the two tall silver lindens by the poultry-yard makes his head ache. We take another path, talking of the book on which I am at work and in which he seems interested.

"Ah! my boy, you are fortunate to be able to invent still."

"What keeps you from doing the same, Goncourt?"

"Age," he says in a grave tone; "a man's imagination ceases to work when he 's as old as I am."

I remind him of Royer-Collard's remark: "M. de Talleyrand no longer invents, he describes his own sensations." But he seems not to hear me and looks about with a preoccupied air.

"What are you looking for, Goncourt?"

"The bench; you know, the bench where we used to sit to listen to your friend Mistral's verses. I noticed that there was always a breath of air there on the most suffocating days."

I lead him to the bench, and we do find there what Mistral would call a *breezelet*, which ascends from the river and stirs the leaves of a grove of young plane-trees on the slope in front of us.

On the two or three occasions when Mistral has visited us at Champrosay, we have always chosen this spot to listen to him, and I recognize the trunk, smooth and straight as a mast, of the tree against which he leaned his tall form as he repeated the ballad of Queen Jeanne's galley-slaves:

> Lau lire lau laire
> Et vogue la galère !

I fancy that Goncourt does not detect, as I do, an echo of the exquisite Provençal refrain in the cool breeze, but he enjoys it none the less and drinks it in with a delight that seems strange enough in a shivering creature who wraps himself up and protects himself in July as in mid-winter. After a moment, he sighs:

"Yes, M. de Talleyrand describes his own feelings, and I would have liked to follow his example and continue to describe mine in my journal; but really people are throwing too much mud at my head. Why, think of the anonymous letters I receive, to say nothing of the others! Even to—yes, like your own experience, my boy, at the time of the *Evangéliste.* I open *billets-doux* all smeared with — What have I done to draw down all this hatred on myself? Tried to illuminate universal falsehood with a ray of truth! And for that I am considered a defamer of character, I am accused of having broken the social pact and am threatened with prosecution. No, I have had enough of my journal, most decidedly, and I am done."

Madame Daudet, coming to sit with us, says to Goncourt, as she turns into the path:

"For my part, I am glad to hear you say so. I don't care for your journal any more; it made you too many enemies."

Criticism of the *Journal des Goncourt* comes with bad grace from me; my own novels, all written after nature, have aroused so much wrath! Nevertheless, I tell our friend frankly that, for several years past, I have felt less free with him. I have seemed to be unable to trust him so fully, to give free expression to my feelings as before. The thought that my every word might appear in the journal embarrassed me, made me ill at ease; I seemed to be talking to the public. He must have thought I was failing; that was the reason.

Goncourt lays his hand gently on mine.

"Be yourself again, little one; the *Journal des Goncourt* is closed."

We sit for a long while on our bench, in the boundless silence of a Sunday in the country. A bell rings in the distance; a bicycler's horn, the cry of a bird pierce the air. I go upstairs to work; he strolls along the lower path, which he calls the curé's path, or makes a few shots at billiards all by himself. He used to love to play with me; but for two years I have been unable to play.

We meet again at breakfast. Goncourt has lost his fine appetite of last evening; he is too thirsty. A burning sensation in two places, the palm of his hands and his stomach, warns him that the dreaded attack is not far away. Doctor Barié prescribes a glass of Vichy Hauterive in the morning, under such circumstances. That suggests a drive for the afternoon; we will all go to Corbeil for the Vichy and return by Tigéry, where the crops are in splendid condition just now. There is one field in particular, a field of potatoes in bloom; a waving sea of light purple flowers, a league in extent — a marvel of beauty. During the latter part of the breakfast, and in the salon while we drink our coffee, we talk of nothing but the festival originated by Montesquiou in honor of Marceline Desbordes-Valmore, to take place to-morrow at Douai. Lucien is anxious to take his mother, who is dismayed at the thought of the fatigue of the journey, the banquet, the platform, the public exhibition. But Marceline is an old friend of the family; my wife remembers going with her mother to see her, as a mere child. Although he has only a vague sort of admiration for the author of *Fleurs et Pleurs*, and often confuses Desbordes-Valmore with Mélanie Waldor, Goncourt intercedes in Lucien's behalf, and the mother decides to start to-morrow morning at six o'clock and return by a night train. But the trip to Corbeil must be made without her, and when Edmond comes down after his siesta he finds only his god-daughter and myself waiting in the landau at the door.

We drive for half an hour along the cliff road between the forest of Sénart and the river, the road which runs through most of my books. A discussion of very long standing between us is taken up at a corner of the forest and accompanies us almost as far as Corbeil. Goncourt firmly believes in posterity; he has worked for posterity all his life; for my part, I never think about it, never imagine what it is like, have no clear idea what it is.

GONCOURT. — What do you write for, anyway? I know you well enough to know that money is not your motive.

I. — Nor renown. To be sure, success has always pleased me, although always dearly bought. But at no time of my life have I been tempted by the laurel wreath. To be a master, the leader of a school, an academician, president of anything under heaven, are things entirely without meaning in my eyes. I write simply for the pleasure of writing, because I feel that I must express my thoughts, because I am a man of keen sensibilities and a chatterbox.

GONCOURT. — Jules was a little like that.

I. — Do you remember one evening at Charpentier's, in the little salon — a dispute on this subject with Flaubert and Zola? I was alone in my opinion against you three, although at heart old Flaubert —

GONCOURT. — Oh! it's a very ancient subject of dispute among artists. There's a long correspondence thereon between Falconnet the sculptor and Diderot.

While we talk, Mademoiselle Edmée sits oppo-

site us, in a white butterfly hat, white dress and
with a little white parasol, contending with the
sun which has designs on her hawthorn-like com-
plexion. At every bend in the road the sun
changes its position, and however she seats herself the child always has a sunbeam in her eye
or on the end of her little nose. Goncourt, with
an umbrella twice as large, which he shifts impatiently from one shoulder to the other every
moment, succeeds no better than his god-daughter
in sheltering himself; he knows no more about
the points of the compass than the child, and I
reflect upon the large admixture of ingenuousness,
of innocence in the character of this observer of
men and things, this subtle mortal whom so many
people accuse of cynicism and inhumanity. Ah!
how little there is of the Goncourt of the popular
imagination in the excellent man whom I watch
as he feels in his pockets for sous to give the
poor at Corbeil, as he goes into the pastry-cook's
and into the bazaar on Rue Saint-Spire to buy
a purse, a basket which Mademoiselle Edmée
desires to present to her governess. The landau
jolts noisily over the stones in the narrow streets
which seem wider and wear a melancholy aspect
on Sundays; the noise attracts people to windows
and door-steps. We stop in front of the drug-
gist's to buy the Vichy; and at a café on the
square for Goncourt, who is dying of thirst. And
while we are being served in the landau, he
glances at the sleeping houses, the silent square,
and mutters in dismay:

"Fancy being obliged to live here! It would be the death of me!"

I. — Of you, perhaps, because you 're a Parisian; but I was born in the provinces. With a home of my own, with love around my table, I should do very well.

GONCOURT. — How could you muster courage to write?

I. — Such work as yours would be impossible certainly; too many of the tools would be lacking. But Kant or Descartes might very well have written their books at Corbeil.

Recrossed the bridge, the Seine on fire; turned to the right through the fields of Tigéry, which slope down in gentle undulations to the forest, in the bright red light of the setting sun. The scene is even more bewitchingly beautiful than I had promised; but I feel that Goncourt admires without conviction, solely to be agreeable to me. This refined product of civilization prefers gardens to the country; and he admits as much to me as we go down from Étiolles, through that exquisite landscape in which his dear Madame de Pompadour lived, those sloping vineyards, of a pale green hue, and the old church-tower rising in the midst.

We return at twilight, just in time to hear the second dinner bell. Much animation around the table. Lucien is triumphant, thinking of the journey and the celebration of the next day. His mother, more and more alarmed at the prospect, tries to take back her word; but she has promised, sworn; she must celebrate.

"Ah! you like poetry, Madame Daudet," exclaims Goncourt with a hearty laugh; "very good! you 'll hear plenty of it."

She does not repine, but the idea of leaving her guest a whole day distresses her.

"Don't be afraid, I will take care of him and so will Edmée," says the grandmother.

For my part, I propose to give him my whole day. Ah! what hard things we will say to each other about the poor women! Goncourt looks forward to it as a holiday. Meanwhile, I notice that he does not eat; barely a little soup and a few strawberries. We shall not avoid the attack. Indeed, he has been like this every summer since he first had trouble with his liver. We have our usual evening session in the salon, cut a little short because of Madame Daudet's early start. Goncourt asks me for a book to take with him to his room. I suggest *Moscou en Flammes*, a passable Russian novel, full of typical details, which, with *War and Peace*, Stendhal's *Letters* and Castellane's *Journal*, completes the picture of that extraordinary episode of the imperial epic of which I am dreaming as the subject of a play for the Châtelet.

"How can one take any interest in countries so far away!" says the mistress of the house, with the little revolutionary air which she dissembles beneath a tranquil exterior. "It seems to me that those things must have happened two thousand years ago."

"Madame Daudet confuses duration and distance. Oh! these poets!" says Goncourt.

"She is right so far as to-morrow's celebration is concerned," adds her husband. "It 's a long way off and it will last a long while."

Upon that cruel jibe we rose and left the salon.

Monday, July 13.

THIS morning when I come downstairs, I am informed that Goncourt has slept poorly; he has taken his glass of Hauterive and requests that I do not go to his room. He will not come down until breakfast.

As he is not seriously ill, I think only of myself and my little disappointment. I had looked forward to a genuine debauch of strolling about on my *Grand's* arm and chattering. It is a fine day. A warm, pink mist rises from the terraces and lawns. It would be very pleasant in the little wood. Luckily the newspapers arrive, those devourers, those slaughterers of time; instead of pushing them aside, as I do on my working-days, I plunge into them bodily; my eyes and my brain are filled with their gray dust. Suddenly the door opens, Goncourt's tall form appears, reaching the lintel. He cannot sleep, so preferred to dress and come downstairs. I watch him as he reads the newspapers, sitting on the divan on the other side of my table; his features are drawn and his eyes yellow. Usually when he has read a sheet, *swept it with his eye,* as he says, he throws it on the floor or on the couch by his side, all unfolded. To-day I am impressed by the care with which he folds each paper and lays it on the table.　I mention the subject.

"I saw that it annoyed you, my boy," he says, with a kindly smile which covers me with confusion.

Ah! pitiful creatures that we are, how cunning is stupidity, how it worms itself into the closest, most affectionate relations!　It is true that all that paper scattered on the floor, around my table, grated on my nerves; but to think that I could not conceal my impatience from him!

"Shall we take a walk?　There's nothing in the papers this morning."

He has risen, put his arm through mine, and instantly, from his gait, from the tone of his voice, I understand that *there is something in the papers.*　Doubtless a line, a sentence on the subject of the Academy.

GONCOURT. — Do you know when the election to fill Dumas's chair is to be?

"October, I have been told, or November. Perhaps even later."

After a few steps he resumes with an effort:

"Are — are you to be a candidate, my boy?"

"If I were to be a candidate, Goncourt, you would be the first to know it."

"What pleasure you give me!" he says, pressing my arm.

We arrive at his bench, the one he prefers this year, and, having seated himself, he continues:

"What can you expect?　After a while these newspaper scandal-mongers make an impression

on one. You cannot help it. They insist upon
it that you have written your letter to the Academy, with a request that it be kept secret until
the election."

"And you were not angry with me?"

Goncourt, seeking a breath of air in which to
hold his burning hands, turns affectionately to me.

"Remember what I said to you ten or twelve
years ago, when there was some talk of your being
chosen. You were already a member of my
Academy, even then; but I urged you, and with
perfect sincerity, to follow your own inclinations.
I still adhere to that. When I was assured that
you would come forward as a candidate for Dumas's
chair, I was deeply hurt, but I remained your
friend, indeed I realized more than ever how dear
you were to me."

"And yet you must have known that, when
you had made me the executor of your will and
entrusted to me the foundation of your Academy,
I would not abandon my post without advising
you?"

The fact is that one day, some four or five years
ago, when Goncourt was not feeling well, he sent
for me to come to Auteuil and inflicted upon me
the cruel emotion of reading to him, aloud, a tes-
tament in which I was named as executor, jointly
with Henri Céard. Subsequently the bungling
of a reporter having banished Céard from the
house at Auteuil, my son Léon had been substi-
tuted for him as executor of our friend's last
wishes. In that document, whose contents were

known to none but the notary and myself, I first saw the statutes and regulations of the Académie des Goncourts. Is it because of the criticisms I made concerning this Academy, the title of which seemed to me a very grave mistake, that he does not care to say much to me about it? I myself am not particularly anxious to discuss it, feeling certain that I shall never be called upon to take any steps with regard to it, as I shall die long before Goncourt. That is evidently his conviction too, as he has associated with me in the undertaking, in the first place Henri Céard, then my son Léon, and quite lately — so I am told — Léon Hennique in my son's place. Why this constant changing? I have no idea. He has always manifested the liveliest affection for Léon, and the last volume of his journal testifies to his appreciation of the boy's talent. He told me two years ago that Léon was one of the Ten. What is the explanation of this change? I shall know one day or another. This is almost exactly what he said to me to-day concerning his Academy. When I asked him if he still clung to the same title, he answered earnestly:

"Yes, my boy; no doubt the word is too solemn for us and is hardly suitable for independent writers, some of whom indeed are soldiers of the vanguard, carrying their weapons as they choose and their tunics over the shoulder. I have thought about changing our title, as you wished me to do, in the direction of simplicity, of good fellowship; I have thought of the *Table des Gon-*

court, the *Prix des Goncourt;* but a scruple has always held me back. My brother and I evolved this idea together; we both worked at the foundation of the Académie des Goncourt; and I do not consider that I alone have the right to change the decisions at which we two arrived. Ah! if Jules were still living, we should have to modify many articles. The course of the other Academy has changed of late years; it has tended more toward youth, toward LITERATURE, as Flaubert used to say; the proof of what I say is that Bourget, Loti and many others were on the list of our foundation before they joined the other, some of them without their own knowledge. For all that, the greater part of the prizes distributed at the Palais Mazarin have no justification. Their Academy either does n't know how to discover talent or does n't take the trouble; often, indeed, it cannot; and our prize of five thousand francs will render noteworthy service. There! Now, let us walk a little."

We walk down the curé's path, and return through the little wood, and all the time he talks about his brother: —

"It 's a strange thing: Jules died in 1870, and for fifteen years, down to 1885, I, who am a great dreamer, never had a dream in which he did not figure. Suddenly he disappeared from my dreams. During the day I thought of him constantly, his memory haunted me as persistently as before, but in my dreams, in my night life, he no longer existed. And that lasted ten years. One night last year my brother returned. I dreamed some silly thing or other, but Jules was in it, and since then he has never failed to appear. Last night again he was with me in my dream."

He said no more. Our steps grated on the gravel, hot with the noon-day sun. In front of the house, in the tall sycamore which rises above the roof on his side of the house and mine, a finch or linnet sang in a whisper, as if half asleep.

"What is that bird?" he asked. "I hear him against my window in the morning. He wakes me, puffing out his little throat, in which the air seems to be mingled with fresh water."

"In the morning about four o'clock. I hear him, too, in my curtains."

And I tell him the story of the blacksmith at the Bellechasse barracks, whom my neighbor Doctor Charcot and I used to hear every morning, each in his study, and whose forge hammer, like a medium of transmission between our brains, beat time for our twofold task, and made us think of each other. "'Which of us will be the last to hear the smith's hammer?' Charcot often said to me, with his stern eye and sweet smile."

"He believed that it would be he," replies Goncourt, to whom I must have told this little anecdote many times; but he makes no sign.

When two persons are and have long been in the habit of seeing each other often, it is hard to avoid such repetitions. And he, dear old fellow, always begins his stories with: "You will accuse me of repeating myself."

.At breakfast that morning there was no repetition of old stories. A small party, but very lively. We talked of the travellers who left Champrosay at daybreak. Where are they now? Taking refreshment in some sub-prefecture to the strains of the local band. Madame Desbordes-Valmore's name led us to Verlaine's, and to the influence which the gentle Marceline's genius exerted upon that refined imp of Satan. Madame A., who has known them both but not at the same time, evokes for us poor Lélian's figure, still a mere boy, when he recited in Madame la Générale de Ricard's salons his pretty Saturnian verses : —

" *Et nous n'aurons jamais de Béatrice.*"

She who was destined to be his posthumous Béatrice died long ago.

I, *abruptly*. — Goncourt, what 's the matter with you? You are not eating.

GONCOURT. — I am not hungry, my boy. If I am very good may I not have a little milk from the cow my god-daughter says is so naughty? Not boiled, but with the chill just taken off?

A large bowl is placed before him, but he finds it too hot, and eventually leaves it and the table, wondering what would taste good. After his nap he comes down, much rested, with less yellow in his eyes. I suggest that we order the horses for a long drive in the forest or in the open country. We can go by the rose-fields of Mandres to bid Coppée *bonjour*, or to taste the delicious Mennecy biscuit beyond the plains of Lisses and Cour

couronne. But neither suggestion tempts him.
It would keep him too long in the carriage; he
can no longer endure drives four or five hours
long as on the day when Madame Daudet, a copy
of the *Mémoires d'Outre-Tombe* under her arm,
drove us through the streets of Savigny, looking
for Henri IV.'s road and the house of Madame
de Beaumont, Chateaubriand's friend.

"Suppose we just go and sit by the river?
What do you say to that, master?"

At Champrosay he frequently calls me "master" (*patron*), everywhere else "Daudet" or "little
one" (*mon petit*), sometimes "Alphonse," but
only when he speaks of me.

"The river it is."

But a forgotten gate-key prevents our going to
the Seine, and we remain in the curé's path,
which the setting sun, intersected by dense lindens, spatters with patches of light.

I. — Then it is true that you don't propose to
work any more, Goncourt? Do you think that
will be possible?

GONCOURT. — I intend to finish my history of
the Camargo, and then to make a very minute
catalogue of the collections not included in the
Maison d'un Artiste. If Antoine produces *La
Faustin* for me, I shall revise a few scenes. And
then — and then, that's all. There is nothing
but my journal that I should have taken any
pleasure in doing. That noting down the events of
life, so varied yet so simple, interests me more than
novel-writing. It's not so with you; I know it.

I. — I am too much of a Latin, I like things
with more construction. For instance, take the
majority of Dostoiewski's books, even the *Kara-
masoff Brothers* and the *House of the Dead.* I
was hardly able to finish them; they are not
arranged enough. It's not my fault, my dear
fellow. When I was a boy, I played morris
under the gate of Augustus, and marbles in the
Arenas or on the steps of the Temple of Diana.

At this point a load of hay passes along the
communal road between the second park and the
path where we are walking. An old peasant,
bare-headed — a round head covered with white
hair — who is driving the wagon, salutes me
through the fence, and I shout to him : —

" *Bonjour,* Père Jean ! "

When Eugène Delacroix lived at Champrosay,
this man was in his service. You should hear
him say, proudly: "I used to fix *Monsieur
Lacroué's* palette." And Goncourt begins to dis-
course upon Eugène Delacroix's palette, with
such learning and energy. To what a unique and
rare conference upon romantic art I have the
privilege of listening! how I bless Père Jean,
to whose chance passing I owe this windfall!
Remain in the park talking delightfully of coloring and light and shade until the dinner-hour.
Return through the little wood and the kitchen-
garden, where the flowers are panting in the
scorching, perfume-laden twilight.

Dinner decidedly depressing. Mademoiselle
Edmée is not accustomed to passing a whole day

apart from her mother. For my own part, it seems to me that three empty places at the table are a good many. We remain a moment on the veranda. The sky is black; a last trace of light lingers on the gravelled paths. From the direction of Versailles, through what is called the Gap of Savigny, come tempestuous puffs, muffled rumblings. I am in a most melancholy mood.

"Well, little one," says Goncourt, taking his place by the fireplace, "I have often felt just as you feel now, when walking in my garden at Auteuil. But you are not alone here and it's only for a single evening, while I have only my collections for company, from one end of the year to the other. They are cold, I tell you, and they don't speak to one every day."

The sincere and heart-broken tone in which he confides to me his unhappiness as a bachelor gives me much pain. I am angry with myself for giving way to this attack of depression, and I pass the evening leading him to talk about his brother, about Jeand'heurs' periwinkles, the evenings at Saint-Gratien in the old days, with Théophile Gautier and the Girauds, and also about our insanely merry parties in Provence, at the Parrocels'. At ten o'clock, when we leave the salon, we are no longer melancholy; I have warmed myself by rubbing him.

Before going upstairs, Goncourt, candle in hand, comes and leans on my table, at which I have settled myself to work and await the return of our travellers by the night train.

"I hate to leave you alone," he says, with his kindly, big brother's smile. "I would have liked to sit up with you; but I feel so tired!"

He goes away, dragging his feet, and I hear him ascending the stairs slowly.

Tuesday, July 14.

"I SAY, little one — "

It is he calling me, in a whisper, as I leave my bedroom, and leaning over the rail at the top of that terrible second flight, which I can only master now with great difficulty.

"I have slept poorly, little one. I am going to pass my day in bed, trying a milk cure. Then a bath on top of it, to-morrow morning, and I shall be quite on my feet again, I am sure."

I am not so sure of it as he is. Milk would be good for him if taken persistently and for a long time; but what troubles my wife and myself above all else is this bath that he asks us to give him to-morrow morning. Goncourt has no bath-room in his own house at Auteuil; or, if he has, it is overrun, like the whole house, by curios and glass-cases. They place a tub in the kitchen and empty it out of the window, so that it disarranges and tires the whole household. And of what would not this Goncourt of the haughty bearing, who is reputed to be an egotist, and who goes down to the door in mid-winter, hardly dressed, to get his newspaper, rather than wake anybody — of what, I say, would he not deprive himself, in face of the thought that his servants might be put to some extra trouble?

Every summer, when he comes to Champrosay, the bath-room is his great delight. He goes into raptures over everything, the hot water, the shower-bath. Unluckily he had a chill there one day, two or three years ago; an attack of fever followed, and ever since we have been very much afraid. But what are we to do? Last year we offended him by postponing the wretched bath. But, who knows? Perhaps he will change his mind between now and to-morrow, perhaps he will feel better. My wife and Lucien, who have been up to see him, found him in good spirits; he made them tell him about the celebration at Douai, the fête of the *Gayants*, the polished addresses of Montesquiou and Anatole France. Several times during the day he sent messages to me.

At dinner we have a guest, a Parisian who has fled from the national holiday. Pass the evening on the terrace. Lowering weather, with a high wind. On the horizon in every direction distant music and fireworks. Goncourt, lying in his bed upstairs, must hear them, brought to his ears by this storm-boding wind, which he abhors.

Wednesday, July 15.

EBNER, my secretary, whose time is so fully occupied on the *Officiel* that he can give me only one day in each week, has come to work with me. We put our shoulders to the wheel in good season. The weather is as it threatened to be: low-hanging, stormy clouds, leaves whirling about as in autumn. Bad weather for Goncourt's bath. This thought suddenly passes through my mind. The servant, when I question him, assures me that everything has been prepared with the greatest care, under Madame's superintendence; moderate temperature, his linen in the thoroughly warmed drying-box. Monsieur Goncourt came down to the bath-room about twenty minutes ago, after passing a very good night. He intends to remain in the water an hour. An hour is too much. I go to the bath-room door.

"Is that you, little one?"

He answers my knock from his bath-tub.

"How are you? I mean to come down and see you when I have had my bath."

"No, my Goncourt, don't come down. You would risk taking a chill in the halls. Do you hear how the wind blows? Go up and bury yourself in the bed-clothes for a while. I will come right up and bid you good-morning. I have Ebner's arm to-day, so I'm not afraid of the stairs."

"Faith, nothing would suit me better than to go back to bed for a few moments. I feel so weak. I have n't spunk enough even to look at my watch, which is here on a chair by my side. What time is it, Ebner? I will stay here another quarter of an hour. You think it's too much? Very good. Perhaps you are right. Send your man to me and I will go upstairs."

Half an hour later I knocked at his bedroom door.

"Come in!" it was his voice, but so changed, with such a far-away sound.

We found him stretched, thrown rather, across his bed, half-dressed, as if he had not had strength to go back to bed when he came up from his bath. The curtains were raised at both windows, admitting the daylight unsoftened, a sort of light that he detests. He complained of a pain in his right side, accompanied by a terrible shivering and cold feet. It was the expected attack of his liver trouble. Oh! he recognized it. And in order that I might not be alarmed, he exerted himself to smile, his teeth chattering all the while. Ebner assisted him to crawl under the bed-clothes. He asked for a glass of Hauterive, and two or three times he failed to find the word he wanted: he said "Fasquelle" for "bottle"; but he noticed it at once, and was the first to laugh at his blunders. We observed that "Fasquelle" resembled *fiasque*, *fiasquette*, the name of the bottle in a wicker case used in the south. Once in bed, under the heavy coverlet, with his curtains tightly drawn, he felt better; the shivering subsided, and his hands were not so hot.

"And the pain in your side, Goncourt?"

"Very bearable. If it increases, I will ask you to give me a prick."

Two years ago, during a very painful attack, one or two injections of morphine had relieved him greatly, but he had never had it injected since and had never done it himself.

"What hard luck, little one," he said, taking

my hand affectionately, "what hard luck always to bring sickness to your house, as if your own suffering were not enough! However, you must take me with all my drawbacks, for I have no one but you, you are my family, my real family."

"Dear friend!"

We talk a moment beside his bed; then he asks us to let him sleep. He did not believe that he could come down to breakfast, but would certainly dine with us.

About one o'clock or half-past one, as I was about returning to my work, Goncourt sent to ask me to come up, saying that he needed me. When he saw me, he began to laugh.

"The dentist's reception-room. When the time comes for me to have my tooth out, the pain stops. I thought I must have a little prick, but the mere sight of you — "

"I will wait, my dear fellow, I am in no hurry."

I sit down on the couch, facing his bed, in the light half-shadow in which his room is bathed as at the hour for the afternoon siesta, and we talk about the fête at Douai, of which Lucien has given him all the details, also about our dinner-party on the next day, Thursday. These Thursdays at Champrosay, the open house, the dinners at which there are sometimes twenty-five people around a leg of mutton and a chowder, the unexpected arrivals, and the terrified excitement of the servants, contrasted with the coolness and ingenious expedients of the mistress of the house, amuse him beyond measure. It is his delight to remain in the salon in the evening, when all the Parisians have gone, and to sip a petit-verre of neat brandy as he recalls words, attitudes, a curl of the lip — so many notes for his journal.

"What a pity that your journal is closed, my Goncourt. There will be crowds here to-morrow, and you would have had copy galore."

"At all events, master, I promise to be here, and to do you credit. I feel better now; I shall not even need a prick."

Those were the last words he ever said to me.

An hour later Madame Daudet knocked at his door. Alarmed by his silence, she entered the room. He seemed to be dozing, but his hands and fingers were moving restlessly as was customary with him in animated conversation, a discussion concerning art.

She speaks to him : —

"How are you, Monsieur de Goncourt?"

"Better, better."

His words come jerkily, his glance is far away. My wife, in dismay, goes to fetch her mother and returns with her to our friend, whose eyes are now closed, his face a deep purple, his breathing labored and stertorous.

For a long time I refuse to believe that it is anything serious.

"It's his liver," I say. "He knows what it is, he just told us."

Ebner, who has been upstairs again at my request, confirms me in my illusion.

"The ladies are mistaken, monsieur, I assure

you. M. de Goncourt is just as we saw him a little while ago, no worse."

But my wife insists, she waxes warm on the subject: —

"I tell you that your friend is very ill. You did n't see him as we just saw him, or you would be as frightened as we are. Send a telegram for Doctor Barié at once, Ebner, I beg you."

Among the numerous physicians who have attended Edmond de Goncourt of late years, Doctors Millard, Rendu, Martin, Vaquez, Barié, he has always had most confidence in the last-named; he has often told us so, and has written it in his journal. And so, when the carriage arrived, about six o'clock, with Lucien and the doctor, we experienced a feeling of genuine relief.

.   .   .   .

"Well, Monsieur Barié?"

"Congestion of the lungs. At his age it 's a very serious matter."

Even in face of this positive statement, this certainty, I was not afraid. It did not seem possible to me. For that shivering which he recognized —

"Was a shiver of fever — a hundred and twenty pulsations a minute. But the fever does n't come from the liver it 's the lung that is attacked."

"Did he take cold coming out of the bath?"

"Yes, perhaps it was the bath — or perhaps a disease that was lying hidden. You say that he was feverish every day. He coughed a good deal last month and complained laughingly of having a wardrobe on his chest and a litter of kittens miaouwing in his bronchial tubes. He must have been ill some time."

All the same there is in this explosion of danger a suddenness which passes my comprehension. To think that only a moment ago he was talking and laughing with me! Now his eyes look without seeing, and when, by applying mustard plasters all over his body and by injecting ether, caffeine, all the most powerful reagents, they succeed in restoring him partially to life, his voice is no more than a distant stammering, painful to hear. Barié raises him for a moment to a sitting posture.

"Come, Monsieur de Goncourt," says the good doctor, shaking him gently, "talk to us a little. Do you know where you are? At Champrosay, with your friends the Daudets; do you know them?"

The poor fellow smiled for the last time, with a movement of the head which seemed to say: "I should think I do know them." Almost immediately he fell back exhausted on the pillow, muttering: —

"Very tired, very tired."

What happened then? There is a dark hole in my memory, dark with that depressing darkness which invades a house with grief, and which no light can dissipate. On such evenings the lamps give no light. We talk low and grope our way about. Should we send for Pélagie, who is accustomed to take care of him? No. He has forbidden her to leave the house at Auteuil, he trusts no one else to look after his papers and collections. Especially at this time, when the roof is off, and the house full of workmen. How excited he would be to see her here when he recovers consciousness; for not one of us, not even the doctor, has dreamed of disaster. Barié, observing our grief, encourages us:

"We will pull him through — surely if there 's no congestion of the brain."

But Madame Daudet is right in suggesting that as a measure of precaution we should notify the family.

Where is the family to be found? We know nothing about it; he mentioned the subject so seldom. His cousins the Ratiers at the Château de Jeand'heurs, Lefebvre de Béhaine, brother-in-law of our friend Frédéric Masson, are the only ones whose names and addresses we have at hand. We send telegrams to them and a messenger to Doctor Fort, the physician at Draveil, an excellent man and careful practitioner, who is to come to receive Barié's instructions and relieve him until to-morrow morning.

In the silence and darkness of the country there is a constant going and coming and rumbling of wheels as on the liveliest Thursdays at Champrosay. At eleven o'clock the doctor from Paris goes away, promising to return to-morrow as soon as he has made his visit to the hospital. He has installed his colleague upstairs beside the patient, whom my wife has just seen — still drowsy and feverish, but calm. He has drunk twice, trying to smile to reassure us and muttering that he is better, much better. Nothing to do now but go to bed, while the doctor keeps vigil overhead, ready to call us at the slightest cause for alarm. I go out on the terrace for a moment. The wind is blowing, sweeping a cloudy sky saturated with storm. The trees in the park stand out a velvety mass as in the *eaux-fortes* of Seymour Haden whom Goncourt taught me to love. Poor fellow! Is this the beginning of a long illness? Are we to be subjected to more weeks of trembling anxiety and suspense, when we have hardly recovered from our intense suffering on account of our child? What **a** year, what trials! However, let us not cry out, let us not complain, so that *no one may know how we suffer.* That is the best way of cheating evil destiny.

Thursday, July 16.

THE clock on the little church at Champrosay has struck twelve times. Everybody in the house is asleep except the physician and myself. Like Macbeth, I have murdered sleep for several years past, and I take a dose of chloral every night. To-night I delay taking it, not that I have any evil presentiments, but the doctor's footsteps over my head engross my thoughts; I follow him to and fro, I see him approach the bed, lean over the sick man, return to the couch, where he stretches himself out and which he suddenly leaves again.

What is the matter? No, it is nothing. And yet, if— Some one is coming downstairs. Oh! the agony of that stealthy step, which comes nearer and nearer. Some one knocks and says in a low tone:

"The doctor wishes Madame to come upstairs at once."

The voice whispers again, still lower:

"Monsieur had better come too. Monsieur de Goncourt is very ill."

What mysterious nervous strength placed me on my feet, dressed in a twinkling, and carried me to the top of that flight of stairs which ordinarily it is almost impossible for me to ascend? His door is ajar, and his breath, a loud breath horrible to hear — of a sort that I have heard on other nights, alas! — reaches my ears in the hall. Is it possible? Can it really be he that I hear? It was he. He was in the death agony, his features motionless, his face bloated and as it were magnified, his beautiful white hair lying like damp silk on the pillow. A moment of frantic grief and terror. I question the doctor. What in heaven's name has happened? Nothing. The night did not begin badly, but suddenly the pulse quickened, the flesh became hotter, the face even more inflamed. Thus far they had been able to make him drink, but now it was impossible, nothing would pass his lips. This is the end. The doctor tries another injection of ether to satisfy us. No, any sort of effort is useless, almost a profanation; the agony has begun. All about

us, in this bedroom of his where everything is
usually so clean and so orderly, the confusion of
death is perceptible already. This doctor, who
unconsciously talks aloud, these open drawers,
these phials and cups on the table, where sheets of
paper covered with his fine, even writing are still
lying about. And still that stertorous breathing, interrupted at intervals, then resumed, but
shorter and more distant after each break, as that
noble mind, that enlightened soul recedes into
the darkness. My wife kneels at the foot of the
bed, praying and weeping; I, knowing no prayers,
have taken his hand in mine — poor hand! all
moist, yet burning hot — and, leaning over him,
my tears mingling with his death-sweat, I speak
to him, very low, close to his ear:

"Goncourt, my dear fellow, it is I. I am here,
close to you."

I do not know if he can hear me, but at times I
fancy that he can, when the loud breathing stops
and his beautiful face with its heavy, drooping
eyelids seems to listen to what I say of his
brother, his brother Jules, whom he loves above
all else. Suddenly his hand, the scorching heat of
which has sensibly abated within a few moments
— his hand is withdrawn from mine, hastily,
almost roughly. The death agony, it seems, is
marked by such spasmodic movements. To me
it was like a hurried departure, when a friend is
pressed for time and abruptly tears himself away
from your farewells. Ah! Goncourt, faithful and
loyal comrade!

How long did we sit beside that death-bed? What time was it when, the tapers being lighted and a rosary placed by his loving friend, my wife, in his beautiful lifeless hands, we returned to our own room, crushed and stupefied with grief? I cannot tell. I know that a ray of dawn was whitening the windows, that I pounced on my chloral like a coward, and that, as I fell asleep, I heard Lucien sobbing in his room below. Two hours later I was awakened by the little bird in the tree near by, Goncourt's bird with his throat swollen with fresh water, whose innocent trills arose joyously in the sunlight. I lay for a moment without thinking, without understanding; and feeling came back to me with memory, cruel memory, when I heard my wife, in a voice broken with tears, ordering the gardener to "cut tall green palms and roses, armfuls of roses, all the roses in the garden."

CHAMPROSAY, Wednesday, August 5, the day of the burial.